The sequel to *Blood Echo*

For Rayne Kennedy, the only Hybrid in Vires, a walled Vampire city in Vermont, life is almost over. Despite the new family and temporary happiness she's found, her vampire girlfriend, Scarlett Pearce, has been given ninety days by the mysterious city government to turn her into a vampire. She's sure her days as a human are numbered.

Scarlett fights to find a way to avoid Rayne's death when her father and society have decreed it must happen. Between new relationships formed, old ones reshaped, and a bloody romp through the city's darkness, Rayne must decide if she trusts Scarlett not to give in to her blood lust. Thrown into the center of an unexpected revolution, Rayne tries to save herself and Scarlett, unsure if her days as a human, and their time being blood bound, are truly coming to an end.

Blood Lust

L.E. Royal

A NineStar Press Publication

Published by NineStar Press
P.O. Box 91792,
Albuquerque, New Mexico, 87199 USA.
www.ninestarpress.com

Blood Lust

Copyright © 2019 by L.E. Royal
Cover Art by Natasha Snow Copyright © 2019

This is a work of fiction. Names, characters, places, and incidents are either the product of the author's imagination or are used fictitiously. Any resemblance to actual persons living or dead, business establishments, events, or locales is entirely coincidental.

All rights reserved. No part of this publication may be reproduced in any material form, whether by printing, photocopying, scanning or otherwise without the written permission of the publisher. To request permission and all other inquiries, contact NineStar Press at the physical or web addresses above or at Contact@ninestarpress.com.

Printed in the USA
First Edition
February, 2019

Print ISBN: 978-1-950412-06-8

Also available in eBook, ISBN: 978-1-950412-02-0

Warning: This novel contains sexually explicit material that is only suitable for mature readers, scenes of bloody violence and death, and references to the abuse of a child by a parent.

Chapter One

"PICK IT UP."

Scarlett watched with lazy eyes as my hand shot forward to grab the apple. I hated her a little for how easy she found this.

"You're scowling, Princess."

I dropped the apple the minute she let me and did my best to straighten my face.

The revelation that Scarlett and I were blood bound was old news, but its implications were still new to both of us. We'd been spending time when we were alone learning to overcome the phenomenon—or trying.

The vampire stretched, reclining before me on the black satin bedsheets, and I wondered if she felt me compelling her at all. I tried to recreate the feeling inside myself from the rare times I had succeeded in bending her to my will. Silently, I concentrated and willed her to pick up the apple.

She yawned.

Raindrops ran down the sleek glass doors of Scarlett's balcony, the sky a dreary gray. Even from the great height of the thirteenth floor, I could see little beige specks below that I knew were actually humans. They came from the outskirts of the city—the Fringe, brought in to work around the decadent skyscrapers that housed Vampire families, like Scarlett's. High up in Pearce Tower we could live under the illusion of safety, for the moment.

Below, the streets of Vires teemed with vampires, Deltas who were genetically advanced enough to walk in the daylight. The non-Deltas would join them at sunset.

A flash of curiosity disturbed me, pulling me back off the dark path I was traveling, thoughts of society in Vires starting to consume me. Without looking, I could feel her watching me, taste her curiosity. Her wish to know what was going on inside my head was clear through the emotional connection we shared. I tried to lock her out, to shield my feelings from her. She tipped her head and when I met her dark eyes, their intensity burned. I figured I was successful.

Pick up the apple.

Her voice was liquid smoke, lingering in my mind, penetrating every corner. My pale hand darted forward and grabbed it again. She smirked. My stupid, smug, beautiful vampire.

My fingers released their grip the moment she bade them to, and the abused fruit fell back onto the sheets.

"Your turn."

I wanted to grumble, to ask what the point was. We both knew I couldn't resist the commands she gave. We also knew she could resist mine effortlessly most of the time. I smoothed my hands over my jean-clad thighs and tried again.

"I'm not resisting you, sweetheart. I haven't felt any compulsion to resist yet." She was amused. It danced in her eyes, in the little tug at the corner of her mouth, but I knew she was *trying* to be diplomatic, at least.

"Why is this even important?"

She had been playful and light-hearted, secretly enjoying the little game we shared. The minute I asked the question I felt her growing cold, uncomfortable. The pleasant hum of her emotions as they lapped at me waned before they shut down altogether.

The subject we were avoiding hung between us, heavy and suffocating. After almost a week of sleepless nights and uneasy dreams I knew sometimes she could share, I was ready to drag it out into the light.

"I don't ever want it to be used against us." She was somber, her expression dark and unreadable.

"Scar, if I'm going to be a vampire anyway..."

She hissed. I prepared to backpedal, wishing I had been a little more tactful, but she was already speaking.

"Why are you so obsessed with becoming a monster?"

"Jade's not a monster and she's a vampire." Dark eyes softened at the mention of her younger sister, one of the people she loved most in the world. Through our connection I had quickly grown to love her too.

"Jade has struggled more than you know." It was cryptic and caustic and an answer that was *oh so Scarlett.*

"You're not a monster, really."

She scoffed.

We were silent for a few seconds, my reply dancing on the tip of my tongue. It was a large part of what had been keeping me up at night, but I was too afraid of her answer to voice the topic.

"Say what's on your mind?" It was only half a question, and I could tell it took some effort for her not to command it out of me. Beneath the cold indifference she had painted on her face, tiny tells and miniscule shimmers of her feelings told me she was nervous.

"I don't want to get old when you'll always be young."

She laughed, and the sound was ever so slightly bitter.

"I'm three hundred and sixty-nine years old, Princess."

I wondered if I would ever stop being staggered by that fact.

"Besides, I don't think aging is something we have to worry about. I'm almost certain you've already stopped, being as you are."

"Hybrids don't age?" My voice was an octave too high with surprise, and maybe a little bit of joy.

We hadn't much discussed what I was, what I had become, what she had made me. Her cool and careful handling of the subject frustrated me, and it gave me the uncomfortable feeling she was making plans without any of us.

"Just a hunch." She tried to curtail me before I got too fixated on the fact. "But if I'm right and age isn't a factor, are you still so eager to be turned?"

I shrugged, unsure.

"Being a hybrid is still dangerous. What if the Government eventually discovers that us sharing blood is what caused this? What if they find out we're blood bound? Wouldn't it be safer if I was less...breakable?"

Even alone in the room I lowered my voice as I spoke. Vires had taught me quickly in the months since my arrival that it was a cruel city. The mysterious vampire Government who ruled were bloodthirsty and resolved in their belief that vampires were a superior species, humans being their chattels—a fact they loved to celebrate. The thought made me shudder.

They had laws, etiquette, and a social structure I was still learning, though I had known their most absolute law since my arrival—once a vampire bites a human, they must be killed. Scarlett had broken this rule with me, and through using her blood to heal me an emotional connection had formed between us, making us blood bound.

Scarlett watched me, her dark eyes following as I smoothed my fingers along tender flesh. The scar on my cheek burned. I forced the memory of being deep in the Government bunker, before the hooded panel of vampires who would decide if I lived or died, away.

"You're so naïve, sweetheart." There was no malice in her voice, only a fond sort of sadness.

"Do you really think we're not breakable? That you can't be broken and bent and used to someone's will as a vampire?"

I guessed she was thinking of her father.

"Why are you so against me being like you?" I tried to keep any accusation out of my voice, to keep my question simple—it had haunted me and caused so much insecurity this last week.

She seemed to consider her response. For a long moment I was afraid she wouldn't answer. Somewhere in the seconds that stretched out between us, I felt her again. Her fear was hot and anxious. Coming from the strongest person I knew, it surprised me.

"You won't be any old vampire. Perhaps if you were just an accidental turn in the Midlands, you could fade into the background, but you're already in the spotlight. You're already a Pearce."

She scoffed, and a little flutter of nerves and excitement flickered in my chest. I was well beyond the age where it was appropriate to be writing my girlfriend's name in my notebooks, but something about sharing her last name gave me the same slightly giddy feeling I imagined it would bring.

She was staring at me and, caught, heat poured into my cheeks.

Her expression cracked into a smile. I smiled shyly back at her, and for a minute our fraught conversation was curtailed, only our mutual feelings flowing back and forth between us.

When Scarlett pulled me across the mattress and onto her lap, I went easily, lying against her chest on the pillows. I couldn't see her face from my position, so I just watched the raindrops chase another one down the windowpane and listened.

"I have no idea what life would be like for you, as a vampire in my family. I can't guarantee my father won't be interested in...making you like me." She paused, and I wrapped my arms around her waist and held her tight.

"You know about the Government standards, or some of them anyway. It's going to kill you to have to whip someone, or beat someone, or kill someone...and eventually it will become the reality of your life, if I change you."

My blood ran cold at the thought. My plan to accept the Government order to turn me seemed more like a nightmare than a solution now.

"I just figured I would be like Jade."

She shook her head, her chin brushing over the crown of mine before I felt the soft pressure of a kiss there.

"Jade is a unique situation, a situation cultivated over years and years of manipulations and different agendas and a lot of blood on my part. I do enough punishing and display enough power for both of us, so she's able to fade into the background some. You know even that isn't guaranteed."

The memory of Scarlett's back split open and bleeding last time she had stepped in to save her sister from the consequences of refusing to act as society said a vampire should came to me unbidden. I didn't want to be the reason she was hurt again, and I knew without a shadow of a doubt she would step in to save me when inevitably I was unable to hurt humans as a vampire.

The solution to our problem was sand, slipping constantly through my fingers; the more I tried to cling to it the faster it fell.

"I can protect you better like this."

The words were well-intentioned, but they rankled anyway. I knew from experience that Scarlett needed someone to protect her too. She seemed to bear so much of the burden from the horrors of this society—the price of her being so involved as a powerful Government figurehead.

"Who's going to protect you?"

I asked the question quietly, my lips against the skin of her neck.

"No one." There was no hesitation in her answer. "But you'll be here whenever it ends, you'll save me."

I pushed up onto my knees until I was straddling her legs, her face between my hands. The words were a statement with the slightest sliver of a question, and her eyes echoed the uncertainty.

"I'll save you."

I wasn't sure what she thought I would save her from, but my reply was strong, sure, determined. I would save her from the dark that so often came close to consuming her. I would try to save her from harm too. I had done it before—or helped at least. I'd stolen the cure to the toxin killing her and the chain of events I'd started sent me spiraling right onto the Government's radar and resulted in the discovery that I was a hybrid.

She didn't kiss me, though I felt the collision of our lips coming, the pull to her overwhelming me. First, her eyes held mine and her presence radiated inside my chest, in my head, my soul. A soft fire glowed bright where we met emotionally. When she did kiss me the fire flared, heating from both sides, love spilling over into lust.

Scarlett pulled away, one arm around my waist and the opposite hand in my hair. She urged my head back so smooth teeth could run rough up the side of my neck. When her teeth became sharp, I ached for her to bite me, even as I flinched. I was well versed with the initial burst of pain accompanying a vampire bite, though I had never experienced it on my neck.

She laughed, that dark coffee and gravel laugh, before her tongue replaced her teeth.

My blood was baying for her to take it. It was undeniably erotic when she drank from me, but it was also romantic. Our connection was renewed and replenished. Something about feeding her lightened my soul, filled me up, and made me content in a way nothing else ever had, or I suspected ever would.

"If you become a vampire, there'll be no more of this."

I smacked her shoulder lightly for the tease.

She flipped us and pushed me back until I fell onto the mattress. She hovered over me, her dark eyes captivating, oddly colored irises, one green one brown, swirling like molten gems as she raised my left wrist to her mouth.

"Still want to be a vampire?"

She was infuriating and beautiful, her hips pressed against mine in all the ways that were too much and not nearly enough. Though the ache for her physically registered somewhere far away, in that moment all I wanted was her mouth.

"I never wanted to. I just wasn't completely against it if it was the easiest solution."

Her tongue felt scalding as it licked a path over the delicate veins across the inside of my wrist. A soft whine slipped from between my lips a few seconds before I sealed them closed, killing the sound.

The tongue became teeth, running up and down over the sensitive area, the single white puncture scar that lived there, aching to be used again.

"Wouldn't you miss this?"

She was still teasing, though I could see her commitment to the cause waning as her lips, teeth, tongue, cheek ran over my arm. I knew her resolve not to drink was crumbling by the second.

I tried to grind out some clever response, but my chest was heaving, my breath ragged with want and all the control I didn't have. We studied each other, her hips grinding down against mine, a delicious backdrop to my focus on her mouth.

"What do you want, Princess?"

It was the first time she had been so bold as to ask, and caught in the moment as I was, I couldn't bring myself to be bashful.

"Bite me."

The words surprised me. They were rich and low and sounded pornographic even to my own ears. I felt her desire rage against mine, and then a sharp sting was followed by the hot wetness of a tongue lapping the single puncture wound on my wrist.

Her eyes were almost black, and swirling. She was torturing us both. Sitting back to grind her body against mine, she let a thick ribbon of blood flow down my forearm, as she held it in her grasp. Finally, she chased it with her tongue.

Drinking hadn't always been like this. At first it was scary, a little uncomfortable, though still somehow sort of satisfying. Now it was a guilty pleasure, as gratifying physically as it was emotionally.

"Scarlett, please..."

A thrill flared hot down our connection at my pleading. I was no stranger to her love of power, but her reaction to it still surprised me. I had too little time to think about it, because, finally, her mouth covered the puncture and she sucked, sending a soft pull through my body. As she swallowed, everything washed backward like the tide. It stole my breath, still. She was beautiful, powerful, and vital in these moments when she needed me, and on some level it satisfied me to no end. The feeling of contentment washed back and forth between us. I tasted her soul, dark and fractured with shards of light so bright they were blinding.

"Open your mouth."

The command snapped me back to reality. Scarlett raised her own wrist to her bloody lips, before opening a twin puncture there which was bleeding.

This was new. Her apprehension twisted around mine, and though I sensed she wanted it, I wasn't compelled to do as she said. The choice was still mine.

I let my lips part slightly in compliance, curiosity winning out over fear. She leaned down to kiss me, her blood-slick tongue pushing into my mouth past my teeth and across my own. We moaned into the kiss, our connection going wild, and I wanted more.

"Princess."

Her voice was breathy against my ear. She pressed her wrist against my lips, which opened on instinct, and then her blood was spilling into my mouth and my head was spinning. She kissed my neck, licked the soft skin there. I felt far away from myself, one hand pinned above my head, her thumb pressed on the wound, the other grasping her arm tight, holding it to my mouth as I sucked. The pull of the tide from the opposite direction was dizzying, intoxicating. I was barely beginning to sate my appetite for her when she pulled her arm away.

She sat up breathless. I watched as she pressed our wrists together, both wounds closing. Hers disappeared into smooth tan skin as if the blemish had never existed. Mine returned to its perpetual little white scar.

With it done she looked down at me, studying me with love and marveling I could feel as much as see.

I flushed, shy in the face of what had just happened.

She laughed a soft breathy laugh, and leaned down. It surprised me when instead of kissing me, the tip of her tongue slicked around my mouth.

"You are beautiful with blood on your lips."

The words were reverent, and I knew they would stay with me. Apparently content with her cleanup, she rubbed her cheek against mine. I pulled her down onto me. The two-way sharing only seemed to have enhanced the affection and contentment she always displayed after drinking.

"I love you."

I twisted my fingers in her hair and tried not to think about the future, about anything outside of right now.

She didn't reply aloud, but I felt the response inside my chest.

You're mine.

"I'm yours."

WHEN I WOKE, the sun was dying outside the windows, brilliant reds and gold behind the wall at the edge of the city. I was still naked, the thrum of Scarlett's blood potent in my veins. Though our connection was quiet, I tasted the darkness she was slipping into.

Pushed up on the pillows, I watched her finishing her makeup in the mirror. Smoky eye shadow, thick black lashes, blood-red lips to match her nails—this was her battle armor, as beautiful as it was deadly.

"Do you have to go?"

When she turned, the eyes of a killer looked back at me, cool and hard before they softened into the woman I recognized.

"You know I do."

The last dregs of her contentment, her softness at our earlier encounter rescinded, leaving behind a nothingness I knew she'd put between us to hide the dark.

She turned back to the mirror to fix her hair from loose waves into soft curls, and I wondered why she went to all the effort.

This had become our routine: long days spent together, and longer nights apart, me sleeping in her bed while she disappeared into the city. She rarely spoke about where she had been. Every day she slipped under the sheets with me at five in the morning, hair still wet from the shower, small in an oversized T-shirt and nothing else, and I knew she'd been at the Punishment Center.

A form-fitting black dress peeked out from beneath her leather jacket, the presence of which told me she would be leaving soon. I rolled out of bed and wrapped my hair into a messy braid, and then tugged on some leggings and a large black sweater belonging to Scarlett.

"I was thinking of making a pie..."

It was a weak play, and I knew she would see right through the offer.

I ached to be able to accept where she went at night, to end the distance my feelings about it put between us. As much as I loved her, knowing she went off to effectively torture people was hard to bear.

"Save me some."

Her answer was cool and clipped and it spoke volumes about her headspace.

Defeated, I trailed after her as she opened the bedroom door. Her killer heels swung from her fingers as she started down the hall.

She paused so abruptly that I ran into her, my shoulder colliding with her upper arm, though she didn't seem to notice. Her biceps was like a rock under my hand as I gripped it to steady myself. Leaning forward to peer into the open door of Jade's room, I tried to see what had caught her attention.

Camilla was over. I hadn't realized, and apparently neither had Scarlett. Jade and Camilla reclined on her bed, the TV playing a movie I didn't recognize. Its blue glow illuminated their bodies pressed close together.

I thought it was sweet, if a little creepy. I cringed internally at the memory that Scarlett and Camilla had previously been...involved. Camilla was drop-dead gorgeous, even by vampire standards, and she and Jade had been growing noticeably closer since the untimely death of Jade's previous almost-girlfriend.

The corny horror music on the TV continued to rise in a crescendo. Jade reached out and wrapped her long fingers around Camilla's on the comforter.

White-hot anger shot through my chest and I'd taken half a step forward, ready to rip their hands apart, before I stopped myself.

Scarlett's eyes were murderous. I tried to force a feeling of calm down our connection to extinguish some of her apparent anger at the situation.

"Cami..."

The vampires on the bed jumped again. I laughed silently as Camilla whipped her hand away.

"Scarlett, come to join us?"

I knew the playfulness in her tone was supposed to hide her true feelings. I didn't understand why they were acting like teenagers who'd been caught in the act. Whatever was happening between them was admittedly kind of odd, but walking on eggshells around Scarlett just made it even weirder.

"No. I'm going to work." Her voice was devoid of emotion, and for a long moment the four of us all held our breath. A storm was brewing, twisting and turning and broiling inside Scarlett, and feeling its perimeter from the outside, I loathed to be there when, finally, it was unleashed.

"Rayne's making pie."

I silently damned her to another death, not in the mood to pull out all the ingredients and go through the motions. I'd only offered the distraction in the hopes of persuading her to stay home, though I was glad for a break in the tension. I made a note to ask her later what had gotten her so upset about Cami and Jade dating.

"I love pie!"

Jade's eyes were like saucers and I rolled mine. I was definitely making pie now.

"Rayne's pie—vampire crack. Who knew?"

They laughed. Scarlett dropped a soft kiss against the side of my neck and bent to put on her heels before she was gone in a blink, the ding of the elevator ringing her out.

The loose hair around my face had just settled when Cami paused the movie.

"Do you want to join us?"

It was an olive branch, but with Scarlett gone and having napped too long during the afternoon, I was restless.

"I think I'm actually just going to start the pie."

"We'll help." Jade popped up off the bed and I was once again grateful to her. I loved her like a sister, part of the emotion mine and part of it Scarlett's, though it didn't matter. She was the one to bring me to Vires and the only one to accept me and understand my relationship with Scarlett and the struggles it brought, no matter what.

Cami seemed less enthusiastic but followed anyway. Though it stung, I knew her disapproval of my relationship with Scarlett came from worry over what it could cost her if we were exposed. Now I was, for all intents and purposes, scheduled to become a vampire. I wondered if that was the reason for her slightly improved attitude of late.

"Peach pie?" Camilla asked.

Although the dessert had been a big hit in the past, it wasn't what I wanted to bake tonight.

"Blackberry... It's Scarlett's favorite." Jade replied for me, as she gave me a sympathetic smile and hooked her arm through mine.

I let myself be towed along toward the kitchen.

Chapter Two

SCARLETT HAD BEEN in a better mood all day. I tried not to think what she might have done the previous night to inspire it, and just enjoy it for the gift it was. For once the hybrid issue, the Government order, felt far away, and after a day of eating too much pie and enjoying a side of Scarlett so seldom seen, I pushed my luck and asked her to take me outside.

By a miracle or something else it worked. We descended the tower via the sleek elevator. The guards at the front desk opened the doors for us as we stepped out onto the sidewalk.

The sun was almost completely set. I marveled at the pretty glow it cast on the city. As much as I had wanted to get out, I was suddenly nervous to be immersed in the culture of Vires again.

"You remember the rules?"

Scarlett's voice was soft, low enough that I had to walk faster to stay close enough to hear her. I felt plain in my jeans and button-up next to the customary skintight dress she had insisted on if we were going outside.

The question caught me off guard.

"Do we still have to? I mean... Can't we be normal seems..."

I was loath to say the word "hybrid" aloud, loath to ruin this rare outing before it had begun.

She shook her head but offered no more explanation. Trying not to let the news deflate me, I nodded my understanding, trusting for now that she knew best, though I planned to ask her reasoning once we got home.

We walked in easy silence between the ominously large skyscrapers housing the Delta families. I looked beyond them to the smaller non-Delta towers, trying to force my eyes not to linger on Chase Tower, which had been my home for my first few weeks in the city.

Beyond the smaller towers I could make out the scattered roofs of buildings in the Midlands, home to the more middle-class vampires. I tried not to think of the Fringe, which lay just past them, inhabited by the humans. Most of them were born here, a life of servitude and being preyed on by the vampires all they had ever known.

Scarlett glanced sideways at me, and I guessed some of my mood had leaked through to her.

"Isn't this what you wanted?"

I nodded enthusiastically before she could change her mind and decide it was safer for us to go back home.

"Yes...Mistress."

The word was foreign on my tongue, but not as unpleasant as it had once been, now I was certain of our relationship beneath it.

Mirth danced in her eyes and I fought the urge to roll mine. Following her as she rounded a corner, the sight of the little market greeted me. It struck me as strange to find the stalls still inhabited. As I studied the clientele frequenting them, their late hours made more sense.

We were browsing one of the closest booths filled with clothes—decadent dresses and fancy pant suits—and for a moment it was nice, easy to forget where we were and all that hung over us.

A pretty, blue sundress caught my eye, plain in comparison to the fancy satin and sheer cuts around it. It was something I might have worn at home, if I'd had anywhere to go other than school.

Scarlett must have followed my line of sight, as she requested—more like demanded—to look at it further.

The younger of the two girls at the stall stuttered a reply, looking as if she was about to burst into tears as she handed over the dress. If Scarlett noticed, she didn't care, busy holding the garment against my body, studying me and it, before she met my eyes and I felt her question. I liked it, the material was soft where it brushed my fingers, but I was embarrassed to have her buy it for me.

"We'll take it. Put it on my account."

The girl took the dress back, folded it and recorded the sale, while Scarlett and I shared a smile that made me warm down to my toes. She was breathtaking. In any other world I would have leaned up to kiss her in thanks, but here I just smiled and hoped she knew.

"Oh, so it's true then, Scarlett, you got yourself a hybrid?"

A hand reached out to touch me before I saw who it belonged to. Scarlett swatted it away before it could ever make contact, and on instinct, I stepped closer to her.

"Hello, Luke."

The man looked to be in his early thirties, a little older than Scarlett appeared. His eyes swirled as he studied me. My stomach dropped.

"Looks human... Smells human."

Scarlett cut him off, inserting herself between us, and forcing him to take a step back. His voice was familiar in a way that unsettled me, though even after racking my brain, I couldn't place why.

"Is there something you need, or are you just trying to get in my way?"

He smiled up at her with poorly hidden contempt.

"My apologies, just a lowly Midlander trying to catch up on the latest and greatest in our great city... Heard all about your new pet hybrid, of course. Everyone has, and how you killed Evan Chase too."

I felt Scarlett's annoyance as he fished for information. The intensity with which he switched between watching her and then studying me sent something cold twisting uneasily into my stomach.

"Sounds like you're all caught up already."

Scarlett turned back to the stall, where the girl was still fumbling with the dress and a bag. She leaned across the table to snatch both and pushed the material inside the plastic without issue before taking hold of the back of my neck. She guided me away without another word to the man, but I still felt his eyes on us as we stopped a few stalls away.

Her thumb smoothed across the fine hairs at the nape of my neck, soothing, though I struggled to reclaim the sense of peace I'd enjoyed most of the day.

Now my focus had been pulled off Scarlett, off the market itself and onto the people inhabiting it, I was aware many were watching me—humans and vampires alike.

I noticed the humans were unkempt, cheeks smudged with dirt, the beige slacks and T-shirts most of them wore setting them apart easily. I noted most of them were not wearing a jacket despite the cooler temperature. Even hidden behind the desks inside the stalls I was aware of them watching me, and as I stared back into each unfamiliar face, they quickly looked away. Were they scared of me now too?

Scarlett dug the pads of her fingers into the back of my neck ever so slightly, bringing me back into the moment. I turned to face the stall before us, boxes upon boxes of produce on display.

"Where do they get this?"

I asked the question half to Scarlett, half to the woman behind the boxes, forgetting myself.

"It's grown in the Fringe, Miss." The older woman curtseyed a little bit as she spoke, "We're selling it on behalf of the Government."

I tried to smile at her kindly, the title she had given me still rolling around in my head. Since I'd entered Vires, I had been forced to use similar titles to address the vampires; it was completely jarring to be on the receiving end of one.

"Someone from the kitchen has already collected supplies this week." Scarlett's voice was cool and disinterested, and she steered me onward, leaving the boxes of cabbages and the rows of shiny apples behind.

We perused a few more stalls and I was amazed at the array of goods on sale. Scarlett explained quietly to me how each stall came to be, sensing my interest. The Government owned some booths and sold produce and items made by the humans in the Fringe. Vampires owned others, the human staff from their tower selling the items they or their masters had made to raise money for their towers.

As we passed a stand selling what mostly looked like weapons, I noticed Scarlett's eyes linger. I didn't want to look, to imagine any of them in her hands, but today had been a gift. Against her original wishes she'd brought me outside, and I wanted to give her something.

"We can look..."

I kept my voice quiet, but I knew she heard. Dark eyes flickered to me, studying me for a moment, searching out my sincerity, before we altered course slightly and headed for the booth.

"Miss Pearce." The woman who greeted us shot to her feet far too fast to be human. I jumped back in surprise, my cheeks flaming. I had been doing better about not getting startled when the vampires moved quickly at home, but out here, I was on edge.

"Shikara."

There was a respect in Scarlett's greeting I rarely heard, and then they proceeded to discuss knives in greater detail than I had even known existed. In my world they were only used to prepare food.

"Would you like to try it out?"

My head whipped around from where I had been pretending to look at the ornate handles on what appeared to be swords. Scarlett seemed to be testing the weight of a smooth silver blade in her palm, balancing it as she moved her hand around.

"Shikara. Vires's official Weapons mistress."

The stall owner took a quick bow in front of me. Looking at her for the first time, I noticed she was of Asian descent, her hair pulled back into a long ponytail. She wore a modern kimono fashioned from a dark material, a belt of weapons tight around her waist.

"I...um, nice to meet you, ma'am?"

Scarlett snickered. When I turned accusing eyes to her, she was busy again with the knife. Given she hadn't jumped between us and didn't seem to mind the woman talking to me, I figured she was a friend.

"Nice to meet you too, hybrid."

There was no malice in her words, just a simple statement of facts. Silence stretched out between us and I wondered if it would break Scarlett's precious protocol if I spoke to Shikara more. Glancing back at the vampire, now spinning the knife around in a way that made me feel nauseous to watch, I decided if she cared she would let me know.

"Where do these come from?"

I indicated the long table of beautifully crafted knives, swords, intricately woven whips and lashes, and many other items I had never seen before and had no name for.

"I make them."

I felt the weight of Shikara's eyes on me, dark and curious.

"After you're turned, come back and see me. I have some weapons that are relatively safe but effective for someone with little training."

Apparently, we just couldn't escape it today. I nodded dumbly and stuttered out a thank-you, not wanting to be impolite.

When I turned back to Scarlett, embarrassed and unsure how to continue the conversation, the knife had disappeared, no longer on the table but not in her hands either.

"Good?" Shikara questioned and Scarlett nodded.

They exchanged something I couldn't see and were saying their goodbyes when we were interrupted by a ringing that had become all too familiar.

Scarlett's voice was cold, brittle as she answered, and I already knew who was calling.

The phone call was over quickly and then she was nodding to Shikara and turning us back toward the tower. My heart fell; our outing was over too soon.

"I have to go to the Fringe, sweetheart. Time to go home."

I dug in my heels, slowing down a little, trying to buy myself some time to talk.

"Can't I go too?"

Realizing my voice was just a little loud, I added a bumbled "*please mistress,*" just in case. She seemed to consider the request, and I was suddenly nervous she would accept. I'd only heard about the Fringe from others, never experienced it myself. I was also acutely aware that a phone call from the Government to send her out there probably meant the reason for her visit wasn't good, and most likely something I didn't want to see.

"There's been some unrest out there, nothing serious, but I just want to walk around and remind them of their place."

"I used to be just like them." I couldn't help but feel defensive at her words despite knowing this was the attitude Vires was built on.

Scarlett shook her head but didn't say any more on the matter. When we reached the front of the tower, rather than taking me up, she summoned one of the customary black cars that seemed to be the Pearces' signature transportation. She opened the back door and waited for me to slip inside.

Through the heavy tint on the windows I looked out into the darkness, hardly able to see anything even under the streetlights.

She slid down beside me, telling our location to the driver before the screen between him and us was raised, and we were alone.

"You were never anything like them. You don't belong here."

She surprised me by continuing our earlier conversation.

I didn't reply, watching the streetlights blur by and become more and more infrequent as we moved from the inner city toward the dilapidated outskirts.

I knew she wanted me to understand; I also remembered a time when she had believed what she did and how she lived was too large an obstacle for our relationship to overcome. I hadn't agreed with her then and I still didn't—she was complicated on so many levels and so was what we had.

I felt the sharp prickle of awareness that I needed to stop torturing her over this. Sometime after we'd discovered I had become a hybrid, I'd finally stopped torturing myself over falling in love with a killer. I just wasn't sure I would ever sleep well knowing what she was doing each night.

Scarlett had the biggest capacity to love and the biggest capacity for darkness of anyone I had ever known.

"Why did you want to come?"

Every word was perfect, steady, and though our connection was silent, I could still feel the pain in them. Like every other creature I knew on some deep level she wanted acceptance of all she was, and I was troubled, uncertain I could ever give it to her completely.

"I wanted to visit the Fringe and see what it's like. I'd like to see where they grow all that food..."

It was only part of the reason, but it was good enough. A line of communication flickered into existence between us, and I felt only slight guilt at my omission.

"We probably won't see the agricultural areas tonight, just the residential. They're mostly out the opposite side." She paused. "I'll take you back during the day to see them if you'd like."

I clung to the olive branch and scooted along the leather seat closer to her. I reached up to touch her cool cheek. Though she let me, she didn't turn to my touch.

"I'm trying."

It was the best apology I had to offer, and it wasn't enough.

Scarlett stared out of the window, her oddly-colored eyes unfocused.

"I love you, Scarlett. I understand, give me a little more time to accept?"

She licked her lips and barely nodded.

"We have bigger problems for now. The city is uneasy, everyone knows about you, which I'd already guessed, but they know nothing of hybrids and it makes them nervous."

I wrapped my arms around her neck and finally, she thawed, reaching for my waist and pulling me closer.

"We'll figure something out."

I tried to reassure her, unsure as I was myself. Even as she nodded, I could tell she was far away, struggling with the burden of finding a solution to my impending death. I shuddered at the thought.

The car rolled to a stop and I followed Scarlett as she got out. Dim lights, spread too far apart, lit the area. Rows of what looked to be garages or outbuildings lined the side of the dirt street.

"What exactly did you want to see?"

Scarlett walked, and I followed, wondering how she stayed upright in her ridiculous heels on the uneven terrain. I was too busy taking in our surroundings to answer her.

I noticed bodies lingering in the shadows, most of them too far away to make out faces or genders. They varied in size, from the smallest children to large silhouettes I assumed to be men.

The eerie quiet of the streets left me uneasy. Lights illuminated the people just enough for me to know they were watching, shining from the dirty windows and holes in the buildings.

"It's after curfew so no one should be outside." Scarlett didn't seem fazed by any of this.

"Why are they then?"

Discomfort followed me as we continued our journey, heading deeper into the center of what looked to me to be little more than a shanty village.

"They're protesting. They want something or are trying to make some sort of statement. Many didn't turn up to the city center to work today. Too many for a mass punishment, or so the government thinks..."

Her tone suggested she disagreed.

"I suppose they think having me walk around might make them reconsider this little coup, a last chance before they take more drastic action."

The bodies lingering in the shadows, pressed against the sides of the run-down buildings, quiet but strong in their presence, took on a new light.

"Hasn't anyone thought to just ask them what they want, wouldn't that be easier than...this?"

Scarlett laughed, the street lamps casting a golden glow that turned her dark hair to shimmering mahogany.

"They don't get to want, sweetheart. If you become a vampire, society will take great pride in teaching you that. And I suspect I'll suffer many pains trying to save you from it."

We stepped into a slightly better-lit area, a large square. I squinted, seeing makeshift benches built from wooden pallets dotting the space, interspersed with what looked like old patio furniture and some miscellaneous objects fashioned into seating.

Scarlett paused on the edge of the space. I tasted the shift in her mood, the skitter of excitement across her psyche, the death of the Scarlett I knew at home in the tower replaced by the predator she had been taught to become.

"Wait here."

I stood rooted to the spot as she took off at a leisurely pace down one side of the square. She slowed past every person, studying them, committing them to memory.

Movement caught my eye. People began to scatter, some walking, some running, some dragging their loved ones with them, all disappearing back into the streets.

One man called an apology as he left, and I followed the sound of his voice, the line of his vision back to a figure that was familiar to me, though I couldn't place her.

I glanced back to Scarlett, who was thoroughly occupied sauntering along the other side of the square saying things I couldn't make out and didn't care to. I moved toward the girl. Recognition prickled at my senses when I saw long brunette hair and a slim but feminine figure. I knew beyond a doubt I had seen her before, but the question was, where?

I stepped around a group of teenagers on my path to her, excusing myself out of habit, sending them skittering away with cries of, "Sorry, Miss," as they disappeared into the darkness between the buildings.

The commotion made the girl turn, and happiness broke through the grim despair that had been seeping into me the longer we spent here.

"Zoe?"

Though there was recognition in the eyes of the girl I had met on my arrival into Vires, they were surprisingly hard. I stopped short on my way over to greet her, suddenly self-conscious as I noticed her tattered clothing, unable to avoid comparing it to the brand-new outfit I wore myself beneath my warm jacket.

"Hello, Miss."

The words were toneless, and I was unsure how to respond. I caught my breath after a second and decided to plow forward.

"How are you? It's been so long."

I ached for any of the camaraderie I had once shared with the girl who had been my first guide in the vampire city, my first friend.

"I've been better."

Her eyes flicked to Scarlett and back to me, wary.

"I...um, why are you all out here? Scarlett said you're protesting?"

She scoffed, the sound so harsh, so juxtaposed to my memory of her that I flinched.

"Yes, we need medicine. It's been a cold winter and too many of our children and elderly haven't made it thanks to pneumonia. See, unlike your nice cozy tower, we don't have heat, we don't have enough coats and blankets, and the vampires keep breaking the windows and doors we cobble together for our houses."

Her voice was full of disdain and it hurt to learn that I had become the enemy. After having listened to her describing the situation, I was embarrassed to say I lived with, and loved, the vampires who perpetuated it.

"Antibiotics?"

She eyed me curiously, glancing at the other humans who stood beside her before she nodded.

"I don't even know where you would get those from here. I'll try to find out, or at least let Scarlett know that's all you want."

Zoe seemed to thaw, slightly.

"Think that will help? We had a nurse down here, she was good with herbal remedies and rationed out the drugs to get us by. Do you know what happened to her?"

I tried not to think about the woman Scarlett had all but murdered to get me back after I was assigned to another vampire family. My silence was my guilt.

"My little sister is dying and she's just one of many. Now you're one of them, if you could do anything..." The first shreds of humility leaked into Zoe's voice, and finally she was something like the girl I remembered. "I would really appreciate it."

I thought about correcting her and telling her I wasn't a vampire but, faced with the awful reality of life in the Fringe, trying to reject the privilege I so obviously had, it just seemed like an insult. So I nodded.

"I really can't promise anything, I don't even know how much Scarlett could do."

Someone scoffed from behind Zoe. Apparently, they were growing braver.

"Your precious Scarlett can do whatever she wants, hybrid, she's the worst of the sick fuckers running this city. Are you really so blonde you haven't even figured that out?"

"Caleb..."

Zoe silenced him.

"We're not going to stoop to their level, and Rayne is at least listening. She's talked about helping which is more than anyone else has. She's not the worst thing inside these walls, even if she is sleeping with it."

Silence stretched out, and I hung my head, my cheeks burning hot in the cool night air.

I didn't hear Scarlett coming, the dirt beneath our feet muffling the usual click of her heels, but the shifting of the little group of people before me alerted me to her impending presence. When I looked up, she was stalking toward us, her dark eyes alight with a sick smile, so out of place in the ruins, the poverty, the depravity, in which we stood.

She studied each of the humans, humming softly under her breath.

"More people out of bed, I've counted over a hundred now. I'd say tomorrow's schedule is shaping up to be quite the marathon."

Nobody spoke. The tension was thick, suffocating, and Zoe visibly warred with herself, her big brown eyes glassy with either fear or determination, I wasn't sure which.

"We just need some medicine, Miss Pearce, that's all we want."

Scarlett surveyed her coolly.

"You have supplies brought out here four times a year by the grace of the government. If you've been irresponsible with them, you have no one to blame but yourselves."

Zoe's hands were shaking at her sides, and her gaze was fixed on Scarlett's expensive shoes.

"My sister is dying. We did try to make the medicine last, but it's been a cold winter and we've worked harder than ever. If the government could find it in their graces to..."

Scarlett waved her words away.

"I'll pass on the reasoning for all this though I should warn you, it likely won't change the outcome. If I was you, or you, or you, Zoe Richardson, I would run along to bed now, and perhaps I'll forget your name when making up tomorrow's whipping roster."

The others had already been backing away, and at her words, some broke into a run. Zoe stood there longer, and I urged her silently to go. Scarlett's curiosity lapped at me, then I felt her excitement stirring in the face of what could be a challenge.

"Mistress..."

I tugged on her hand, and she turned to me, her dark eyes blazing brilliant and terrifying.

"Goodnight, Zoe."

I tried to cue her into action.

"Yes, goodnight, Zoe." Scarlett echoed my words though her tone twisted them into something I worried I would hear in my nightmares.

Finally seeming to come back to her senses, Zoe fled, leaving us alone.

"They just want medicine to save their family, Scar, why is that so much to ask?"

The words poured out, hastened by my frustration and lack of understanding at this whole stupid thing.

"It's not my call, sweetheart." She licked her lips, whatever had woken inside her still dying as she studied me.

"And if it was, would you give it to them?"

I squared my shoulders and held her eyes, pulling our connection tight and tasting her surprise at the question. I tried to be patient as she searched herself for the answer, my breath billowing out in thin puffs of steam, warm air in the cold.

"If you wanted me to, then yes."

It was a half answer at best. I pressed.

"And if I wasn't in the equation?"

"No."

Anger flared hot in my chest. She scoffed.

"You can't be mad over something that isn't reality. You asked, and I was honest."

I took a deep breath, ignoring the way the cold air was starting to burn the insides of my nose.

"But if it was me or Jade or Cami, would you get the medicine?"

She didn't seem to follow the jump. Her brow furrowed as she reassured me.

"Of course, always. You know that."

"So why not them?"

An unsure smile tugged at her lips, as if she didn't quite believe I was being serious.

"That's not how the world works here. Helping them does nothing to benefit my family or me. In fact, it only puts us at risk. It's a huge display of weakness. When you lived beyond the wall did you dedicate yourself to saving every laying hen living in horrible conditions, every dairy cow in poor health?"

I turned around and stomped back in the direction we had come from, needing time. Scarlett gently took hold of my arm.

"I am not your damn dairy cow, Mistress."

I spat the last word, and I couldn't remember a time I had ever been so harsh with her.

I felt apology, her need to explain herself, but one thing Scarlett understood well was the need for space. She gave it to me, walking beside me in silence as we made our way back to the car.

"I'm sorry I keep disappointing you, Princess."

The words were sincere. She kept her eyes away from me as she opened the car door for me. I paused before I slid inside, trying to find something to say. The truth was, she did disappoint me. I understood why she was the way she was, how she had become like that, but I still wished she could be more compassionate toward humans. The logical voice in my head told me if she did, it would be at the expense of her safety and the safety of everyone in the tower.

It was an impossible equation with no easy answer, and Scarlett was still waiting politely for me to get into the car, her chin tipped so I couldn't see her face.

"I understand why you're like this, but I wish things were different. I wish Vires could be different."

She looked up and there was remorse in her eyes, something she rarely displayed, despite her far worse crimes.

"I offered to take you back."

She was dejected and pitiful, and I launched forward and wrapped her in a hug, because damn her and her huge stupid heart and sadistic vampire tendencies.

When I pulled back, there was the slightest wetness in her eyes.

"I don't want to leave you, Scar. I just wish we lived in a world where you didn't feel like this was necessary."

She shrugged, and I felt her uncertainty. I knew she doubted her own ability to live in a world without this, which was sad given that inside the tower, she did it every day with our little family effortlessly. She was happy.

"Will you come home tonight?"

I hated to unleash her on the city like this, for her sake and its.

She nodded, and I tugged her down into the car.

We were silent for the ride home, her head on my shoulder and my fingers in her hair.

I wondered if I would ever find a way to stop hurting her, to find a balance, a way to make peace with this. For the first time, I wondered if there was another option, if we could somehow survive here without Scarlett having to be a punisher. A little voice inside me asked the question that scared me most of all.

Even if she could stop, would she want to?

Chapter Three

IT WAS A few hours before sunrise when the guards came. I tried not to remember Scarlett's threats, clever at first, careful and calculated. As it became clear they were going to take me anyway, she devolved into a desperate snarling mess, ready to take on all comers in her gray plaid pajama pants and bare feet.

Camilla had barely held her back, all but ushering me onto the elevator with the guards, Scarlett raising hell behind us. I didn't recognize any of the men who had come for me, and all we were told was I was to report to the bunker for testing to further knowledge of my nature as a hybrid.

I had tried to use our connection to restrain her, to stop her from getting herself into even more trouble for the sake of saving one of us. I was unsure if it had worked, or if she had been logical beneath the emotion and let me go; I knew for sure Cami hadn't been strong enough to hold her back entirely.

The urge to let her anger at the situation consume me had been strong. Incensed as she was, there was no filter, and as I was tugged toward the elevator, I felt it all; her rage followed closely by her desperation. The fear of losing me ran deep down into her soul.

I stared at the concrete wall in front of me, a lump in my throat as I tried not to think of her, of home, of Jade and Cami, and our life. I worried about the tests, tormenting myself with gruesome scenarios where the truth I was a hybrid because I shared Scarlett's blood would be revealed. This terrified me more, because it would mean death for us both.

I took a deep breath, blowing it out over dry lips and trying to curtail the panic that was threatening to take over.

The air got to me the most, deep inside the underground bunker; it was thick, stale, the smell of rust and chemicals permeating it to the point that breathing felt hard. It had been months since I was last in the bunker, months since the endless days, maybe weeks spent in my concrete cell waiting for Scarlett to find me, but I remembered. I was so naïve then. I knew nothing of Vires, little of the vampires and less about the Government. I tried to console myself with the fact that this time I was far more informed, though I wasn't sure it would be enough to save me.

I felt like at any moment I might choke, run out of air, yet I kept on breathing and the moment never came.

The steel door to the small room opened, and a man dressed in the uniform of the bunker guards walked toward me without a word. Taking my arm, he hoisted me from my position on the floor to my feet. I let myself be moved, trying to ignore the hammering of my heart. My mind cycled rapidly through things, places, and people. Anything to focus on to be anywhere but here, though every one of them was too painful to think of, when I wasn't sure if I was about to lose them.

I chastised myself for that line of thinking, following easily as I was towed along, having already learned it was best not to resist.

We stopped at another door. Fingers blurred over a keypad, too fast for my eyes to follow, and then we were stepping inside.

The sight that greeted me was jarring. A long workbench was lined with machines of various sizes, pipettes and beakers, and what I recognized from my high school science lab as a centrifuge, all laid out and ready for use.

A woman approached, nodding politely to the guard who released me with a shove, seemingly transferring me to her custody.

"This way, please."

Her tone was polite but firm. She reminded me of the busy school nurse at Jaffrey High whom I had spent so much time avoiding during my school career.

I followed as she led, her black flats and white lab coat making her look very professional. She took me to the back of the laboratory and gestured for me to take a seat on one side of a desk, before she sunk down on the other. I could tell from the movement, too graceful, too lithe, that she was a vampire.

"Rayne Kennedy?"

I nodded, watching fascinated as her fingers moved over the touch screen of a tablet computer, faster than was humanly possible. Somewhere in the back of my mind, behind the anxiety, the fear, I wondered where they got this kind of technology.

"Have you ever been bitten by a vampire, Rayne?"

She asked the question in a monotone, clearly reading from a script. Despite that, I had to take a deep breath to calm myself enough to answer, to lie.

"No, ma'am." Politeness seemed appropriate. She had treated me with respect and I hoped it might foster some kindness in her later, for whatever tests had to be performed on me.

"Do you have vampire abilities, speed, strength, enhanced vision, hearing?"

She trailed off and I shook my head.

"Do you crave blood?"

My mind wandered without my permission to Scarlett's bleeding wrist in my mouth, the satisfaction, the gratification, the headiness of it. I cleared my throat.

"No, ma'am." I hoped I wasn't blushing as hard as I thought I was.

The tests were mundane in comparison to what I had imagined, in comparison to the last time I was here and one of the hooded Government members had decided to find out if I had vampire reflexes by striking me, leaving the scar that still lived on my cheek.

A male scientist joined us, and I tried feebly to catch a ball thrown so fast my eyes couldn't even see it. I also tried to move out of the way quick enough to avoid being hit by it. Again, I failed.

I was a little bruised but mostly okay, though the next test worried me more than the others had. The vampires brought out a steel box, placed it on the table we sat around, and opened it to reveal a silver block. The female scientist asked me if I could touch the metal, a pair of thick gloves already encasing her own hands and arms. I figured it was silver, surprised to learn the myth was true.

Tentatively I reached forward and pressed the pad of my index finger to its surface, holding it there. I waited a few long seconds for it to hurt. It didn't. I thought the metal ought to feel cool, but it was warm against my skin.

"Any burning, irritation, pain?"

I shook my head at the bespectacled woman, deciding the less I told them about myself the less they could use against me, or Scarlett.

"Pick up the block, please."

I did so, holding it in the palm of my hand. The longer it was in contact with my skin it seemed to warm more. After what felt like thirty seconds or so, it felt hot, and I started to worry she was going to make me hold it for so long it would burn.

"Put it back in the case."

Forcing myself not to sigh in relief, I did, setting my warm hand against the cool steel tabletop and hoping that concluded the testing.

A flash of pain, anger, darkness, rushed through me and knocked the breath out of me. I leaned forward and clutched the edge of the table until it had passed and I could breathe again, until the urge to tear the lab to pieces and fight my way out of the bunker to find her died. I hoped we were through because I needed to get back to Scarlett. The feedback I had just received left me sick, hot dread coiled in the pit of my stomach.

I raised my eyes to see the two vampire scientists staring at me expectantly.

"Sorry, thought I had to sneeze."

I wasn't sure where the excuse had come from, but although they continued to study me, it seemed to satisfy them.

"Carl will take a blood sample, then we have one more test before you'll be escorted to the surface, Rayne."

I nodded my understanding, struggling to hold my already frayed nerve. Trying to keep the fear off my face, I rolled up the sleeve of the shirt I had on. Thankfully I'd been dressed when they arrived, or I imagined I would be sitting before them in my pajamas.

I chose the right arm on instinct, eager to hide the scar on my left wrist, where Scarlett drank from me. She had been smart from the beginning, never leaving twin punctures, never using my neck, I hoped it would be enough to save us, but dread was already seeping into me.

The last time my blood had been tested here the scientist performing the test had faked the result, denying I had been bitten by Scarlett in exchange for me keeping the secret of crimes committed by his son. Scarlett had since killed both the scientist and his son, so while there was no one left to expose us, there was also no one left to lie for us now the test was being repeated.

I felt a sharp prick as the needle touched the crook of my elbow, and I jumped. The male scientist looked up at me, shaking my arm gently in his cool fingers before he laid it back on the desk.

"Try to relax, please."

I nodded, the macabre scene from the last time I was here playing over and over in my head. The row of six hooded figures sentencing me to death for stealing the antidote which saved Scarlett's life; the scientist saving my life by revealing I was a hybrid with Delta genes and so should be punished as a vampire; Scarlett ending his with one swift, bloody snap.

The needle slipped into my vein and I kept my eyes on the wall, on the floor, on the lab equipment humming close by, anywhere but on that damning little sliver of metal.

I both regretted and rejoiced in the fact we had shared blood recently, anxious that somehow it would make the result more likely to confirm Scarlett's guilt, but glad that if we were about to be caught, we'd been together so intimately one last time.

I forced myself to get a hold of my thoughts, to swallow down the tears crawling up my throat. It wasn't over, and until it was, I had to keep my head.

My arm stung as the needle was removed. I watched him drop my blood onto a small glass slide, much like the one the previous scientist had put his own blood on to cheat the test. My stomach dropped, and I looked away, wanting to hold on for just a little longer to the fragile happiness we had found—me, Scarlett, Jade, even Camilla—before it was all torn asunder by the Vires Government, again.

"Her blood reacts to the silver, but it's slight. Probably not enough to cause a full reaction."

I whipped my head back around to where the scientists were taking turns hovering over a microscope. Hope shot hot into my chest, and I tried not to cling to it. When they tossed the slide and the vial of my blood into a trash can marked "biochemical waste," it flared. I was dizzy as relief consumed me. Maybe we were going to be okay; maybe I would make it home.

They pored over another slide, talking quietly, back and forth between them, though I heard the confirmation that I had in fact stopped aging. Being eighteen forever was a pleasant surprise.

"The final test is a set of eye drops. Head back, please."

God, I hated eye drops! Nerves about what exactly they would do to me twisted my guts. Fear helped me find my courage.

"What's in the drops, if you don't mind my asking, ma'am?"

The woman paused for a second, before thankfully, she explained.

"There's a silly story about holy water causing a reaction among vampires—not true but derived from the fact that water from a specific ocean can be harmful to us. The drops are from that ocean, diluted down greatly. In a vampire's eyes they would cause a temporary blindness, fifteen minutes maximum."

I was pretty sure I couldn't cheat that test, but I hoped, like the speed and strength, this particular vampire quirk had bypassed me. I tipped my head back as she hovered over me, blinking the first two tries before she was finally able to get one fat droplet into my right eye. I squeezed it closed until the left was done too.

"Can you see?"

Blinking away the excess liquid, I nodded, relieved. Everything was still blurry, but the more I rubbed my eyes the more my vision cleared. The liquid that had seeped onto my cheeks and smeared the back of my hands made them itch. I forced myself not to scratch.

After a quick series of *"how many fingers?"* I was cleared to go. This time, the guards who came to fetch me, hopefully to take me home, greeted me with the traditional black cotton bag over my face. I guessed the first set hadn't for fear of Scarlett's reaction.

I floated along, bounced between them, stumbling up a flight of stairs and bumping into their bodies, an ever-moving stone prison around me. I breathed a sigh of relief, tasting the freshness of the air as we stepped out of the bunker. It was cool on my cheeks, even through the bag. Pearce Tower was familiar to me: the ding of the elevator, the hushed greeting of the doormen, the smell of the thirteenth floor when we arrived home.

The fabric was tugged over my head and Scarlett's hands were on my arms. She was hissing, the sound still strange to me, caught between wanting to kill the men who took me and checking me over. The elevator dinged and, glad the guards were gone, I sagged forward and let her hug me tight.

We stood there in the foyer for a moment that seemed like forever yet passed in the blink of an eye. Relief finally, truly, settled over me at the realization I was home, and it seemed our secrets were still our own. Her hair was soft on my skin, and her body against mine was cool and so familiar. She was breathing, sharp puffs of air against my cheek. Though she was doing her best to hold her emotions back, I felt her relief at my return, and the fear at what they had found, nipping close at its heels.

When finally, her grip loosened, I stepped back, reaching out for her arms to steady myself. I blinked hard again, my eyes taking too long to adjust to the bright lights of the hallway. I missed Scarlett's arms entirely, my fingers grasping at air, but she held me around my biceps, keeping steady on my feet.

"They didn't find anything terrible."

I blinked hard as I spoke, conscious of the sound of Cami and Jade talking quietly somewhere behind Scarlett. The secret we were blood bound was one we kept from our family as well as the Government and city as a whole.

Cool fingers were on my face and I tried to stand still, growing increasingly concerned when, blink after blink, my vision didn't clear.

"They put some ocean water in my eyes."

Scarlett hissed again, and I cut her off.

"No, no, it's fine, it was really dilute, and it didn't affect me to start. I guess it's just a delayed reaction. I can see, it's just...blurry." I left out exactly how blurry.

"What else did they do to you?"

Jade was closer now, her hand squeezing mine. I squeezed back, eager to reassure her.

"Mostly testing my reflexes, testing how my blood reacted to silver, and my eyes with the water."

"Did they hurt you again?" Scarlett's voice was coarse and fraught. I looked at the pale blur I knew was her face, knowing she was remembering the last time my reflexes were tested in the bunker. It had left me with a scar even her blood couldn't heal.

"No, nothing like that. Catching a ball, dodging it, that sort of stuff."

"Why don't we get Rayne to bed, or at least the sofa? I'm sure the vision issues will wear off soon, but we may as well sit while we talk. It's been a long couple of hours."

Cami's voice was closer, and tension hung in the air after she spoke. Scarlett was rigid beneath my hands for a few long seconds before she agreed under her breath. She led me in a direction I could vaguely make out as being toward the living room.

She tugged me down, guiding me to land on the sofa beside her. I pulled my knees up to my chest and leaned back against the cool familiarity of her body. Her arms closed around me, her lips brushed softly against my ear, as she told me in a quiet voice how worried she was.

I tried to kiss her lips, catching what felt like the corner of her mouth before someone sat down, yanked my sneakers off my feet, and tossed them to the floor. I knew it had to be Jade. The thought of Camilla touching my shoes was comical.

"So what else happened?"

Jade's voice was soft and patient, careful, and between her tone and the tension in the room, I knew they had all expected the worst. I imagined Scarlett had handled the situation pretty poorly while I was gone, though the air was so fraught it seemed to be more than just that.

"I went down there, they did the tests..." I tried to look around, searching among the blurs for Camilla. I found her vague outline in the recliner across the room.

"The only really notable thing was they said for sure I'm not aging."

I tried not to sound as pleased as I was by the news. Jade squealed, ecstatic, though it died quickly.

"That's wonderful, Rayne, I was worried but... I don't suppose it matters, you would have stopped soon enough anyway."

I internally cringed at the mention of my scheduled turning, unsure how Scarlett would handle the subject on the back of an already rough day. She continued to thread her fingers through the ends of my hair, my back against her front, her other arm around my waist. She clung to me in a way that hammered home how truly scared she had been when I was taken to the bunker, yet her reply still sounded lazy, devoid of the tension I felt from her.

"Not necessarily."

"Vampires don't age, Scarlett." Jade was almost laughing, I guessed she thought her sister had just spaced out, but Camilla was deadly serious when she spoke.

"They do if they're never turned to begin with. Tell me you're not thinking you can fight this too?"

Scarlett was quiet behind me. The room was quiet.

"It's a death sentence. I don't see a way to avoid it, unless you know something we don't, and why? She's safer, less fragile as one of us, and you can be with her without the constant fear of being found out."

There was something careful and slightly distant in Camilla's voice behind her ever-present abrupt honesty.

"Safer from whom?" Scarlett's tone was icy, and my thoughts flitted to Wilfred Pearce, to the hooded vampire Government. They owned me now as a human, as a hybrid, but as a vampire I would be duty bound to do their bidding or die.

Everyone else must have made the jump too. The room was silent, and Camilla stared at me.

I blinked, startled then relieved to realize my vision was clearing up.

I cleared my throat, suddenly shy in the face of breaking the heavy silence we all seemed to have submitted to.

"I think my eyes are getting better. Hold up some fingers, Cami?"

Three long slim fingers popped up, followed by two, then five, and each time it was easier to count them. Still smiling from my success, I scooted forward and turned to look at the woman I had ached to see since the elevator doors had closed behind me that morning.

"What happened?"

My voice was high, and pitchy with surprise and worry. I shot up to my knees and turned to face Scarlett. I knelt in front of her on the sofa and reached up to touch the dark bruise beneath her left eye.

"It's nothing." Her tone was final, and at any other time I knew she would be avoiding my eyes. Today she stared back at me, and I searched brown and green for any traces of what had happened in my absence, remembering the sudden pain that had stolen my breath for a few seconds in the bunker.

"Did they come back while I was gone? Did you try to come and get me?"

I stuttered out the questions one after the other, beyond upset that she was hurt and still trying to fit together the puzzle when half the pieces were missing, withheld by her apparent desire not to share with me.

"It wasn't the Government, sweetheart. Can we leave it at that, please?"

I knew she was trying. Her jaw was set, she was irritated by my questioning, yet she kept her words pleasant, ever so slightly beseeching.

"You're hurt." My tone was soft, careful but unyielding.

I searched her face, which was becoming clearer each second as the eye drops wore off.

"Was it...your father?"

My mouth asked the question as my brain formed it, and this time she looked away, confirming the answer for me.

Jade caught my eye and nodded ever so slightly before her brown eyes fell to the floor.

"I have to go to work."

Surprise that she was leaving me so soon shot through me. Instead of following, I let her go, only then noticing she was already changed into her typical outside clothes, makeup and hair fixed perfectly.

"You could stay tonight. Rayne just got back and it's already late!" Jade called after her, voicing my thoughts. I knew first hand that Scarlett struggled to deny her sister, but tonight she was resolute.

"Perhaps if I'd been working more to begin with, she wouldn't have been taken in the first place."

The words were sharper than she usually used with Jade. I could sense her restlessness, the storm rising inside her and her desperation to get away from us all, to a place where she could unleash it. I was ready to tell Jade to let her go, but Camilla spoke first.

"She has a point, Scar. No need to bite her head off."

Scarlett's dark eyes burned, and her fury was hot. For a split second I worried I would lunge across the coffee table and strangle Camilla myself. As quick as it came, the emotion left me, though I knew from looking at her it still raged inside Scarlett.

"Don't you dare defend her to me. I spent my entire life defending her. Your sudden interest in getting into her bed doesn't give you the right. She's a child."

She spat the words. Jade looked like she was going to cry, and I was torn between watching the car wreck taking place before me and comforting her. I couldn't feel anything from Scarlett down our connection, but I knew she needed to leave, now.

Camilla was on her feet and stalking toward us, so I jumped to mine, my vision blurring at the edges ever so slightly before it cleared again.

"Rayne's a child. She's eighteen years old. Jade's nineteen and she's been nineteen for how many years? Pot calling the kettle wouldn't you say?"

"I trusted you. I let you into this family, and this is how you repay me?"

Scarlett was winding up, and as much as I trusted her, as much as I knew deep down she loved Camilla and had put herself in harm's way for her and her siblings multiple times, she wasn't in a place to have this conversation right now. The tension I had walked into on my return from the bunker started to make sense.

"Cami, maybe we should do this another time..."

I tried to interject but it was too late.

"I just didn't expect this from you. Now I'm unavailable you suddenly want my little sister?"

Scarlett didn't seem to notice me, intent on getting answers from her former lover.

"Oh please, get over yourself, if anyone is jealous here it's you! Why can't you see that we're happy? It was unexpected and unplanned, but we work in a way you and I never did—maybe because Jade's not psychotic!"

"You don't even know her!"

The volume was rising, and I stepped between them, one hand on Scarlett's arm. I pushed her backward gently, hoping she might go with me to our room, anywhere. She didn't budge. It crossed my mind to compel her, but as livid as she was, I thought better of it.

"Scarlett, stop it, please!" Jade shot to her feet. "Cami, you too. Scarlett, I love you, you're my big sister and I need you, I will always need you, but I care about Camilla too. She's right, this is still new but we're happy. I never meant to hurt you."

"I'm not hurt, I'm worried." Scarlett's voice thawed. Much of the venom seeped away but it was still cool, hard.

"Maybe we can take a break to think about what's been said here, and talk some more later?" I tried tentatively.

Scarlett studied Jade and then stared Camilla down for a few more seconds. Camilla looked back, unflinching.

"Be safe tonight."

Scarlett's words to me were quiet, and her lips lingered against my cheek for barely a second before she was gone. I didn't hear the elevator ding.

"Did she leave?"

Jade nodded.

"Window." Camilla supplied as she rolled her eyes. "Someone's feeling dramatic."

"Were you guys fighting while I was gone?"

Camilla nodded. Jade slung her arms around my neck.

"I'm so sorry, Rayne. You've had a horrible day, and you come home to all this. Scarlett's just...being Scarlett. She never wants me to grow up."

"Well, her and Cami did used to be...a thing." I tried to be tactful. "I can see how it's maybe hard to hear you two are dating now?"

Camilla glared at me.

"On the flip side, I'm happy you guys are happy," I added, guessing my question would remain unanswered.

"We just need to give her time," Jade concluded sadly.

I untangled myself from her and plopped back down on the sofa, tired from the events of the day—night—and anxious about the hell I knew Scarlett was creating wherever she was.

The thought spurred a memory.

"There was something I wanted to ask you guys about. My friend from the Fringe needs some antibiotics. Her sister is sick, a lot of the people out there are. Where do you get drugs from?"

"You don't." Camilla cut me off. "It's not your business, don't make it."

She got up, clearly still irritated from the exchange with Scarlett, and disappeared down the hall in the direction of Jade's room.

Jade seemed glad of the distraction.

"We have a lot of medicine here in the tower, and we never have issues getting more."

"Do you get sick?" I couldn't help but wonder.

"Not often, but the staff does, so... We could get some, but I've no idea how we'd take it to them. I hate to think of them suffering out there." She paused. "And I would like to look for Christian, just to know she's okay."

Jade's inclusion of herself into the plan made me nervous and it soothed my anxiety about trying to accomplish it alone.

"Couldn't we get into trouble for this?"

She nodded. "Probably, but we could make up a story, maybe that we visited the Fringe and dropped the pills by mistake or something?"

"I think they need more than a bottle or two."

Her hazel eyes were determined, alight with the adventure I knew she craved but so seldom got to have.

"We can figure something out."

Loath to deny her and loath to spend my evening alone wondering what Scarlett was doing, I nodded my agreement.

Chapter Four

SINCE MY RETURN from the bunker, Scarlett had been fanatical in her quest to avoid turning me, convinced now that we were running out of time. She was right; we had little over two months left to complete the order, though as the unrest in Vires around my existence as a hybrid grew, it felt shorter and shorter each day.

She was gone more than she was home, leaving me chronically lonely, homesick for her, for the messed-up simplicity that had been our life before the bottom fell out, again.

She kept her emotions away from me always, and I only had an insight into her turmoil, her determination to overcome this, and her fear of failure when she sat down to play the piano early in the morning after she returned home and thought I was sleeping.

I missed her, and I ached for her, for her to spill my blood and her own, for her to let our connection flicker back to life. For her cool body against mine to be peaceful not tense while she lay there lost in her schemes.

She'd kissed me goodbye and disappeared into the elevator a while ago, leaving me lingering in the living room, staring at her piano, replaying the many memories we had together with it and searching for a solution of my own. Anything to take some of the weight.

Jade appeared in the doorway already wrapped in a heavy winter coat, fur lining the hood and a thick scarf peeking out from its collar.

"Do you think it would really be so bad if I just became a vampire?" The words tumbled out.

I knew we ought to focus on the task at hand, but I had gone so far down the road of what-ifs and how-abouts that I had to see this train of thought through. I trusted Jade enough to share it with her.

"I don't know." She unzipped her coat and sidled over to the sofa. She sat down opposite me as she sensed my need to talk. I let out a breath I felt I'd held for days, because finally, finally I was going to talk about this rather than chasing it around endlessly in my head.

"I think it would be complicated in a different way than your being a human, or I guess a hybrid now, is."

I nodded for her to explain.

"I mean, your relationship with Scarlett would be no big deal and we wouldn't have to worry all the time about you getting squished or bitten or just...dying."

I couldn't help but giggle.

"Gee, thanks."

She laughed, an apology in her lingering smile.

"I mean, you are sort of breakable..."

In comparison to the vampires, she wasn't wrong.

"So that's the pros of turning me. What are the cons?" I wanted to hear it from someone else's point of view, someone a little more impartial, more reasonable, than Scarlett.

"Well..."

She hesitated, and I could tell she was choosing her words carefully.

"You're already kind of famous in the city. Everyone is eager to see what you'll be like as a vampire since you're the only hybrid in so long, maybe forever."

I doubted Scarlett and I were the first vampire and human to ever share blood as we did but said nothing.

"Then there's the fact that you're associated with Scarlett. They probably expect you to be like her, or maybe they want to see if you end up like me, for all intents and purposes a failure in their eyes."

She laughed a self-deprecating little laugh and I reached out to take her hand and squeeze it in mine.

"Jade, being a good person, having a moral code, and caring about the fate of those around you doesn't make you a failure."

"As a Delta vampire in Vires, a daughter of the most powerful family in the city, no less, it sort of does."

The words were sad, and I knew she was right. She cleared her throat and returned to her explanation.

"Aside from the Government expectation, there's my father too. He's the one who set Scarlett down this path. He's tried the same with me, though she never really let him, and eventually I became more useful as a means to manipulate her than I ever would have been as someone like her. He'll probably be interested in you too, for one reason or another."

I nodded.

"That's what she's so afraid of, isn't it? That's why she's completely against turning me?"

Jade shrugged, her lips tugging down at the corners. I knew the sisters had been distant recently, perhaps more so than they had ever been, and I knew it was hurting them both. They needed to resolve the Camilla issue soon.

"I don't know. I think so, but there's also the fact you probably won't live up to what the Government hopes for you and that's not going to lead to anything good. Plus, I think she sort of loves you for your humanness."

That made me smile. I wanted to ask what she meant, but it didn't seem like the time.

"I'm just worried she's making herself crazy trying to figure this out. She's gone all the time doing who knows what. When I asked, she said her reputation is going to be important and that we're going to need *power and fear,* and anything else we can get if we're going to find a way out... I believe her, but part of me also thinks she's just using it as an excuse to take everything out on people..."

I was saddened by the thought, saddened by the knowledge that Scarlett was out in the city right now punishing and torturing, and more than likely having a wonderful time doing it.

"It's probably both," Jade agreed grimly.

I loved her in that moment. I had loved her long before I really knew her well enough, thanks to Scarlett's feelings for her reflected to me because we were blood bound. But now, she was one of the few people, maybe the only person in the world, who understood what it was to truly love Scarlett Pearce.

After a long few seconds she broke the silence.

"Are you ready to go?"

I agreed though in reality I wasn't ready at all.

"Do you have it?"

Long slim fingers reached into her left coat pocket. She pulled out a sandwich bag stuffed with large white pills, before producing another from the right.

"Wow...and no one will notice they're gone?"

She shrugged.

"Maybe the head of staff, but she'll just order more and probably assume they got misplaced or someone took them without asking. Word shouldn't get back to my dad or Scarlett, we should be good."

"So, we just take a car down there, walk around some. If anyone asks, we were going to see what all the fuss was about. You hide them when you can, and I let Zoe know?"

Jade nodded, standing and zipping up her jacket. "Yep, sounds right."

I got to my feet, letting out a long breath and reaching up to bop her nose with a fingertip as I went, creating a much-needed break in the tension, I went to fetch my own coat, glad that in the midst of all the mess, we could at least get the medicine to those who so desperately needed it.

THE CAR RIDE was mostly silent. The standard issue black car with dark tinted windows took us out to the Fringe at Jade's request. Unlike when I rode with Scarlett, the divider between the front and the back of the vehicle stayed down. Maybe Jade was too polite to raise it. Either way, we had no time to talk.

Jade asked the driver to wait, and then we slipped out, boots crunching in the few inches of snow that had settled over Vires the previous night. It was already dark, the sun long gone down, and I tugged Jade close to me. Linking my arm through the crook of her elbow, I wondered if I had been wrong to bring her here. The echo of Scarlett's feeling for her sister, the unconditional love and the overbearing protectiveness lingered in me, clouding my own feelings. I had to tell myself to shake the thought off and focus on the task at hand.

"So, we'll walk a little, hide it, find Zoe, or Joseph, or someone, then we'll go back to the car, go home, and never say a word about this."

My breath billowed out in clouds. When Jade replied no vapor escaped her lips.

"Yes. Cami said she wouldn't be back from her thing until midnight at the earliest, so we should have plenty of time."

I squeezed her arm and we continued down the streets. Jade led me easily. Everything looked the same, especially under the thin covering of snow, and I knew without her I wouldn't be able to find my way.

"Where is everyone?"

Jade's voice was quiet, hushed now. Some of the little shacks had dim light shining from inside, some were totally dark, but unlike my previous visit, the streets were empty.

"I don't know. Let's check the square, and if no one's there we can just leave them somewhere?"

Jade shook her head.

"The humans have a tough life here, and there's corruption inside the Fringe as much as there is in Vires as a whole."

When I looked at her, questioning how she knew such a thing, what she even meant, she shrugged.

"Christian told me. They have so little and they trade and barter a lot. Imagine if the wrong person found all those pills, imagine the kind of prices they could have people pay to help their sick loved ones. We have to make sure they get into the right hands."

I agreed instantly.

We turned a corner and the brighter lights of the square up ahead greeted us, bodies already visible silhouetted in its glow, and lots of them.

"Wow, the protest ramped up..."

I barely got to finish my sentence. Jade tripped, making me jump, the eerily dim lighting and the forbidden nature of our visit getting to me. Luckily, I caught her using our joined arms.

"Sorry."

I was about to brush off her apology but something more pressing caught my attention. A foreboding energy radiated from the gathered crowd. My stomach sunk from it, the lead of nervousness settling heavy inside me.

Jade tugged my arm and I slowed my pace, moving quietly to lessen the crunching of the snow beneath our feet as we approached the edge of the crowd.

Jade heard it long before me, stopping in her tracks. I tugged her forward, determined to find Zoe, Joseph, Christian, anyone we could trust, and drop our cargo then leave.

I heard her voice before I saw her. Scarlett's voice found me through the bodies and we ground to a halt again. We stood on the edge of the square. I couldn't see her through the throngs of people. The sparse lights illuminated Jade's pale face as we stared at each other.

"We need to go."

She looked sick, and I wondered how much more she had heard that my human ears couldn't detect.

"Scarlett?"

I asked the question I already knew the answer to, wanting absolute confirmation, hoping, somehow, I was wrong.

She nodded.

"She's... Rayne, we need to go. We shouldn't be here, she'll be so upset if she finds out, and neither of us needs to see this."

Her big hazel eyes were beseeching, her cold hand tugging lightly on mine, urging me back to the car. I thought of other brown eyes, in the cell across from mine in the bunker, keeping me sane, explaining how the city worked, hateful and guarded as she explained she needed to save her sister.

"I have to help Zoe. You go back."

My blood turned to ice at my own words. As much as I meant them earnestly, I dreaded that she would leave me here alone.

"I'm not leaving you," she hissed. "Let's just find someone quickly and try to stay on the edge of the crowd?"

A scream ripped through the air, followed by another, and another. By the time the final one had died to horrible hacking sobs, I was shaking, adrenaline, fear, repulsion taking me over.

"Okay."

I tried to steel myself, to disconnect myself from the fact that it was the woman I loved at the center of the crowd, probably with a whip, a knife, a cane in her hands, eliciting those sounds from some poor soul, and probably loving it.

As we moved around the perimeter of the square it was quiet, unnervingly so, more than it should be with so many bodies packed into a small space. I spotted a trend. The outer ring of the crowd appeared to consist of the elderly and children. Jade seemed to notice it too.

"Anyone we need is going to be further in. They put the old and young furthest away from her." The realization shattered me.

Her words were a whisper, and I saw so much of my own emotion reflected in her eyes. We just had to finish this, finish it and get out. I squeezed her hand.

"Don't let go of me?"

She nodded and before she could protest, I pushed forward, squeezing between two small bodies and journeying inwards, until we were close enough that I could hear Scarlett speaking.

"By my count that's twelve, and still my audience breaks curfew. Who's next? Eeny, meeny, miny...moe."

Her laugh was so foreign to me but still familiar. It turned my stomach. There was a scuffle up front, and I tried to look for the source of it. I tried not to hear, but it was impossible. We were about four rows back from her now, and I was glad my short stature meant I still couldn't see her if my eyes did wander.

"Rayne."

I jumped at the sound of my name, gripping Jade close to me, before I saw Joseph looking down at me with wide eyes. His dreads had grown back some, though they still stuck out awkwardly after Scarlett had chopped them off. I tried not to stare at the spot on his chest where I knew she had left those awful words.

"Rayne." He was shaking my arm lightly. "She's got Hannah, Zoe's sister."

Dread swallowed me.

"The sick one."

"No, she's the middle sister. She's got her, Rayne."

He was looking at me like he expected me to do something about it, and my heart thumped hard, battering against my ribcage, bruising me from the inside.

"Okay... Okay."

I turned to Jade.

"Give him the pills."

She fumbled twice with her left pocket and, impatient, I reached into her right. I yanked out the overstuffed bag and shoved the package of pills into Joseph's hands.

"Call this off. Get everyone inside?"

He nodded, making a request of his own.

"Help her, please?"

A scream ripped through the air. Trying to cement my resolve, I headed for the center of the square, ready to meet the side of Scarlett I tried so hard to forget.

"You can't!"

Jade hissed the words in my ear, dragging me back with an arm around my waist. I struggled in her grip, but she was too strong.

"Jade..."

She cut me off.

"You're still lower status than her, even as a hybrid. If you disobey her in public, she'll have to punish you, or make a scene. If she doesn't, she'll end up in trouble."

Crap.

"We got them the pills, we did that. They're leaving, she won't hurt anyone else, but we have to go, right now."

She was frantic, and I clung to her hands, shimmying out of her grip though I stayed right in front of her.

"I owe Zoe, okay? I have to try."

She was shaking her head, and I understood. From her perspective this could only end horribly, but I knew something nobody in Vires did, except for Scarlett and me. Maybe, just maybe, it could save Hannah.

"It's not worth it. We did good, we got the pills."

Jade's panic felt far away, as I planned my next move. Zoe's guarded eyes, her calling me "Miss," the look of disgust on her face haunted me. I loved Scarlett, despite this. I understood why she had come to be like this even if I couldn't condone it, and a part of me loved her darkness, her depravity, her brokenness, but seeing it enacted turned my stomach and filled me with guilt. I loved her, but I was nothing like her, and I would save Hannah and prove that to myself, and to Zoe, even if she would, hopefully, never know I was involved.

"Go back to the car."

"Are you crazy?" Jade tightened her grip on my arm.

"Jade, please don't force me." I searched her dark eyes, appealing to her morals, and as I knew she would, she released my hand.

"You two have enough coming between you right now, don't add this. Go back to the car, please?"

A fat wet tear rolled down her pale cheek and I forced myself to hold strong.

"Go before Camilla gets home. I'll be there soon, okay?"

She lingered for a moment longer, her shaking hand tight around mine before, finally, she let me go. In a second, she was gone.

I surged forward. There was no time left to think. Hannah was crying, loudly, and nothing I could do prepared me for the sight that greeted me.

She was sitting in the stained red snow, a long deep cut across her chest, maybe a lash, her dark hair disheveled. Horrible strangled sobs racked her body and her hands covered her face. Around her there were several red, slushy piles where the snow had been stomped into the ground. In one of the piles, a body lay, unmoving.

Scarlett stepped toward Hannah and into my focus, beautiful and macabre in her black dress and black leather jacket ensemble. Her bloody bare feet and crimson hands turned the picture to one of horror.

"Please..."

The crush cleared rapidly. A few bodies lingered around me, though I hardly felt their presence.

When Hannah moved her hands from her face and held them up in surrender, a long dark gash ran from the corner of her mouth down to her chin. The bloody knife was still in Scarlett's hands.

"Don't you want to match?"

Her back was to me, but I heard the thrill in her voice, rich and dark with an edge that chilled me to my bones.

Hannah was stuttering out her response, but Scarlett didn't seem to care.

"But you were so brave, coming out here, leading this great, big protest." She punctuated every plosive heavily, taunting her, as she crouched before the girl who couldn't have been older than me, in the snow.

"You wanted attention, well, now you have mine."

She leaned in so close to her that for a second, I thought she was going to kiss her. My body seemed to move of its own accord, pushing through the stragglers until I could see Scarlett in profile, the pad of one finger running down the knife's edge, as she inhaled deeply at the scent of all the blood.

Gore stained the cheek I could see, and when she pulled back, I forced myself to focus, to concentrate and try to calm myself enough to compel her. I ended up screaming at her mentally to stop.

"It's important we finish what we start, and you started this, so now I'm going to finish it." She raised the knife.

She hadn't even noticed me.

"Smile, Hannah."

Hannah screamed, and I felt like the sound was my own, all the breath leaving my lungs as the knife continued to move up and up and up to her face. I silently begged Scarlett to stop, in the same second that I cursed her and damned her. I wished for her just for once, to fight the darkness. I could be happy, if she could only stop.

The knife dropped from her hands. I sucked in a huge breath before it billowed back out of me, smoky in the cold air.

Mismatched eyes found me immediately, and even from twenty feet away I could see they were alight, bright and full with the thrill of it all. She reached for the knife and it was easier this time to stop her. Her hand stalled halfway there, and she growled.

Determination shot me in the chest and squared my shoulders. I could do this; I would stop her.

Hannah's sobs were the only sound piercing the night, the square all but deserted now, the white snow sullied, ground under too many pairs of boots.

Scarlett's frustration flashed through me, chased by her blood lust, her hunger for it, the sick pleasure still alive in her chest from a night of tormenting and maiming.

Her voice was in my head telling me to leave. I knew I could resist, because now it *counted*, and I was right. Her emotions railed against me, telling me to stop, to kneel, but I stood my ground until Hannah's sobs quieted to heavy, wet-sounding pants, blood seeping from her mouth grotesquely with each breath. Scarlett's eyes never left mine.

I felt her betrayal and it almost cracked me. She reached for the knife again and took it into her hands before I controlled myself, and though she held it, her arm stayed down at her side.

"Seems like it's your lucky night, little girl."

She hissed the words and even without feeling her, I knew she was livid.

Scarlett released her hold on the neck of Hannah's shirt, tossing her back into the snow like a doll, and she lay there. I had to fight my own mind as memories assaulted me: another state, another town, another life, where I was the one on the floor.

"Princess." She swaggered toward me, her eyes bright. A game was still afoot, and Scarlett was still playing. I didn't fear her directly, but I feared for our relationship, depending on how this night concluded.

"Scarlett." The strength in my voice surprised even me, and she smiled, reaching for me tentatively down our connection. When I reached back it blazed, the flames swallowing me and stealing my breath.

A tanned hand was extended to me, that wicked smile still kissing her mouth beneath wild eyes and cheeks stained in blood. I understood her as much as I didn't know what to make of her in that moment, but after a few seconds, I slipped my hand into her waiting one anyway.

With a whoosh I was swung, spilling through the air before I landed on her back, and then I was flying, her dark hair tickling my cheek as she ran. I gripped tight around her neck, my heart beating hard, not slowing down even by the time we scaled the side of the tower. The experience was particularly terrifying, despite the vise grip that closed over my hands, holding me in place, until we hurtled up onto the balcony and then into her room.

She closed the large French doors behind us, shutting out the frigid air of the city, and turned to me, breathing hard.

Her irises swirled, one brilliant green the other brown, and we studied each other across the space for a moment, standing three feet apart.

Slowly, our connection fluttered back to life, and I hadn't realized she had been quiet, too preoccupied with running, which at vampire speed was more like flying.

Her anger found me first, hot and vibrant, slick and spilling into every part of me, all-consuming. Beneath it, when I finally wrestled it aside, the thrill of her evening lingered. She watched me breathe it in, the frenzied, heady rush of power, the breaking, the blood.

I surged forward and kissed her hard, bruising, unsure if the desire was mine or hers. Now it was happening I had no desire to stop, to go back, to think or talk about everything that had unfolded since Jade and I had gone to the Fringe.

She cupped my face in her cool hands, and I twisted one of mine in her hair. I pulled her head back harder than I had ever dared or thought to and pushed her back until she was sitting on the bed. She smiled up at me, that same wicked grin, and I hated it as much as I wanted to taste it. She grabbed my wrist and pulled me closer. She didn't stop when our bodies collided, pulling my arm up to her mouth and opening the scar on my wrist in a way that was more painful than it had ever been. I grit my teeth, and watched my own fingers close tight around her neck.

"Now yours."

My voice was dark, demanding, and she panted under my grip despite having no need for air. She sank her teeth into her own arm, leaving less of a puncture and more of a bloody tear. She looked up at me, a challenge in her eyes, blood dripping down her fingers and onto the bedsheets.

I tugged away, holding my own bloody wrist, and crawled up the bed. I settled near the pillows, fascinated with the feeling of leading this strange dance when she followed. She took my wrist, killing the thought to resist as she pulled it to her lips. Her tongue played around the wound, lapping up the blood that spilled but not taking more.

Our connection cleared, static leaving it every second. I loved her and loathed her and wanted to consume her completely. I jerked her wrist up to my mouth and took a huge swallow, sucking hard on the gash her teeth had made. The blood made my head spin. She was still licking around my wrist, her dark eyes transfixed on me, as if she was waiting.

I pulled my arm away from her and kissed her, pouring every little bit of the conflict, the disgust, the guilt and the anger I felt into it, because she was terrifying and dark and twisted, and I loved her irrevocably. My tongue was in her mouth, my lips between her teeth, and she was pliable, yielding in a new and satisfying way. I hiked up her dress, barely breaking from my assault on her mouth, her neck, her bloody cheeks, to drag the tight material up slim thighs before I shoved her underwear aside to feel her. She was warmer there, slick and wanting, and I shoved two fingers into her, pulling back just in time to see her eyes darken almost to black.

This wasn't me, but it was. Somewhere on some base level, it was everything I needed, perhaps to process, perhaps to understand, perhaps just to live through this moment, through once again being confronted with the parts of Scarlett I tried to hide from myself.

She watched me watch her, bringing her own bloody wrist to her mouth. Those motile dark eyes dared me. I pressed into her harder.

When she moved her hand away, I smelled the blood, saw it in her mouth, around her lips, and dribbling down her chin. Goose bumps rose across the tops of my arms. Struggling for a second before I found my balance on my elbow, I wrapped one hand tight around her throat, the other still between her legs, before I leaned down to claim my prize. It was rust and saline and something else entirely.

After I had swallowed it down my tongue lathed her lips, her face, her chin, my grip forming a vise on her neck while my fingers pushed into her. My thumb had been rubbing her and I pushed down hard, eager for a reaction I couldn't name. The moan that spilled into my mouth was long and loud and unbridled in a way I had never heard from her. I was an instant addict.

I was losing myself to this, to the hot, sentient need just to have her, to own her and bend her, and understand her. To believe just for a moment that this could last. Perhaps I could be strong enough to make her stop her sadistic ways, perhaps I could be dark enough to join her.

Struck by the thought, I yanked away from her and climbed off the bed, stumbling on my feet. Her silent question chased me, a sliver of insecurity that pained me and gratified me in equal parts.

I shrugged off my coat, kicked off my boots, jeans and underwear, and rifled through her nightstand until I pulled something else up my hips, something she had worn for me before but never the other way.

"Okay?"

I growled out the word, hating to ask. I just wanted to have her. I was already climbing back onto the bed as she licked her lips, eyes lingering on the toy between my legs before she nodded. She moved to sit up and I pushed her back down, kissing her hard.

One hand moved between our bodies, the other pulling me forward, her nails digging painfully into the soft flesh of my behind as she guided the toy inside her. She bit my lip hard and I tasted my own blood. I wanted to hurt her in that moment, and it terrified me, sobering me from whatever frenzied haze we were in so much I stopped moving, panting down at her, scared.

All her insecurity assaulted me, her wondering, her fear, and I couldn't understand how she could ever believe there was a world where I wouldn't want her. As broken as she was, laid bare underneath me, her dark hair spilled on a black pillow, there was something so beautiful about Scarlett off balance.

I let the moment linger, studying her. I pushed back so I was kneeling between her legs, and the first slivers of panic radiated from her.

I raked my eyes down her body, the dress hiked up crudely around her middle, the scrap of black lace she passed off as panties stretched and shoved aside, the slick purple dildo still buried in her.

"What do you want, sweetheart?"

They were her words in my mouth, but I felt no bashfulness at using them. She squirmed beneath me. Her discomfort tasted like ash in my mouth and I swallowed it down, consumed by the sudden confidence I had found in having the tables turned.

I already knew what she wanted. Her desire burned against mine and my stomach clenched at the mere thought, but what I wanted more was this: Scarlett deconstructed, Scarlett laid open, Scarlett for once in a position of insecurity. I wanted her to trust me, and tonight, I wanted her to belong to me.

"You."

The word was coarse, breathy and broken.

I ran my tongue along the pad of my thumb before I lowered it to rub against her, bumping the toy still inside her. Her hips canted, and she keened softly under her breath.

"What do you want?"

I rubbed her slowly, torturously, refusing to move more than that. The fire in her dark eyes flamed, and I could feel on some level she ached for this too, needed it, found it cathartic as much as she feared it the loss of control.

"Fuck me."

It was a command uttered through gritted teeth, and I laughed, the sound seeming strangely foreign even to me. Moving back ever so slightly, I let the dildo fall out of her. It landed wet against her thigh, and I marveled at the slickness that chased it.

"What do you want?" I asked her for the third time, painfully aware this was a pivotal moment in our relationship. Though I didn't understand my desire for it, I knew I needed it, absolutely.

"Fuck me...Mistress."

The last word was a whisper. Her eyes were round and kissed with the first wetness of tears. Something shot through me and I almost moaned at the feeling. I jerked my hips forward, bumping the head of the toy against her, and heard the breath rushing out of her lungs.

"Again."

I rubbed her slowly, pushing the toy along sensitive flesh but not inside.

She whined softly, the first beautiful note in a symphony I had somehow suddenly learned to conduct.

"Just...fuck me? Please?"

She was almost begging, her eyes dark but soft and her hips twitching.

I laughed, slicking my tongue over my lips because I longed to taste her like this, but first, I wanted to hear her say it.

I pinched her hip hard and she moaned long and loud, grinding down against the toy, almost enough to push it inside her before I moved back.

"Scarlett." Her name was heroin on my tongue. "Lie still, look me in the eyes and ask me for what you need."

She hated that word, *need*; I could feel her objection to it choking me, but now, like this, she did need me. And as quick as the fire came, it died, and she was still beneath me, breathing hard for five long seconds into the silence.

"Please, fuck me..."

I pushed the tip of it into her before I pulled it out. Her head was thrown back, a sound lost between pain and pleasure leaving her lips as I watched her stomach muscles clench, still rubbing her slowly.

When she looked back at me the eye contact was electric, and I could already taste the high of my victory.

"Fuck me...Mistress."

I was on her within a second, kissing her mouth, her tear-damp cheeks, and rocking my hips into her over and over and over.

My mouth moved against her ear as her nails clawed at my back, and I listened to my own voice telling her I loved her, telling her that she was mine, and I felt the words echo, engraving themselves on my soul.

She went rigid underneath me, and then her body was slack. I shoved a hand down between us and carried on, rubbing her and moving over her until she came for me again and then again, and finally, I was too exhausted to carry on.

I tried to shimmy out of the harness, but gave up, collapsing half on top of her as she clung to me.

Her cool fingers struggled with the straps. She was still shaking as I buried my face in her neck. She finally got the thing off me and wrapped her arms around me tight. We clung to each other and I loved her. As much as I wasn't ready to process so many things that had happened, so much of what she had done, she was small against me, soft and open, and she was everything.

She turned my bloody wrist over and rubbed her own against it. I knew when she was done we would both be healed and only I would keep my scar.

Her fingers were soft through my hair, as sleep came to take me. The last thing I heard was her whispered apology.

I WOKE UP stiff and sore, blinding white light streaming in through the balcony doors. I looked to my left, and Scarlett blinked back at me with wary dark eyes. Her face was still bloody. The events of the previous night rushed back to me, a horror reel: Hannah and her screaming and blood on the snow. The memory spilled into something darker, something more erotic, as I recounted Scarlett's oddly colored eyes swirling like galaxies, looking up at me, and *please, Mistress.*

I was slightly embarrassed but strangely unashamed. I knew we had so much to talk about, so much to work through, but more than anything I wanted to know where Scarlett was at.

"You okay?"

My voice was scratchy with sleep and I cleared my throat, sure I looked positively terrible with my sex-ruffled hair and the blood still caked on my chin, a mixture of hers and mine. Scarlett was a vision, as always, dark hair and tan skin and the aloofness she wore almost constantly.

"Are you?"

I nodded, and she relaxed against the pillows slightly.

"Shower?" I questioned tentatively, as I reached for her at the same time. I tasted a little of her mood, careful, pensive, before it shimmered away, and she was pulling me to my feet. I followed her, unbothered by my nakedness, and waited patiently while she shed her remaining clothes and stepped under the hot spray.

The water ran pink. The blood faded from her face and she reached up to wipe the last of it away. She stepped into me and we ended up hugging, my chin on her shoulder, her body small against me, bare in every sense, and I knew this was our healing.

Finally, we parted, and I watched her through the steam, missing her cool body against the heat of the water, as she washed her hair. Free of makeup, free of pretense, she was the woman I loved. Last night had driven me deeper, forcing me to confront the side of her I hated. She turned to wash her front under the water, and I studied the thick scars she used to be so secretive about. They were displayed to me now in a move that had become easy, where once this kind of vulnerability was earth-shatteringly hard for her.

I thought of Wilfred Pearce and what he had done, how he had twisted her and who she might have been before him, without him. He was a distant specter, hovering near but far, and I knew eventually he would make his presence felt again in our lives. I knew Scarlett feared that day even more than I did.

She was soft like this, small and battle-scarred, I thought, but something dark lived inside her, something sadistic and power hungry, something that had been there too long, or she loved too much, to ever eke out. Like most creatures she craved love and acceptance, and I knew I succeeded in providing her with only one of the two. Flawed as I was, she loved me unconditionally and without restraint.

Last night had been a bloody, filthy romp through the world in her shoes, a taste of the darkness out of her mouth, and with it had come a new understanding. I could understand that she was trained, abused, brainwashed to become an enforcer for the Government. I could even understand that over many years, my lifetime multiple times over, she had learned to enjoy the role. The broken had become the breaker, and she was committed to never going back. As much as it made me feel guilty, dirty, from the very first night she had appeared in my life, I had been drawn to her dark side as much as her light. A moth to her flame, a lamb to her lion, because split bare, with caked blood under her nails and death in her eyes, she was a force of nature. I'd never thought to run, just hoped I'd be lucky enough to have her crash over me, and she had.

I loved all of her, but I didn't think I could ever accept what she did, maybe because of my own personal guilt, maybe because of my morals. I would never watch her hurt people with pride, or affection, yet that was exactly what she had been trained to do. It was how she had lived for so long, one of the main ways she gained approval from her father, and society.

She turned to me with water dripping from her thick dark lashes, looking innocent, washed clean of her sins from the previous night.

I let her switch our positions, my hands resting easily on her cool hips while she washed my hair, rubbed the last of her blood from my face. When she kissed me, I let myself float away from the questions, from my worries, and met her halfway down our connection, warm and soft and unusually shy in the face of our mutual feelings.

She pushed me against the cold tile of the wall, but made love to me gently, kissing the echoes of the previous night from my skin, righting the balance of our relationship though I knew something had shifted irrevocably.

We didn't talk, we just felt. Being close to her soothed me, left me breathing easier as I followed her through the motions of dressing, letting her kiss my cheek, running my fingers through her still wet hair, before we made our way out into the hall on our way to breakfast.

Jade looked up from the bar in the kitchen, a tall glass of orange juice in front of her untouched, her skin paler than usual, heavy circles under her eyes tinged red.

Scarlett moved to the refrigerator. Guessing she was making breakfast today, I sat down beside Jade, muttering a quiet good morning.

"You look terrible, when was the last time?" Scarlett demanded without looking up.

Jade let her head fall onto one arm that rested on the counter.

"I don't want to talk about it."

Scarlett cracked eggs into a pan, and I watched the exchange between the sisters with interest, glad they were finally communicating.

"Well, we can talk about it or we could talk about what you and Rayne were doing in the Fringe last night."

I groaned inwardly. I had been so sure Scarlett hadn't noticed Jade before I sent her away.

"I took some medicine to my friend, Zoe. Her sister is sick—not the one you left mauled in the snow, the younger one."

There was a trace of confrontation in my voice I hadn't meant to put there. It was a discussion I had hoped to avoid, at least until after breakfast, still content with the glow of the shower in my system, but I was loath to let Jade take the heat for what had essentially been my idea.

The eggs sizzled in the pan, and Scarlett turned from them momentarily, no doubt surprised by my interruption, though she let it pass.

"So when did you last drink, Jade?"

Finally, her earlier question made sense.

"I'm fine, Scarlett, please..."

Jade did sound sick, and as much as I understood her reluctance, I began to worry for her too. I had noticed she was pale last night, but preoccupied with our mission, and the fallout when it all went to hell, I hadn't thought much of it.

"How often do you guys usually have to um...drink?"

Scarlett snickered, and Jade thumped her head on her arm, mumbling something under her breath.

"It's different for everyone, Princess. For pleasure, often, for sustenance, very little. Jade gets by on about once every few months, though she is an extreme example."

"And what about you?"

She drank from me a few times a week, but I was suddenly insecure that she was also getting blood elsewhere, and somewhat confused by my own jealousy over the thought.

Scarlett flipped the eggs onto the plate and the toaster popped. A second later I jumped as a plate was set down before me, and one before Jade, then Scarlett was leaning against the counter, amusement in her eyes as she studied me.

"Every few weeks, but again, I'm an extreme example, opposite end of the spectrum though." I knew she'd felt my jealousy. I forced myself to hold her eyes. Her fondness for me washed over me.

For a moment I tried to do the math, tried to work out how many humans per year it would take to sustain the vampires of Vires, knowing each one except myself was killed after they served their purpose. I didn't even know where to start.

Finally, her dark eyes let me go and she turned back to her sister.

"We can start doing the dispenser in the fridge again if you like, I'll buy you another sippy cup, but you know eventually you're going to have to drink something publicly, even if you can't handle the cleanup when you're done."

Her voice wasn't unkind, it was matter of fact, and I was surprised again by how easily she talked about life or death, about killing someone. In moments like this I was reminded we were a different species entirely.

"Why does she have to do it publicly?"

I was curious.

"It looks bad for me to be bringing her blood. Drinking is one of our basest requirements and instincts. People will talk, eventually the Government will notice, and the last thing we need is more involvement from them right now."

I glanced at Jade. Her eyes were still closed, head still resting on her arm, and she was apparently ignoring her sister's words, and her breakfast.

"Who even are the Government, and why do they matter so much?"

It was a question that had never occurred to me, but now I wanted to know. In the real world, my world, the system of law and order, of government, it made some sense. There were standards and consequences, but here, I only saw standards. Scarlett had overpowered large groups of Government guards on multiple occasions, and I wondered what consequences they could offer to her as the strongest vampire I'd ever met or heard of. Jade coughed beside me, uncomfortably.

"Jade can explain it better. Eat your eggs."

With a wink that killed my appetite for food and replaced it with something else entirely, Scarlett went back to cleaning the stove. I studied the backs of her bare legs, visible below the sinfully short shorts she had chosen to wear today while we were at home. She was playful, content, which was the last thing I'd expected this morning after my using our being blood bound to stop her from hurting Hannah last night, plus the recent reveal that she knew Jade had been in the Fringe with me and we'd been taking medicine to the humans. The sex *had* been fantastic, though. I smiled to myself, stabbing some eggs.

"No one really knows who the Government are. We sort of lost track over the years."

Jade finally raised her head, and although she still looked unwell, she seemed revived by the chance to talk about something she was clearly interested or at least had some knowledge about.

"There's six positions on the council, and basically the story is that not long after the city was formed these six vampires gave up everything. Like, their families, their life outside the tower, everything, to become the leaders of society. The idea was that by giving it up they could be impartial, and not have their views tainted. They would be purists, if you will, single-mindedly guiding us all on the best course of action for the city, and for us as a species."

She rolled her eyes at the last part.

"Why does anyone even obey them?"

Scarlett scoffed but carried on cleaning the stove, not even turning around though Jade and I both studied her back.

"To start, they have the numbers. Almost all the vampires in the Midlands work stints for them as guards, then there's a number of prominent Delta vampires who also work for them. And there's Scarlett."

Jade looked as uncomfortable saying it as I was to hear it.

"So, if another vampire breaks the rules...."

"Most cases the penalty is more reasonable: fines, confinement in the bunker, sometimes doing tasks for the government or helping them accomplish a certain goal. There's no book of play, no hard list of sentences for each crime, it's all at their discretion, and that's where it gets so hard."

"They're everywhere, sweetheart." Scarlett cut in. "They control everyone and everything in this city, right down to the eggs on your plate."

"But you've overpowered groups of their guards multiple times." I spoke my earlier observation aloud.

"I'm a special scenario, but not unique. There's always more guards, more pawns to die for them, but why bother? They snatch you or Jade, hell, even Camilla, and I'm their willing puppet. They've been playing the game too long not to know how to win."

The thought made me uneasy.

"But nobody knows who they are?"

Both sisters shook their head.

"So, I'm going to be a vampire then..."

I searched Scarlett's eyes, uncertainty and a new wave of fear washing over me as, for the first time, it started to sink in that my life as a human would soon be over.

She looked back at me, cool and hard, and for a moment I felt her wish to ease my fears, to comfort me, before our connection blinked out.

"What makes you say that?"

"You just said it's impossible to win."

"I said they know how to win, I never said it was impossible to beat them."

I looked to Jade when Scarlett glanced away, and Jade shrugged, before she turned to her sister.

"Scar, how exactly are you thinking you can avoid turning her? I love Rayne, and I don't want Daddy...messing with her either, but I don't see how we have a choice. The whole city knows."

Though I couldn't feel her emotions, I knew Scarlett was slipping into that dark and brooding place she often went when we lay together at night and she thought I was sleeping.

"She's probably right. I don't want you to get hurt for me, and I don't want to be something for the world to use to control you."

Jade flinched beside me and wished I had been more tactful.

"You'll be that either way, Princess." She ground out the words. "I love you, and here that's nothing but another weakness to be exploited, a hand to be played and taken advantage of."

Definitely dark and broody.

"I'm just trying to say I can handle it, your father and the Government. I don't want you driving yourself crazy or doing anything stupid trying to fight something if it's inevitable."

Despite my words I wasn't strictly sure I was 100 percent ready to say goodbye to my human life completely. The reality of being a vampire, of having to drink from people, kill people, still tormented me, though I was finally beginning to accept it as my fate. I wouldn't let Scarlett destroy herself trying fruitlessly to save me.

"Maybe it would be easier?" I suggested gently.

"No." Her dark eyes burned mine, and I felt it all in that moment: her fear, her repulsion at the idea, the call in her blood and her willingness to wage a war to save me.

"Scarlett, you said yourself the Government rarely loses. How much are you willing to lose to try and stop this? You know they won't end at just hurting you if you disobey them," Jade chimed in, tentatively.

"If I can't beat the Government, I'll just have to take them down."

It was sweet treason on her tongue, the first clean breath of air in months as her scheme was finally uncovered. I felt everything she felt, her elation at finally having a solution, the thrill of the destruction she had to bring, and the absolute terror this kind of revolt inspired in her.

"I don't want you to fight a war for me." I shot off my stool, the metal feet screeching violently against the smooth tile. Jade jumped beside me at the volume, her juice sloshing over the sides of the glass and spilling on the counter.

"I don't want to be a vampire, but I don't want to lose you. I can't lose you, or see you get hurt because you're trying to save me. Turning me is the easier alternative."

I was arguing for my own death.

"Not for me." She hissed the words and then she was gone, only the breeze gently lifting the ends of my hair left in her wake.

"That went well."

Camilla strode into the kitchen, dragging along a boy I didn't recognize.

"We'll definitely have to kill him now he heard all that, but first, drink up."

She dragged him around the bar and shoved him in between mine and Jade's stools. I immediately got up, stuttering my way through excusing myself. Jade looked horrified, and I walked out to the sound of them arguing, my breakfast forgotten, bile in my throat as I left the boy to die.

IT TOOK ME a full half hour to find Scarlett, and when I did, she was on the roof still in her ridiculously short shorts and T-shirt, sitting on the edge of the wall, looking bound and determined among the soft blanket of snow covering the world around her.

"Is all this because you won't...want me like that?"

Tired of holding things in, of letting what-ifs and maybes and insecurities eat me from the inside out, I asked her for the truth. I had felt her revulsion in the kitchen, and I wondered what about me she wouldn't like if I was a vampire. It was easier to throw myself at this than to think of what was happening in the kitchen.

"It has nothing to do with that. Go back inside, please."

She glared at me from her perch. I knew that she knew I was absolutely freezing, in a T-shirt myself, and dark blue jeans. Thank God I had stopped to grab my sneakers.

"Just help me understand why. Why go to war over this, why try to take down an organization that has controlled you all your life?"

Scarlett stood up and stalked toward me. She opened the door back into the tower and waited for me to step inside. I held my ground, and she held hers.

Finally giving up, rolling my eyes, I stepped into the admittedly warmer hall, though I turned right back to where she still stood, door in hand, and waited for my answer.

"Because I love you."

It was only half a reason and I was about to tell her as much before she spoke again.

"And I never want to see you end up like me."

Chapter Five

HAWTHORNE TOWER WAS stunningly beautiful and, it turned out, only two towers away from Pearce Tower, which explained how Camilla was always at our place so much.

After a tense few days it was nice to be able to forget. Scarlett was losing herself in her insane quest for power and this even more insane scheme she had to destroy the Government.

I had heard Camilla arguing with her in the early hours of the morning, and I had shared Jade's dread the nights she'd crawled into Scarlett's bed with me long after Scarlett had left for the Punishment Center.

Nobody spoke about it, but it hung over us all, and I was sure it was what had prompted Camilla to invite all of us to dinner with her family tonight, an invitation that had taken copious begging on my part before Scarlett would accept.

The décor was a little much for my taste, designer this and that, expense for expense's sake. Their human workers dressed in fancy pressed tuxedos and elegant cocktail dresses that seemed bizarre, now I was accustomed to our tower workers and their beige clothing.

"I like beautiful things. If I have to look at them, I may as well enjoy." Camilla had shrugged and then given Jade a look that had made even me blush. It was true, all the servants here seemed to be beautiful, and Jade was practically a model, shy and awkward as she was, even by vampire standards.

I never did find out what had transpired in the kitchen between them that day, and the fate of the boy, but Jade no longer looked like death. I figured it was resolved and tried not to think of it further.

Scarlett twisted her fingers in the hair at the nape of my neck, and I turned to look at her, drinking her in, enjoying her in her sleek black evening dress. We had all dressed for the occasion. I was wearing something Cami had brought for me, a soft deep blue number, while Jade had on an emerald green gown. I vaguely wondered if Camilla had provided clothes for all of us for the occasion, before I was lost again staring at Scarlett, noticing her irises were just barely beginning to stir.

Music crackled to life, filling up the opulent sitting area we had moved to. I had never been fuller, after an elaborate meal I hadn't been able to finish, though somehow I found room for my dessert and half of Scarlett's, which she'd spooned into my mouth indulgently. I really liked the cake.

"Shall we dance, darling?"

Cami took Jade's hand, and I giggled at the corniness of the gesture.

"Are you kidding? Do you want her to fall and break something, or worse, herself?"

There was no malice in Scarlett's tone, but it was still cool. Things had begun to smooth over between her and Camilla. I couldn't say mend because I knew Scarlett was still unhappy with the relationship, though I honestly did wonder if she would ever believe anyone good enough for her sister.

Camilla ignored her, giving Jade a dazzling smile and promising to lead as she pulled the reluctant vampire to her feet.

I watched them sway together and couldn't help but think they did look beautiful; both tall, slim, glamorous. I loved Jade and worried for her too, but I knew she could do far worse than Camilla who was brutally honest and a little bit shallow, but also loyal and loving beneath it.

"Maybe give them a break, just a little?"

Scarlett harrumphed, and I knew it was unlikely, though I could feel her softening as she watched Jade laughing, head thrown back in glee as Camilla twirled them effortlessly.

"Do you want to dance, sweetheart?"

I was still smiling at the scene when soft lips kissed the skin just beneath my ear. I shook my head, enjoying just being with her, our time together seeming entirely too short over the previous few days.

She twisted her fingers into the ends of my hair, and rested her chin on my shoulder. I let my eyes close as we sat there on the sofa, cheek to cheek. I imagined that this could be our life: dinners with friends and family, laughter and dancing and light. If only it could be this simple.

Scarlett jumped away from me a split-second before the door to the room opened, and I turned to see a rather portly older man, totally bald and bursting from his three-piece suit, making his way toward us.

"Scarlett!"

He seemed thrilled to see her. Her reaction to him was unreadable, though as he plunked himself down on the sofa, forcing his way between us and clapping her on the back, I sensed her mood darkening, and her anxiety at not being near me.

"Mr. Hawthorne."

She was cordial, and the old man laughed jovially.

"Call me Harry, Scarlett, for Pete's sake! I've known you since you were in diapers."

She laughed, as awkward as I had ever seen her.

"Yes, sir, Harry."

"Good, good. Now, tell me, how are you? I did hear about your hard work in the Fringe. I know people talk but I think it's absolutely wonderful that a young lady is up to the task, putting some of the young Delta men to shame if you ask me!"

I carefully pressed myself back against the arm of the sofa, feeling suddenly small, transported back to my high school days where I wished for nothing more than to be invisible, unsure how to navigate this new unknown variable in a society as dangerous as I knew Vires to be.

"Daddy, stop harassing Scarlett," Camilla cut in.

Her hand was still loosely entwined with Jade's, both their eyes bright with happiness.

"Camilla, my love, you look just like your mother in our younger years. And little Jade, you're all grown up and finally out of the tower! I was most happy to hear you two have become such good friends."

He gestured between them and I cringed.

"I remember a time Scarlett and Camilla were the same way!"

I wondered if he knew exactly how great friends either of the sisters and Camilla had been.

"Daddy, Jade and I are dating."

He looked up at her, his puffy cheeks and piggy brown eyes making me seriously question where Camilla got her good looks.

"That's wonderful, darling. Perhaps you could take your sister on some of these dates too. She's awfully stressed now the baby is due any day, she could use some time with the gals!"

Jade's cheeks were beet red, and Scarlett was barely containing her laughter.

"Daddy... Jade is my girlfriend..."

He was still nodding along.

"We're involved..."

I watched the train wreck that was happening as Mr. Hawthorne seemed more and more thrilled with each development in Jade and Camilla's "friendship."

"Harry," Scarlett cut through, and I could tell she was choking down her laughter, her voice thick and throaty. "They're not gal pals, they're girlfriends."

He nodded some more, and she sighed, the humor falling from her face.

"They fuck, sir. Loudly."

She gave Camilla a withering glare, delivering the news with a dryness only she could possess in a moment like that, though I vividly remembered the two separate occasions I'd had to drag her off the thirteenth floor before she burst into Jade's room and ended up coming to blows with Camilla for "defiling" her sister.

Harry's mouth formed an O, and he clambered to his feet. He clapped Camilla on the back.

"Right then, darling, very good. I'll...er...let Mommy know. You girls enjoy your night."

He was clearly flummoxed by the news, but I admired his grace and was pleased he hadn't reacted negatively; he just seemed surprised.

As he moved to leave, he seemed to notice me again.

"Oh Scarlett, you brought your hybrid. She'll be a beautiful vampire, magnificent. When will you turn her?"

And just like that, the good mood wilted.

"I've not set a date yet, sir." All the levity had left Scarlett's voice and I ached to have it back, to return to the comic relief we were all enjoying just a few moments before.

"Well I for one can't wait to see her. Goodnight, girls, Camilla, do keep the noise down tonight if you decide to stay home."

He gave the two of them a pointed look before he disappeared, and the minute the doors closed behind him, even with the mention of my turning hanging over us, I couldn't help but break out laughing. It wasn't long before everyone else in the room joined me.

WE LAY IN bed, a content silence between us, the ghost of emotions washing back and forth on an easy tide as we were each lost in our thoughts. For my part, it was the perfect end to what on the whole had been one of the best evenings we'd had in a while, only made better by the fact that tonight, Scarlett had stayed home.

My mind roamed, wandering back over the evening, amusement still tickling me at Harry Hawthorne's blundering misguided enthusiasm, before something struck me.

"Scar?"

She looked up from where she had been staring at the wall, still combing her fingers through my hair.

"What did Harry mean when he said Cami's sister was having a baby in a few days? Is that possible? I mean, can vampires have children?"

Surprise shot through her followed by a carefulness that made me instantly curious. I tugged harder on our connection, prying, though it quickly snapped and went silent and I knew I'd been caught.

"We do have a way to reproduce, yes, but it's not what you're thinking."

I was immediately interested. A distant thought of Scarlett holding an adorable little girl rose from somewhere unknown before I shoved it back down, too embarrassed and conflicted to even assemble my feelings on the subject.

"How so?"

"We can no longer reproduce sexually after we're turned, so it's all done in the lab. The geneticists take genes from both parties and incorporate them into blank embryos. You can choose girl or boy."

"Wow..." I wasn't expecting that, though I knew Vires was a society heavily invested in advanced genetics.

"Then is the baby grown in the lab or...?"

She studied me.

"Why are you so interested in this?" It was an honest question, and despite the subject matter it didn't feel loaded, but something in her eyes made me careful with my answer.

"Just curious. I'd like to know how you came to be."

She nodded and returned to her explanation.

"The embryo is carried to term by a human surrogate. It's customary to kill the surrogate after the birth, to avoid later conflict or confusion."

I preferred my lab idea so much more.

"So that's how you were born? And Jade?"

She stiffened at the mention of her sister, which seemed strange to me.

"Yes, we're born as human children and turned at a time of our parents' choosing after we turn seventeen."

I let the information wash over me.

"Was Jade made differently?" Her jaw clenched, and I backtracked. "You just seemed tense when I mentioned her. If you don't want to talk about it, wait... Is Jade...your daughter?"

For a minute the pieces fit.

"Of course not. She's my sister." There was a long pregnant pause before she spoke again. "I've never told anyone in the world this, but we have different fathers."

I reached up to brush some dark hair back from her face, a silent thank-you for the trust.

"How? If vampire babies are always planned and conceived in a laboratory, was it intentional?"

She shook her head.

"There was a mistake at the lab, and a huge cover-up afterwards. I only found out two years ago when I worked my way deep into the bunker and was finally able to find the records there."

She hesitated. I let her take her time, sensing there was more she wanted to share and willing to wait.

"The wrong DNA was used when they made Jade. I don't know much else about it other than the scientist responsible was killed, probably by my father, and my parents have likely known all her life. It explains why he's always been so hard on her and treated her as a failure. In some part."

"Does Jade know that you're half-sisters?"

"We're sisters." Her tone was absolute. "She's been my sister since the moment she was born, nothing will ever make it to a lesser degree, but no, she has no idea and I'd like to keep it that way."

I squeezed her shoulder through the thin cotton sleep shirt covering it and leaned over to kiss her softly at the corner of her mouth. Anxiety still radiated off her.

"I promise you I won't ever repeat this."

She nodded.

"Did you find out whose genes they accidentally used?"

The emotional ricochet from the question was huge before she locked it down tight. I still felt the echoes of her war with herself over whether to tell me.

"Promise me you'll never tell?"

I promised her sincerely.

"April, Cami's younger sister, is the same age as Jade. They actually share a birthday."

My mouth fell open.

"It's possible Harry Hawthorne is the...donor." She muttered the words with a grimace.

"So Camilla is...oh my God."

"She's not her sister." Scarlett corrected the words I hadn't said. "Blood doesn't make a family."

"That's why you were so against it?"

She sighed heavily.

"One of a few reasons, but like you've told me so many times they're happy. They're never going to find out. That information will never see the light of day. If it did there would be a massive loss of trust in our reproductive process and it would rock the city. Can you imagine the uncertainty of everyone wondering if their child is really their child? They really care about something as stupid as genes. The government would never let it get out."

I was three steps behind her and still bowled over by her admission that Camilla and Jade could be biological half-sisters, her earlier resistance to their relationship suddenly cast in a whole new light. I felt guilty for the times I had prodded her over it. I couldn't imagine how lonely it must have been for her, fighting that fight for a reason no one else understood.

"I'm sorry I didn't respect how you felt about their relationship."

She shrugged. "It took me a while to come to terms, yes, but honestly, why shouldn't they be happy? Besides the fact that Jade is a child and Cami is...Cami. Why is it wrong, who says, society? The same society that would say the fact I love you is also wrong?"

I wrapped my arms around her neck and hugged her close, closing my eyes and listening to the sounds of her unnecessary breaths. I needed a moment to process, and she gave it to me.

When the shock passed, I was struck by something else.

"Scarlett?"

I pulled back and she kissed my lips softly, humming her response.

"Thank you for trusting me."

She kissed me again. A little uncertainty and unease still lingered over the decision, but for the most part I was pleased she didn't regret it.

"You're mine, Princess, always."

I rested my forehead against hers.

"And you're mine."

We soaked up each other's presence, moving away from the weight of the admission. I knew I would have to mull it over more later to make peace with my feelings on it.

"I don't want to lose this."

My back was pressed against her front and she leaned up on her elbow. She dipped to kiss my cheek then my temple, the fingers of her free hand playing with the hem of my shirt by my thighs.

"Your heartbeat, your warmth, the smile that doesn't know the real weight of the world."

My stomach plummeted as I realized she was talking about not turning me.

"I just want you like this, forever."

She whispered the words and I swallowed down the trepidation, and the rush of longing, they brought.

"You have a plan?"

I could already sense she did.

"Yes."

It was one simple word, but it changed everything. Finally, defying the government wasn't just an idea, a crazy scheme she was courting. Now she had plotted a course, and I knew she would see it through.

"You know the saying, if you can't beat them, kill them?"

"I don't think it..." I sighed. "I mean sure."

I turned in her arms, looking up at her, thinking again how bizarre it was that this small, soft woman who adored me was also a merciless killer.

"I haven't been able to find a way to avoid turning you and maintain the life we all have now, to stay in their good graces."

Dread nipped icy at my fingers, my toes, and I was glad to be receiving this news while she held me, or I knew I would be panicking so much more than I already was.

"I'm going to take them down from the inside. It's time for a revolution, a new world order."

A touch of the fanatic slipped into her voice, traces of the woman she was at the punishment center, in the square that awful night. The thrill of destruction darkened her eyes.

"How would you even start? You have no idea who they are?"

She shook her head.

"That doesn't matter. Outside of the bunker they're nobody anyway, they said goodbye to family and anything else I could use long ago. I have to get them from the inside, and I will."

She scared even me a little bit sometimes, reclined in bed snuggled close to me, soft fingers comforting in my hair while she whispered about death like a dream.

"What will happen to Vires? Without any structure wouldn't society collapse?"

She laughed.

“My sweet, naïve princess. When one power falls, another takes its place, and when I do, we’ll never have to worry about anything again.”

Every quote I had ever heard about how power corrupted came back to haunt me, and I was terrified to lose her to it completely.

“Sweetheart, I’ll be fine.”

She misread my fear as concern about her physical safety, and I let her.

“First, I need to get into the archives, do some digging, which involves going deeper than I ever have, but people in the bunker know me, and my reputation. It shouldn’t be an issue as long as I’m not caught by any of the council.”

Now I was scared for her.

“Scarlett... Don’t you think we should think this through a little more? Maybe we can talk to Cami and Jade...”

“No...” She cut me off. “Camilla and Jade stay out of this, you stay out of this, I’m telling you because...we’re partners.” I heard my earlier words to her repeated back, tentatively. “I should share these things with you.”

She was trying, and it was as sweet as it was heartbreaking. I just wished she’d also got the memo that huge, life-altering, and possibly life-ending, decisions were supposed to be shared too. At least she’d had the courtesy to tell me about what I believed more and more was a suicide mission.

“I’m scared for you.” I wasn’t ready to beg her, but I knew her, and I knew now her mind was set and a course charted she would be chomping at the bit, eager to set to running it.

“Rayne...”

She waited for me to look up at her.

"I can do this. I've trained my whole life for it, without ever knowing. My father taught me how to serve the Government, but in a way, he taught me how to break them too. I know more about how they operate and have access to more of the bunker than anyone in this city, I'm the only one capable of this."

"I'm not worth your life, Scarlett."

I closed my eyes, feeling tears stinging them, not wanting to cry on her. To me, this felt more and more like a goodbye I wasn't ready for and was powerless to stop.

"You are my life."

It should be cheesy, but coming from Scarlett, wonderful, crazy, intense Scarlett, it was the sincerest thing I had ever heard.

"We need you." I tried.

"And I need you, as you are, not twisted and turned and destroyed. I will not let them destroy you."

I realized with sickening dread that I was not going to be able to talk her out of this.

"When were you planning to go into the bunker?"

"Tonight."

The word echoed, bouncing painfully around my insides, and the feeling of impending doom that had blanketed me became a raw, urgent panic.

"I'm not ready, can we just...not tonight? Just promise me not tonight and we'll talk about this some more tomorrow?"

She ran soothing fingers up and down my bare arm and studied me with dark eyes full of love, and something else I couldn't read.

"Fine. We'll talk tomorrow, okay?"

I let out a breath. It almost felt too easy of a win but, desperate to escape the panic images of her caught by the Government inspired, I took it.

"Okay."

Her presence, our connection, grew heavy, relaxed, content. I told myself it was the relief of having one more day to try to avert this disaster, though really, I knew she was lulling me. I let myself go, wrapping my arms around her and settling myself half on top of her, just in case.

Chapter Six

IT WAS JUST beginning to get light outside when I woke. I searched the cool sheets for Scarlett.

My eyes shot open. I already knew she was gone.

I whipped the sheets off my body anyway, jumped to my feet, and banged through the door and out into the hall. I skidded into the kitchen, my socked feet having too little traction to slow me from the dead run I was taking around the house to look for her.

She wasn't on the thirteenth floor, and I burst into Jade's room without knocking, frantic. Shock and panic made my brain take too long to catch up with my body. Jade squealed and yanked the covers over her naked body. Camilla sat there, in all her glory, hands on hips, pissed.

I stared.

"Do you need something?"

Cami looked at me like I had lost my mind, and she wasn't totally wrong.

"It's Scarlett."

The prospect of trying to explain it all was daunting, but somehow, I garbled out my story and how I was sure she had left to go to the bunker already.

"Shit."

Camilla raked her hands through her mussed hair.

"Darling, we need to get dressed."

She tossed some clothes at Jade, and within seconds they were both standing before me fully clothed. I envied their speed as my brain grappled to wake from the pleasant slumber I'd been enjoying just minutes ago.

"Come on, she may not have left the building yet."

I didn't know if I truly believed that, but I clung to it as the truth desperately, not ready to accept that Scarlett was really gone on this crazy mission and I might never see her again.

We hurried to the elevator, Jade towing me along by my hand. My inferior human legs weren't able to keep up with vampires on the edge of using their supernatural speed, not to mention both of them were at least a foot taller than me.

The ride down seemed to last forever.

"Why didn't you tell us last night? We could have talked to her or tried to reason..."

Everyone in the tiny metal box knew reasoning with Scarlett would have done no good, but I understood Camilla's need for an outlet.

"She asked me not to, and I did make her promise she wouldn't go last night. I thought I had time!"

Cami scoffed.

"Typical Scarlett. Ran off before you could try to stop her. Unbelievable."

She burst out of the elevator with me and Jade on her heels.

"You."

She approached one of the guards who snapped to attention.

"Ma'am?"

"Scarlett Pearce, did she leave this morning?"

He nodded. "About half an hour ago, give or take."

Damn her, damn her, damn her.

Jade gripped my hand and Camilla turned to us.

"Go back upstairs, I may be able to catch her."

She said no more—we were all conscious of our company—and then she was gone.

We stood there for a few long moments, the doorman hovering awkwardly, both Jade and I shell shocked, rudely interrupted from entirely different pleasant activities to deal with this.

"She's going to die."

Jade was staring out of the doors after Camilla. Coming to my senses, I tugged on our joined hands and led her back across the elaborate foyer to where I could call the elevator.

The ride back up felt surreal, and it dawned on me that I had stood in the lobby in nothing but my underwear, a big old T-shirt of Scarlett's, and a pair of fluffy black socks. I couldn't even care.

Jade seemed to be in shock. Deciding I was going to be in charge until Camilla came back, hopefully with Scarlett, I tried to busy myself with that rather than the worry threatening to overtake me.

I dragged Jade to the kitchen, telling her softly to sit down at the bar while I put the kettle on to boil, glad to have something to do.

I wanted to tell her it would be okay, but neither of us knew that, so we listened to the water bubbling in silence.

The tea was cold in front of us by the time the elevator dinged, Jade's cheeks wet from the silent tears that had streamed down them. For my part, I was numb.

Camilla appeared in the doorway of the kitchen, alone, dark eyes blazing, and my heart sank.

"All we can do is wait for her to come back," she announced grimly, lifting her chin just a fraction more than usual. The move told me she was as worried about this as the rest of us.

"She'd already gone inside, and I didn't have good enough reason to be able to follow. People already think I'm bizarre, running around like this, with no makeup on."

She sniffed, and I couldn't help but think she looked oddly cute in her tight jeans and thin cashmere sweater, though it was a far cry from the opulent designer attire she usually donned for the outside world. Much like Scarlett, she had a public persona she clung to.

"So, while we're here anyway, with nothing to do but wait, why don't you tell us again what she said last night before she ran off to...do this."

She stopped herself, but I still heard *her death,* loud and clear in my head. Camilla tried to backpedal.

"For a complete idiot, she's smart. If anyone can pull this off, it's her."

I nodded, numb.

"Maybe Rayne should put on pants first?"

Jade finally spoke, and I looked down at my own bare legs. So did everyone else in the room.

Camilla rolled her eyes.

"We'll be in the living room once you've managed to dress yourself."

I sidled off to do as I was told, trying not to linger in the bedroom that smelled like Scarlett. Her things were all around me, so many memories of my life with her; so many of the very best parts of it involved that room.

My face was pale in the bathroom mirror, my hair mussed. I gave up on trying to smooth it out, brushed it through quickly, and fastened it into a long braid at my back. It struck me how much I had changed during my time in the city. Gone was the deadness in my eyes that had stared back at me in New Hampshire. I was alive now, living, breathing and feeling, with so much to continue to live and fight for. As much as life in Vires was a roller coaster, and as far from perfect as it was, I knew I would never go back, not willingly. I grabbed a thin sweater that came down to my thighs and tugged on some black leggings, before I rushed back to the living room, not eager to be alone with my anxiety for too long.

Cami and Jade sat huddled together on the sofa, talking quietly. I tried not to dwell on the information I had learned about the two of them last night. I saw the similarities now—the slim, tall figure, Amazonian good looks—or perhaps I was just convincing myself they were more alike than any two other tall gorgeous women because of what Scarlett had told me. I was lonely for Scarlett as I perched on the edge of a recliner.

They turned and fixed their dark eyes on me.

"Did she say exactly what she was hoping to find?"

I shook my head.

"Just that she needed more information so she could take them down from the inside."

Camilla hissed something that sounded a lot like *stupid*.

"And what does she plan to do if she succeeds? Hooray, we get to keep Rayne as a breakable little human, but what then of the city and society?"

"That was what I asked her. She told me she planned to take the Government's place."

Tense silence followed the admission, and no one seemed to move. Jade was the first to come back to herself.

"I don't want her to do this, but that could be good, right? We could change things...things could be better, for everyone. We could finally get away from all the stupid barbaric tradition and move forward."

Her excitement at the prospect was growing, but I just didn't share it. Cami held my eyes. The wariness in those dark irises told me she wasn't so convinced of Scarlett's good intentions either.

"That or the power corrupts her completely and she goes to a place none of us can get her back. She's come close before, don't forget. Wasn't that why you concocted your hairbrained scheme and brought Rayne here in the first place?"

Jade deflated momentarily before she seemed to reason her way around that particular piece of our history.

"That was different. She met Rayne and was in love with a life she thought she could never have, so yes, it made her dark. She was taking out her anger and all her conflicted feelings in her work. Now she has Rayne, and she's loved, and she has her family. It's different."

It was a nice ideology, but I just didn't know if it was true.

"And what about recently? You know she's been immersing herself in it again, she's gone more than she's home."

I hated to disappoint Jade, but all of us needed to approach this with our eyes open.

"This is nothing compared to before." Camilla cut in easily. "She's lived all her life under someone else's control. Give her the leash and one of two things will happen. She'll rise above what she is and maybe evolve and move the city toward progress, or she'll get drunk on the power and dive down darker than any of us have ever known her."

The thought was chilling.

"She's a good person." Jade was offended, and Cami placated her instantly.

"I never argued that, but she's broken, Jade, everyone in this room knows it, and somewhere along the way, that became a part of her. She loves power as much as she loves any one of us. Yes, she will beg and crawl and bleed to save us, but she always rises, I think she always will rise. Take your father and the Government out of the equation. As much as I love her, she's my best friend and I want to see her free, but I fear the world she would create, or what would become of her as she tries to find a new outlet."

I scrubbed hard at my eyes. I wanted to believe in Scarlett, believe her to be capable of doing the right thing, though I didn't really know what the right thing was beyond stopping the murder of innocent people.

"Don't you think we're getting ahead of ourselves? This is all some distant what-if, assuming she defeats the Government and it all goes as she plans. Shouldn't we be more concerned right now with the current suicide mission, not to mention the multiple future ones she's no doubt planning. How're we going to stop her?"

They were busy avoiding looking at each other, Jade picking her nails.

"We can't physically stop her..."

It occurred to me that I could, maybe. I was able to use being blood bound to influence her that night in the Fringe, though whenever we practiced at home I never could. I couldn't rely on it, and even if I could, I wasn't sure I wanted to. I would probably compel her to save her life but taking away her choice in anything sat extremely heavy with me. I knew if it happened it would be a last resort and never something I had planned to do.

"We're just going to have to talk to her and treat her like the reasonable creature we all know she isn't," Cami decided.

"Talk to me about what?"

I had never moved so fast in my life as I did then. I rushed from my chair and launched myself at her, my arms around her neck, breathing her in, the faint scent of the stale air in the bunker still clinging to her skin. Snow was melting in her hair and on her clothes, on her silly leather jacket that was too thin for the weather, and I clung to her, silently rejoicing a million times that she was okay.

She kissed the top of my head and set me back on my feet. I got one good look at her, inspecting her for any signs of harm and finding none, then all my sweet relief at her safety dissolved into anger.

"You promised!"

Heels clicked against the floor for two steps as she moved past me, before they were kicked off and she sunk down into the recliner that was previously mine.

"Did I? Think back."

She'd promised not to leave last night and left first thing in the morning instead. She'd planned this, used some stupid technicality to avoid waiting, and gone and risked her stupid self anyway. I was still seething, trying to form words.

"I'm guessing from the death glare and the sad eyes you shared our conversation with Jade and Camilla?"

"I was worried you were going to die!" I spat the words out as she regarded me coldly.

"She was scared for you, Scar, we all were."

Jade came to my rescue, appearing behind me and tugging me back to sit on the sofa. She threaded her fingers through mine in a show of support.

"So, care to share what happened? I assume you weren't caught given that you're here, alive."

Scarlett opened her mouth to reply to Camilla before she paused, her head tilted to the side slightly, then raised one finger to her lips.

It was bizarre, and my heart picked up at the strange sight, suddenly nervous.

"I just can't eat fillet again, Cami. Cook always overdoes it anyway."

Something flashed between them, and suddenly, they were two different people.

"Then how about veal? We could always dine at my place. You know my father would be thrilled to see you and perhaps April's baby has come?"

The elevator dinged.

"If the baby had come the whole city would have known about it by now. They talk of nothing else in the market, I don't think there's a stall she hasn't commissioned for some thing or another for it... Oh, Father."

I hadn't heard his footsteps, but Wilfred Pearce stood in the doorway, leaning heavily on his cane. His dark eyes were as bone chillingly cold as I remembered them.

"Wilfred, it's lovely to see you again, sir!"

Camilla was animated and fake, more like the woman I had experienced whenever we were outside the tower, all designer clothes and prim propriety, a heavily exaggerated version of herself.

Jade smiled at the man though it looked more like a grimace. It pretty much summed up how I felt about him too.

He looked at each of us in turn.

"Good to see you, Camilla. Excuse the interruption, Jade. I have some news to share with you. Join me for dinner tonight on my floor?"

The room was quiet for a moment before Scarlett and Camilla spoke at the same time, both eager to excuse her. Something was happening that I didn't understand. After giving Camilla a withering glare, Scarlett tried again.

"Jade has dinner plans tonight."

He turned on her. Something in his expression made me want to stand between them.

"Really? Well perhaps after dinner then, or maybe right now. You and I could possibly have discussed the matter instead, but you were occupied when I needed you this morning."

He knew. I had a sinking, crushing feeling that he knew about whatever Scarlett had been prying in.

"I was working."

She was outwardly cool and impassive, and I suppose in her focus on keeping her physical composure, she let down her walls emotionally. The amount of fear she had for the man terrified me.

"Deep in the bunker? Not your usual place to work." He turned to Jade beside me. "Jade, let's go."

She got dutifully to her feet and Camilla jumped up after her looking obviously rattled. The thin veil of pretense everyone in the room was clinging to shimmered and seemed about to shatter, as I understood Jade was being threatened.

Scarlett stood too, inserting herself between Jade and her father, looking supremely confident for all the unrest choking her. It was making me feel sick to experience it second hand.

"I'm available for the rest of the day. Whatever it is, I'll take care of it. Let Jade enjoy her dinner date with the Hawthornes. April invited her; perhaps she had the baby."

The room was silent while he considered it for a long moment.

"I suppose that's best. We wouldn't want Jade to be missed. Next time you disappear into the bunker I'm sure she and I will get our chance to spend some time together."

It was a warning. Scarlett's jaw was clenched tight. Camilla smoothed her palms over her jeans. She grabbed Jade by the hand, trying and failing to be casual about pulling her back down onto the sofa, and away from him. Cold eyes followed the movement and my stomach plummeted as they landed on me.

"And what of your hybrid, Scarlett? Still human, I see. I look forward to meeting her as a vampire."

His gaze lingered on me in a way that made me uncomfortable. His appraisal of me felt like a physical violation.

"Soon," was the only response she gave, already back in her heels and heading out of the door. My eyes flitted to find hers, dark and anxious, as she waited for her father to follow. He studied me still.

"Are you ready to join us, Rayne?"

The question paralyzed me, and I stared up at him dumbly. Scarlett's voice in my head took over and I lowered my gaze and dropped my head respectfully, as was her will.

"Yes, sir. It will be an honor."

The words were not my own, but they seemed to appease him, because when I looked up, the two of them were gone.

Jade spoke first.

"He knows she's been looking into things she shouldn't."

Cami nodded grimly.

"She's going to get herself killed if she insists on seeing this stupid scheme through. There has to be a better way, a smarter one."

I cleared my throat, finally leaving my head where I had been reaching for Scarlett. A stone wall between us again left me to wonder what exactly Wilfred Pearce wanted from her. The dark bruising under her eye, thick scars across her back, all plagued my mind.

"Is he going to hurt her?"

Jade shook her head.

"He doesn't usually. Not often, anyway."

It wasn't really comforting but it was all I had, so I clung to it.

"So how else do we take down the vampire government besides killing them all or whatever Scarlett has planned?"

I asked the question, trying to distract myself, bone shatteringly tired and done with missing her, with wondering where she was, with worrying myself sick over her. I just wanted her here, safe, pressed up against me. I regretted my earlier anger. No matter how much her clever evasion of my promise still rankled.

"Killing them is probably the only way." Camilla was musing aloud. "But perhaps there's a smarter way to kill them, a cleaner way."

"Poison?" It instantly popped into my mind.

"We're mostly immune, though we all know a certain family who dealt in vampire-harming serums."

My mind went back to the Chases, Evan and his father Mark, the latter of whom had made a serum designed to kill a vampire over time, as well as an antidote. I had almost died for stealing it for Scarlett after she was infected.

"Scarlett took the serum to the government. It was part of her big play to get Rayne back," Jade supplied, the plan beginning to crumble before it could form, but Camilla seemed determined.

"But perhaps that wasn't all Mark Chase made, perhaps there's more. Drew, Evan's older brother, runs the tower now. He's a drunk and he's been besotted with me forever. I think it's worth looking into."

Only Camilla could have the confidence to declare someone besotted with her. Regardless, I nodded my agreement.

"A backup plan if nothing else. Couldn't hurt."

Jade looked less optimistic. I wasn't sure if it was because of lack of faith in the plan, or the fact Camilla was probably going to flirt her way into Chase Tower and to answers.

"Do we mention this to Scarlett? Maybe she can help, or focus on this which seems kind of doable, rather than getting herself killed snooping in the bunker."

Cami shook her head.

"She won't listen. There's no guarantee this will work, and she's too tunnel vision right now to slow down enough to consider it."

"She's single minded in protecting what she loves." Jade sounded sad. "It's her greatest gift, and her biggest flaw. Right now, she's hell bent on saving you from becoming like her. If we tell her she'll only try to stop us."

I let out a breath.

"So, we keep it a secret."

Cami repeated my words.

"We keep it a secret, for now, until we know if anything will come of it."

Chapter Seven

THE FEELING OF being watched had followed me all morning, the fine hairs on the back of my neck raised, goose bumps rising across my skin. I missed Scarlett. She'd returned from her business with Wilfred and spent only a few hours this morning entwined with me in the sheets before she left.

I couldn't escape the memory of her big dark eyes begging me to let things rest when we talked, but she gave nothing away. She had been warm and more loving than I had expected, and in favor of enjoying that, I greedily hadn't pushed talking. At least she wasn't hurt from wherever Wilfred had taken her.

The thirteenth floor was eerily quiet, lifeless without Jade's comfortable presence, Camilla's laugh, Scarlett's fingers on the ivory keys of her piano. Something told me this would be my life more and more over the coming days. Camilla was obviously shaken by Wilfred's sudden interest in using Jade to deter Scarlett from whatever she was doing in the bunker. The pair of them had blown out of the tower as soon as the sun was up, and I had a feeling they wouldn't be back until much later in the day, if at all.

"Rayne."

I shrieked, jumping to my feet and whirling around, my heart slamming against my ribcage and making it hard for me to breathe.

Wilfred Pearce stood beside the recliner I had just been sitting in. I wondered how long he had been there at the same time as I wondered why he was here. I was horribly, acutely aware of how utterly alone I was. He could take me back to the bunker, he could turn me, he could kill me. I fought to get myself under control, panic rising in my chest.

"Hello, sir."

I dropped my head as I remembered Scarlett commanding, and tried to think back over the protocol we once used when she was my mistress in public, eager not to offend him and spark anything more unpleasant.

His outfit of dark jeans and a black button-up tucked in at the waist was different than those I had seen him in previously. Somehow, it reminded me of the tight dresses and leather Scarlett donned for the outside world, for business. My stomach rolled again.

"Finally, you seem to be unoccupied." I heard the true meaning in his words–*finally, he had me alone.* "Come, we have much to discuss."

He began to walk, slow enough for me to follow, and I was surprised to see he did use the cane he always carried. It was a strange paradox. This man was the monster under the bed of the biggest monster in Vires, but for all intents and purposes he seemed old, fragile.

I trailed along behind him, warring with myself, trying to find my voice to ask if I could go get my shoes. The words wouldn't come so I stepped into the elevator barefoot and in only jeans and a sweater. I hoped we weren't going out in the snow.

He pressed the fifteenth-floor key with one weathered finger, illuminating it, and I stared at it as we ascended. I had never been on the floors this high up Pearce Tower, and I had no idea what was up here to gauge what might be about to happen to me.

We stepped out and I followed him down a long hall. This floor was as silent as ours today. No staff moved between the closed doors we passed. Even the air was still. Dread swallowed me. He opened the last door at the very end of the corridor and we stepped inside. I was surprised to be greeted by a sitting room.

A large fireplace sat below a huge television, a small coffee table between two recliners nestled in front of it, with a mini bar close by. Off to the side, the room opened into a larger area, housing what looked to be a kitchenette. A small table was pushed up against the window that showed me only sky from where I stood, but I knew would look down over Vires in its entirety.

"Please have a seat, would you care for a fire?"

The question surprised me, and I was almost lulled into feeling more comfortable. Almost. I considered my answer carefully.

"Whatever would please you, sir."

He didn't respond, but he did light one anyway and I was grateful. As I sunk into one of the seats, I realized this wasn't really a living room, but more of a meeting room. I wondered what business he had with me.

"So, tell me about yourself."

He lowered himself down into the chair before me, and again, I was confused by how aged he seemed. His salt and pepper hair had not thinned, but deep lines were etched at the corners of his eyes, and across his brow.

"I'm eighteen..." I wasn't sure where to start or what to say. Honestly, I didn't want him to know anything about me. "I came from New Hampshire, where I was in high school."

He watched me, impassive, attentive though I knew my mundane facts bored him.

"And what do you make of our magnificent city? I'm sure society is very different?"

"Yes, sir." That was an understatement. "I think the city is beautifully built and this society has so many intricacies I'm still learning. I feel privileged to have Scarlett to guide me on how to fit in here."

His eyes lit.

"Scarlett herself is an important part of Vires, a pillar of society some may say. Have you seen her work?"

"Yes, sir."

His tone was light and curious, but the dark undercurrent didn't escape me. His glittering black eyes reminded me of Scarlett's when she held a whip in her hands.

"And what do you make of that, Rayne?"

His use of my name unnerved me. It was something that had always made me uncomfortable, it always felt too familiar, too personal, almost accusatory coming from anyone but Scarlett, and perhaps Jade and Cami now. From Wilfred, it was worse.

"It amazes me and frightens me, sir." My admission was quiet, and he tipped his head waiting for me to go on. I didn't have enough time to lie. I was scared to say what she did revolted me, which it did on some level, so I went with the truth that I was still struggling to accept it.

"It's beautiful like a car wreck. I feel like I should look away but sometimes I can't. She's alive when she's doing that in a way she rarely is outside of it."

I couldn't bring myself to meet his eyes.

"She is incredible." Pride was evident in his voice. "But she wasn't always. Like anything, talent must be nurtured. Once upon a time, Scarlett was much like yourself."

Those words got my attention, and when I raised my eyes up to his, he gave me a smile that chilled my blood.

"I'm sure you have strong feelings for my daughter, Rayne. She owns you, yes, but I see she has personal interest in you beyond her usual toys. She got rid of the nurse to acquire you, and I can assure you that little fixation was quite the journey in itself. Soon, she'll turn you and you'll become one of us. You'll no longer belong to her, per se."

I didn't know what to say in response.

"I suppose my question for you is this, what kind of life would you like for yourself in Vires?"

Everything was starting to feel like a trap. I defaulted back to protocol and tried to defer my own choice to him.

"I'll be honored to become a vampire. I think it will make for a wonderful life."

He nodded, some of the pretense slipping.

"Yes, yes, but what kind of vampire would you like to be? Obviously, you are a Delta, science has already proven that, and obviously you will be a Pearce. The very first hybrid ever discovered, manifested into one of us, of course you belong in a powerful family, but answer me this. Will you be another leaded weight around my daughter's neck, one more thing for her to hide in this tower, or will you stand up beside her and help her weather the storm of her noble service to the city? Will you revel in it by her side and finally set her free from the last constraints holding her back?"

I wasn't 100 percent sure what he was asking me.

"Scarlett won't love you forever, Rayne. There have been others before you, and there will be more in the future if you let her outgrow you. You are unique in that you have something none of them did—the ability to be a true partner to her. She's hardwired to care for things weaker than herself. It's a compulsion I never could break."

He spoke about it as if Scarlett's compassion, as selective as it was, was a burden.

"But you have the unique opportunity to become a vampire, to have a lifetime that spans alongside hers, to rise to the top of the city beside her and keep pace with her. I can help you do it, when the time comes, but you must want to learn. Jade taught me that."

He was waiting for a response and I was still stumbling through the information he had poured on me. I tried not to let his pointed statements get inside me, tried not to imagine the throng of girls Scarlett had kept in my place. I had met her most recent girlfriend, Aria, first hand when Scarlett was involved with her, though she seemed to be more of a pet than a partner. I was sure I looked the same through an outside lens. Insecurity seeped through my cracks, the cracks left by a life of being nobody before Scarlett found me.

"I'm not sure I could do it, sir."

I surprised myself with my honesty, but Wilfred just leaned closer, as if he was on my side. The lines blurred.

"I like you, Rayne; I like what you could become for her, for our city. You have potential where her previous distractions had none. You will either be great beside her or be the tool that finally drives her into greatness, and a darkness none of you—not Jade, not Camilla, not you—will be able to follow her into, or divert her from. The choice is yours."

The words stunned me, because in that moment they rung with a truth I didn't know how to deny. I could never be a murderer—I didn't want to be. My sense of identity, of self, fought to the surface, past Wilfred and his smile full of promises, past my love and undying need to be with Scarlett, and to be everything she needed. I wasn't a sadist, I didn't believe in hurting people, in denying them basic rights, in using and abusing them at will because of some assumed status. Like Jade I believed there was another way the vampires could live, that Vires could work, without this.

"Let me help you decide. Don't touch anything. I'll be back to collect you later."

He got to his feet and I sprung up after him, suddenly terrified of what he was leaving me to. A firm hand on my shoulder pushed me back down. I almost reached for Scarlett, screamed down whatever connected us, remembering how she had come when I'd needed her before, but I held myself back.

If she burst in now it could reveal too much, and it would no doubt not end well for her with Wilfred. I had to ride this out a little longer and hold my nerve.

He reached for a remote I hadn't noticed, and the TV clicked to life, static filling the screen. He hit play, and was gone, the remote vanishing with him.

"What's your name?" Wilfred's voice asked off the screen before it cut to a little girl, sitting on a sofa. She had dark hair and two differently colored eyes that I would recognize anywhere, despite the roundness in her face, the gap between her teeth. She looked about five.

"Daddy..."

She laughed. He repeated the question.

"Scarlett Elise Pearce."

"Very good, and how old are you, Scarlett?"

"I'm six and...just six."

He hummed out of view.

"And when you grow up, what do you want to be?"

She played with her fingers on the table, the first tiny tells of apprehension.

"A Delta vampire?"

It was more a question than a statement of desire, but Wilfred's disembodied voice was pleased.

The next video was not shot on a sofa. The room was cold, clinical, concrete walls and floor, a steel table, which a preteen Scarlett perched on. The change in her was drastic, and already the beginnings of the aloofness, the moodiness I knew so well was on full display.

"How old are you, Scarlett?"

This time Wilfred stepped onto the screen, the cane absent, though he looked to be the same age as he currently appeared. Somehow, he seemed in better health on the recording.

"Fuck you."

The response surprised me. It was quick and vicious and came with a venom that was absolutely jarring from the mouth of a child.

Video Wilfred flashed so fast that the camera and my eyes couldn't follow him, but when he stilled, he was lowering his cane, and Scarlett was spitting blood out of her mouth, tears in her eyes.

"I'm eleven, today." She said the words like a curse.

"And why are we here?"

"Because you're a psychopath?"

He waited, patient, and I held my breath for her answer. This all felt like an invasion, like it wasn't mine to see. I looked around for another remote, studied the front of the TV, wondering if there was a control up there which I could use to stop this, before her voice distracted me.

"Because I will be a Delta vampire, belonging to the most powerful family in Vires, and I have to learn to act accordingly."

"Good." The praise was clipped. Wilfred disappeared again. When he returned, he dragged a red-haired girl behind him of similar age to Scarlett. She was dirty and marked as distinctly human by the tattered beige rags clinging to her slim form.

He tossed her onto the floor at Scarlett's feet, disappearing again before something else was thrown. It landed beside the redhead with a soft slap.

"Today, Scarlett. Now. This is your last chance."

Finally, the girl on the screen seemed to break from whatever was keeping her still.

"I'm not going to whip Jessica, you idiot! She's my friend! I did your stupid training, I learned the weapons and the politics, but I don't want to hurt anyone."

Wilfred took a seat, just barely on camera. He looked bored in his black button-up and black jeans ensemble.

"Pick up the whip, Scarlett."

She folded her arms.

"You've taught me many things, darling, and I foresee over the years you will teach me many more as we go on this journey together, but would you like to know what lesson you have given me today?"

She didn't reply but he told her anyway.

"In order to learn to break, one must first experience brokenness."

This seemed to shake her.

"Daddy... I just want to go back downstairs...please?"

For the first time she looked and sounded her age, and my heart broke.

"Do you care about Jessica?"

She nodded.

He stood and crossed the space in two strides. Two sharp movements and Jessica was dead on the ground, her neck broken in a move I had seen Scarlett herself use since. The symmetry was sickening. Scarlett screamed an awful wail, which ended when Wilfred grabbed her by the hair.

"Humans are food. They are labor. They are a resource. They are never friends."

She cried, silent hacking sobs in his grasp.

"You will be great, Scarlett. Greater than me, than your mother, than almost anything in this city, and that begins today."

He tossed her forward and she landed. I was reminded again of her humanness, long dark hair falling over her face as she fell hard on her hands. The whip cracked across her back before she could get up. I knew the screaming would haunt my dreams. Tears were wet on my cheeks. I shot to my feet, desperately searching for a remote, for a plug, for anything to turn it off, to make it stop—for Scarlett's sake and for mine. I didn't want to see this, it wasn't Wilfred's to share, and although I knew he was responsible for the thick scars on her back, I had never dreamed his actions were as brutal as the video depicted.

I rattled the locked door, tried the windows. The horrific soundtrack of her screaming and crying went on, filling the room, until finally it stopped.

The next video was no better; the same little girl with dead eyes being asked to pick up the whip again, only this time when she refused, Wilfred produced a much smaller child. Scarlett's strangled proclamation of *Jade*, the strings of begging that followed, identified her as her sister. I guessed this was the day Wilfred found her weakness.

In the end she agreed, Jade was taken away, and she swung the whip clumsily, feebly, with not an ounce of the finesse I had seen from her, crying horribly the whole time.

Unable to escape, I resigned myself to watching this, and sat back down in my seat, my chest hot with hate for Wilfred Pearce and what he had done to her.

The tape wore on. She got better, more indifferent. There was less crying and less begging and more blindly following orders, though there was no trace of the satisfaction, the enjoyment, the blood lust that she would come to display later, yet.

The next poignant clip was of a teenage Scarlett in the very room I sat in. It was disorienting.

This time it was a blonde woman who looked to be in her late twenties who accompanied her.

"You understand sex, Scarlett?" the woman asked.

I could see teenage Scarlett's cheeks color.

"You understand that when two people find each other attractive, they fuck?"

Scarlett just swallowed hard, trying to avoid the attractive blonde's eyes.

"Sex can also be used as a weapon, it's a powerful one, or as a way to make a living, or to gain control. It's part of the adult world, and it's something you need to understand."

She leaned in and kissed Scarlett on the mouth. It was grotesque and terrible, and I only half understood what was happening. I wanted to look away, but I was caught.

It continued until the woman raised one hand, red manicured nails perfect, and palmed Scarlett's barely rounded chest through her shirt, and finally, Scarlett jumped away, cheeks flaming.

"Jenna... I don't..."

"Do you like boys?" Jenna asked.

Scarlett's reply was mumbled, too low for me to hear.

"Your father thought not. This has to happen, sweetie, we both know that."

Scarlett started to cry.

"Do you think I'm pretty?"

Jenna grabbed her by the hand and yanked her back down onto the recliner I was sitting in. I jumped off it instantly, sick to my stomach.

"Don't fight, just let me make you feel good, okay? I can make this good for you, someone else might not have."

Scarlett cried the whole way through.

She cried when she was left alone afterward, her jeans still discarded on the floor, her knees pulled up so her forehead rested on them.

"You're a woman now, Scarlett," was all Wilfred had said when he entered the room to stop the camera. I wondered if he had watched all along, bile in my mouth.

The videos got darker, bloodier, and I cried while I watched until my eyes ran dry. Scarlett whipping, Scarlett cutting, Scarlett branding and burning and breaking. There was none of the joy in it, but she began to show some proficiency at the simple act. They flitted to her as a twenty-year-old already working in the punishment center.

Somewhere between the screams, I fell into a fitful sleep. A nightmare reel played behind my eyes, Scarlett and me changing places in Wilfred's sick games. When I woke it was to the sound of her voice singing softly, and I almost cried with relief. I needed desperately to touch her, hold her, just know she was okay, whole somehow still, even as fractured as she was.

Her voice was coming from the television, a soft haunting song leaving her lips, the macabre scene displaying the punishment center, bodies at her feet, and bodies strung up on poles. She was barefoot and bloodied, and this video seemed more recent because some of her showmanship, her love of it all had begun to creep in. The song stopped, someone cried out, and she moved through the room like a tornado of death.

I shot to my feet when the door banged open behind me. Scarlett crossed the room too fast for me to follow, then the TV went silent.

Turning to me, she held up her hands. She approached me slowly, wary.

"Princess?"

I ran to her and she held me tight.

"Did he hurt you?"

I replied against the soft skin of her neck, still cold from the world outside.

"Will you get in trouble for being up here?" I pulled back to look at her, checking her over silently for any signs of damage.

"No, he told me to come fetch you. He's not exactly playing his cards close to his chest right now."

She tugged me out of the room, pulled me up into her arms when she noticed my bare feet, and carried me easily down the hall to the elevator.

We didn't speak until we reached our room, the thirteenth floor still silent as she moved us quickly through it.

She set me on the bed and closed the door, locking it, before she turned back to me.

"He locked you up there and had you watch me...working, all day?"

I understood her nervousness now, her worry that her father had driven a wedge between us by showcasing the very worst of her. Instead, if anything, he had fostered a clearer understanding of her in me, by showing me exactly how it had all begun. I knew she would be devastated that I had seen the tapes. She was immensely private. I wondered if she even knew the man who had forced it had so meticulously recorded her transformation. She deserved the truth.

"Actually, they weren't just working videos, there were some from when you were younger."

The life drained from her face, and she was frozen for a long moment. Though I couldn't feel her I knew she was uncomfortable. She hated to be seen as weak; it was still difficult for her to be vulnerable, even with me, and the recordings displayed her at her most exposed.

"Oh."

She glanced at the door and I knew she was debating leaving again. I ached for her to stay; I missed her, needed her, needed something to hold me down, anchor me in the storm that was gaining intensity around us.

"He offered to help me become like you, to teach me how so I could work beside you, rather than being just another burden for you."

She hated the thought. The weight of her disdain for it, her desire for me never to go down that path, felt crushing. I scrubbed my eyes to try to clear my head. It was easier as she realized she was influencing me.

"And did you accept?"

I hated this, her careful distance. I just wanted her close, safe, whole. I needed it, to run my hands over all her broken pieces and check everything was still in place after the devastating spectacle of the impromptu video marathon.

"Of course not."

She hovered, and Wilfred's words rang in my ears. Was I already too late? Was this quest to save me already driving her to places too dark for any of us to get her back? I couldn't deny that she was obsessed. Chasing down the idea, barreling toward an undoubtedly bloody, messy climax none of us could divert her from. She wouldn't stop until it was done, until she had the power to subvert the order and keep me as I was. Or until she failed.

I wanted her to stay, desperately. I wanted to find her again in the noise that surrounded us and taste her on my tongue.

She appeared beside me, her dark irises just stirring to life.

"Careful, princess."

The warning was soft and breathy, and I realized I had compelled her.

"Sorry."

I wasn't, but she kissed me anyway, soft and slow, and it was everything I needed and not entirely enough.

"Your voice is in my head..."

She whispered the words against my lips. I pulled back, surprised, tangling my fingers in her loose curls and reveling in her presence. The phenomenon of her speaking to me in my mind wasn't something that had ever run both ways before, as far as I knew.

She lowered her lips to my neck and kissed the sensitive skin there. My body sang, and I blushed in spite of myself. I wanted to reconnect with her, I wanted her soul laid bare so I could count the pieces, and I wanted her cool fingers to smooth over the cracks I could feel beginning to show in mine.

"If it wasn't my greatest wish to keep you safe..."

She kissed and then nipped the soft skin at my neck. My tears dried on my cheeks from the horrors on the fifteenth floor turned to summer rain.

"I would bite you, just. Like. This."

She mouthed my neck harder and I ached for it.

"Is this what you want?"

She was whispering against my skin, and as much as I was confused by the sudden erotic turn the day had taken after what had happened to me with Wilfred, I welcomed the escape. For once, I just let myself go.

I told her yes, a million times in my thoughts and only once out loud.

She moved away to rummage through the nightstand. My heart rate spiked, images of what she kept there already assaulting me. Scarlett turned and gave me an amused look, her tongue running slick over her lips as she followed my train of thought.

What she produced instead of a toy was a single razor blade.

"My teeth and nails will mark your skin. This won't, and my blood will heal you afterwards. It's your decision."

The little metal blade scared me. It was a foray further down the rabbit hole I was already dangerously addicted to, but the thought of her mouth on my neck, sucking, licking, taking from me, was glorious in a way, and my wrist wasn't enough anymore.

I was already breathing heavier and she moved closer, hovering in front of me, watching me reverently with sharp eyes. Scarlett brushed back my hair with slim fingers. Her love for me shattered over me. Our connection was there, warming me, but I wanted it to burn.

I nodded. Her fingers slid from my hair around my neck and she squeezed, I watched her mismatched irises swirl in response as I struggled slightly to breathe until she let me go.

One quick movement set a long white line across the inside of her tanned wrist, before it filled in red, and then crimson began to leak from the edges. I took it before she offered it, tugging it up to my mouth and lathing my tongue along the wound. She hissed at the sting and then was quiet. She crashed over me like the rain in a lightning storm. I tasted it all, her vulnerability, her fear at what I had seen, the raging desire to keep me human, to protect me and for her own selfish reasons because this was something she never wanted to miss. I wanted the same.

With the fingers of her free hand, she pushed me back onto the pillows. They pushed up my shirt and ran over my hipbones, up over my breasts and around the column of my neck. She squeezed again, and I ran my tongue across her wrist, tasting her desire, the edge of darkness that spilled into her veins before she pulled her arm away.

"I want you naked, sweetheart."

It was a simple request. I stripped down until I was bare and lay back on the bed. She removed her own clothes slowly, blood from her wrist dripping onto the sheets, into her hair, over her body. The sight excited me more than I ever would have believed blood could.

"Use me, Mistress."

The words surprised me, and she swallowed thickly. It took me a minute to realize they had spilled from me at her bidding.

"I love you, Scarlett, drink from me, have me..."

I repeated the sentiment in my own words this time, because I wanted what she wanted, if not in exactly the same light. She crawled up the bed to kneel atop me, the blade still in her hand. I tried to ignore the anxiety its presence put in my stomach.

My fingers ran trails up her sides, over the curve of her waist to the tips of her dark hair. She was wet, I could feel it on my stomach even through the black panties she still wore.

She fingered her bleeding wrist and brought the digits to her mouth, licking them and sucking them in a show that was completely pornographic, pouring gasoline over the fire of everything I ached for.

"Do you want more, Princess?"

"Yes, Mistress."

The answer was easy, and her eyes flamed in response. I could give her this. On some level I loved it too. I wanted her to own me, to belong to her always.

She lay down on top of me and raised her wrist to my lips. I took it greedily, my other hand on her backside, pushing her into my rolling hips. The little cut didn't bleed as much as her usual messy wounds there did, a fact that frustrated me as I sucked hard.

She whined softly, grinding down against me. I was torn between the want to kiss her lips, devour the needy little noises she was making and to keep drinking, tugging the blood from her veins.

She yanked her arm away, biting my neck hard enough to make me moan, not entirely in pleasure.

"Ready?"

She held up the little razor, shining in the late afternoon light.

My heart beat hard with fear and adrenaline.

"Yes."

I held my breath, and when she leaned down, I closed my eyes.

It wasn't the sharp bite of the razor that kissed my skin, it was a long swipe of her tongue, the graze of her teeth, the pressure of her lips, until all I could feel was the raging need for her to bite me.

"Please, Scar... Please." I clung to her.

It happened fast. Her mouth was gone, something cool in its place followed by the sting of cold air on the fresh edges of a wound, and then her warm wet mouth covered me again and I was lost.

The tide washed over me as she took, and I pulled her arm up to my lips, my teeth mauling the cut she had left there until it bled for me again and we were totally connected.

She pushed her free hand down between us, three fingers pressed into me, and the sharp burn of them was followed by a wave of slick pleasure that made them easier to take.

She fucked me as we drank, long and slow and deep. I came so hard my jaw was slack, the pressure of her hot mouth over my neck, making it the most intense orgasm I had ever known.

I felt the heavy weight of her in my head, the claiming in her voice as it echoed the word *mine.*

She pushed back into me again, this time with more force, and I cried out, a cry she broke from drinking to swallow. She stretched me more than she ever had, four fingers inside.

Blood was hot down the side of my neck; it soaked the pillow beneath me, my hair, and I vaguely wondered how much I had lost, though any real care was secondary to more carnal things. I trusted Scarlett and I was addicted to the taste of our blood mingling in my mouth, as she forced her tongue into it.

Her fingers curled inside me and I came again hard, exaltations of "yes, Mistress," spilling loud from my lips.

I was sore when she pulled out of me, but not tired. I wanted more.

Forcing my limp body to sit, I lifted her wrist to my neck. When I pulled it away, my blood had closed the gash on her arm, but my own still bled over my shoulder.

She smiled wickedly, and I panicked for just a second before she leaned over and took the razor blade from the nightstand and slashed a long vertical cut down the smooth column of her own neck.

The blade fell to the floor as I tackled her onto the mattress and climbed on top of her, my own bloodied throat forgotten in exchange for hers. The blood in my veins sung as my lips closed on the cut that was bleeding heavily for me.

"Sweetheart..."

She tried once to divert me, her pleasure at my reaction, her satisfaction, dark and dirty and depraved at the way I held her down. It overtook her concern for closing the gash on my neck.

I bit at her throat, sucking, licking, drinking, consumed with having her, devouring her, belonging with her. Wilfred's words were present yet far away, but I let myself go. Like this I was enough for her; I was as dark and filthy, dried blood streaked down my chest, matted in my hair. I felt her desire for me, her wonder at me. Deep down, as much as she wanted to save me, keep me untainted, she was curious about me as something of the dark.

"Princess..."

She groaned, and her hips bucked up to mine, her shoulders lifting from the bed. I shoved her back down, slicking my tongue greedily over her bleeding wound.

She fumbled beside me, her head turned away. I ignored her, content to rock my hips down hard on hers, already cruising pleasantly toward another high. She pushed me back. Something cold slipped between my legs, pressing at the apex of my open thighs, then it was inside me. I looked down between us and watched her guide the business end of the toy into herself.

I twisted my fingers in her hair, pulling her head up and stopping the movement.

I studied her face. She wanted it, she dared me.

"So needy." I enunciated each word, letting myself slip back into the place we had both so enjoyed last time.

Her dark eyes burned up at me, defiance and submission in one smoldering look.

“Tell me you need me?”

She did.

I pushed my hips forward, using one hand to feel the thick toy slide into her.

“Let me hear you.”

I felt the command as I gave it but didn’t have time to worry over the ethics of it, already diving back down to her neck.

She writhed and moaned beneath me, she begged and cursed and told me she loved me, and she was my needy little whore. Everything spilled out, and I tasted and felt it all in tandem, hurtling toward another orgasm.

I pressed my lips to her ear.

“You’re mine, Scarlett. Always.”

She came, agreement on her lips, and I followed close behind. When we finally sagged, spent and sweat-soaked, I was light-headed and tired.

I heard her sharp intake of breath when she pulled the toy out of her, jolting it inside me and sending aftershocks skittering through my veins. Warm wetness pressed against my neck, the sheets rustled, and I was aware I had stopped bleeding.

She tugged me closer to her.

“Look.”

It was a simple command and I opened my eyes to follow, finding hers in the large mirror that sat on her vanity at the end of her bed.

The two of us stared back, tangled together, eyes bright, hair mussed, my pale skin and her light tan, both covered in blood. The sight of it matted into my hair was particularly unsettling, but I couldn’t deny, together like that, we were beautiful. I knew she was thinking the same.

Her hand journeyed down my body and I whined softly as she went to remove the toy. Sensing my tenderness, she left it in place, her eyes meeting mine again as she licked her lips and then disappeared. I watched in the mirror as she went down on me, her mouth cool against my abused flesh, and overly wet, slicking over my tender parts, lubricating me.

It was erotic somehow to see myself, my blue eyes dark, nipples hard and straining, legs spread unabashedly as a gorgeous woman worked me closer and closer to coming again.

I jumped when she slipped the bulb out of me, the pain edging me closer.

She looked up in question.

"Don't stop."

She lowered her head again, and I was surprised to feel something enter me. I whimpered lightly, but her tongue lathing over me soothed the temporary burn.

"Let me have you, Princess?"

Powerless to deny her, I spread my legs wider. She knelt before me, ushering my back up onto the pillows before she settled over me, taking the bulb into herself.

"Watch."

The word was whispered, dropped with a kiss onto my ear, as she started to touch me. Sore as I was, I was soaked from the attention of her mouth, and I did my best to keep my eyes open, to do as she said. I watched her back muscles move, the bob of her backside, her long tan legs resting inside my open ones as she pushed us both to one last long, slow orgasm.

Her nose brushed the crook of my neck as she slipped out of me, and I heard the thud of the toy hitting the floor before she was winding herself around me.

I studied us in the mirror. Scarlett, the most beautiful creature I had ever seen, in this world or mine, and me, still the same plain girl I always was, though I looked healthier now, my figure fuller than before, my skin brighter. The evidence of someone finally caring for me showed in my appearance.

She pressed her lips just below my ear.

"You're exactly right for me."

It was everything I hadn't known I needed to hear.

"Make me a vampire?"

The request surprised me, but it didn't scare me like it once might have. I tried to explain my sudden desire.

"I can't lose you. I want this with you, forever. We can work out the rest."

She was rigid in my embrace.

"Scarlett. Just this time, let me save myself?"

I clung to her tight, and she clung to me, and I wondered exactly what turning me would entail, if it would hurt.

She leaned up on her elbow.

"You'll have me forever, Princess, I promise. I don't have to end your life to give you that." She kissed me softly. "You're mine, and I'm yours, and we're exactly right for each other, just as we are. I'll give you the city, and when it's done, your heart will still beat harder every time I look at you."

Chapter Eight

I FELT A little awkward in Hawthorne Tower. I could tell Jade did too. The atmosphere was lighter than at home, and the human staff were far better dressed, and obviously better treated. I just felt like I didn't quite fit.

"Cami has always been a little jealous of April." Jade leaned over and whispered the words to me quietly as we sat in one of the many grand sitting rooms, waiting for the aforementioned vampire to return with said sister.

"She laughs it off and Scarlett likes to tease her about it, but I think it's sort of sad. April always admired her growing up, idolized her. So of course, because all Camilla wants, really, underneath all her pretense is a family and a dozen kids, April wanted it too. She just found the right person sooner."

It was sort of sad, but it raised a question that made me uncomfortable, beyond the fact Jade still seemed like such a child herself at times.

"Do you want kids, though?"

She nodded. I wondered what Scarlett would make of that, if she would let them go through the process of having babies together, even though if what Scarlett said were true, and biologically, they could be half siblings. They were so happy it seemed cruel to tell them, though I wondered if it might come up anyway during the process.

"I know that probably seems crazy. My family life isn't exactly awesome, but Scarlett raised me well, and the family

I chose is great." She gave my hand a quick squeeze. "The thought of raising kids here terrifies me, but it is my dream someday to have one, maybe two."

The admission was shy, and I squeezed her back.

"You'll be a great mom, and I'll be the cool aunt."

She smiled, though there was a question in it.

"You don't want any kids?"

I laughed.

"With Scarlett? I don't think that's in our future."

She was somber as she looked at me.

"Why? Do you think she would be a horrible mother? She raised me, and I like to think I came out sort of okay..."

She trailed off hurt, and I backpedaled.

"No, Jade, of course that's not it. You're amazing, and I know she has a big heart, I just... Do you think she would want that?"

Honestly, it was hard for me to really, truly imagine it, Scarlett and diapers and spit up, but Jade's face lit up.

"She loves kids! She's great with them. She's never actually said she wants her own, but she never thought it would be on the cards for her. But now who knows?"

The thought made me uncomfortable, because I certainly didn't. I had always imagined I might have a family one day, but then I'd always imagined it would never actually happen either. Before Scarlett I was just the invisible girl, and with her, she was the sun, so big and bright that she bleached out everything else, and I hadn't thought much beyond just hoping for a life with her, forever.

"Who knows."

I echoed Jade's sentiment and was still playing with the idea shyly in my mind when, finally, Camilla reappeared.

"Here's my nephew!"

She was carrying a bundle of blue, adoration shining in her eyes as she sat beside Jade and me on the sofa, taking a tiny hand between two fingers carefully.

"Isn't he precious?"

April appeared behind her, towing along a little girl who looked to be about five, a toddler on her hip.

"Jade! Oh my God, it's been forever, and now you're dating my sister!"

Jade laughed and got up to hug her, the children greeting her with choruses of "Auntie."

"And you brought Scarlett's pet. This one's the hybrid, right?"

"Actually, A, she and Scarlett are together. More girlfriend, less pet kind of together."

April's only response was, "Wow."

"Nice to meet you." I forced myself to find my voice, eager to fulfill my role as *more girlfriend, less pet*.

April smiled. She was dark-haired where Camilla was a lighter brunette, but they shared the same tall stature and large, dark eyes.

"Nice to meet you...?"

"Rayne," Jade supplied helpfully, fussing over the older child.

"Where's Scarlett today?"

"She had an errand to run. She said she'd join us soon."

April nodded, tugging the younger girl off her hip and putting her down on unsteady legs.

"Mia, who's your favorite Auntie?" Cami asked her, already beaming with pride as the girl wobbled her way toward her. She shrieked something that sounded like "Auntie Cami," and Cami cheered. It was strange to watch her like this, all her perfect pretense gone, baby spit up on her designer dress and a smile that didn't just reach her eyes, it illuminated them. Jade sat beside her and they cooed over the baby, sharing a look that made me worry we may have to address the possible genetic situation sooner than I previously thought.

A woman slipped quietly into the room. She wore dark jeans and a loose blouse, but her demeanor told me she was human.

"April, it's so distasteful to have the help around when company is here," Cami chided.

April huffed.

"Excuse me for caring more about my baby than your social etiquette, Cam. Breastfeeding is good for him."

She took the baby from her sister's arms. The tension between them was palpable. Cami watched with longing as the baby was passed to the human woman, who seated herself on a chair furthest from us all and lifted her shirt to feed him.

The love in her eyes when she looked down at the baby told me she had been the one to carry him, the fullness in her figure becoming apparent now. Sadness clawed at my chest as I remembered what Scarlett had told me; once she was no longer useful, she would be killed to avoid any confusion in feelings later. I noticed Jade was oddly stiff beside me, and I was sure the empathetic younger Pearce was thinking about the same thing.

"What did I miss?"

Scarlett appeared in the doorway, and I noted she'd been home to change, most likely meaning her work day was a messy one. Her cheeks were as colored as I'd ever seen them, probably from a combination of the cold outside and our intense blood sharing the previous day.

The toddler wriggled away from Cami and started bumbling toward her. The older girl was already there, babbling up at her with big, adoring eyes.

Taking pity on Cami, Jade struck up a conversation with April, and some of the tension in the room cleared. I only half paid attention, busy watching Scarlett with the children. They clung to her as if she was the last piece of candy in the world.

She sat on the floor with them, talking and listening carefully. The younger girl, Amy, played with the crimson fingernails on one of Scarlett's hands, while Mia stood beside her, arms around her neck, telling a very long story with their faces ridiculously close together. I couldn't help but smile as Scarlett crossed her eyes and added a line.

She was good at this. She was happy like this. Jade's words earlier made sense, and I wondered how this person could live inside the same shell, the same soul, as the woman who dominated the punishment center, who treated extreme displays of violence like an art form, and destruction like a divine experience.

I loved both parts of her, for better or worse, but I couldn't deny that part of me, a larger part than I was brave enough to admit, wanted her like this. Soft kisses and long days spent together at home, that big genuine smile on her face with little arms around her neck. It sounded like a fantasy, like a fairytale, where the darkness we delved into together in bed might actually be enough to sate her, and beyond that, we could have normal lives.

Someone tapped me on the knee and I jumped, glancing down to find Mia looking up at me, a determined frown on her face.

"My aunt says...you falled from heaven and did it hurt?"

I gave Scarlett a look over the little girl's head. She winked at me and turned on the godforsaken smolder that melted me every time.

"Your aunt is very cheesy. Can you tell her that?"

Her eyes lit up, and we seemed to have struck on a common interest.

"I likes cheese. Who you?"

"I like cheese too. I'm Rayne. Who are you?"

"I'm Mia."

She considered me for a moment them stuck out her hand.

"You play with us, Ray?"

Jade "aww"-ed beside me.

I took the sticky little hand and followed her dutifully back to Scarlett, who watched the entire thing, looking me up and down as I walked across the room in a way that made my cheeks flame.

"Best wingwoman ever!"

She gave Mia a high five they had to redo twice because the girl kept missing and pulled me down beside her.

"Dis you wife?" Mia asked, and Scarlett turned to look at me, long and hard, as she answered.

"No...not yet, but she is mine."

I think my heart stopped beating, and I know I stopped breathing because Scarlett's voice was soft in my head. *Breathe, Princess.*

Mia was prattling still, Amy had Scarlett's fingers in her mouth, gnawing them like a bone, but time was frozen for us, and all I heard, saw, felt was her shy desire, her endless longing for me. It was mutual, and it consumed me completely.

Cami yelling maturely for us to get a room broke the moment, and my cheeks flamed red as I finally took a breath. Jade was smiling in a way that told me she had heard some or all of the exchange, and it only made me more embarrassed. I studied my shoes and let Mia tug on what she called my pretty hair.

Despite the woman in the corner who disappeared once the baby was fed and didn't return, the outing turned pleasant with Scarlett by my side. I discovered it wasn't just Hawthorne Tower's opulent décor that made me feel out of place; it was the sheer normalcy, the illusion of regular society, that seemed to live here. We talked and laughed, and played with the kids, and for a while, I could forget I was in Vires, I could forget the love of my life was a sadistic, power-hungry vampire. For a while we were just Scarlett and Rayne, in a world where Scarlett had implied she intended to marry me one day, and maybe we could have a child of our own and live happily ever after. It was too clean, the path was too straightforward, it was too light, and it just didn't feel like my life.

"Come for a walk with me?"

She pressed a kiss beneath my ear, and I swore she sensed my need to take a breath. I nodded and let her haul me up from under a disgruntled Mia as she detached Amy.

"Go give Auntie Cami a big kiss!"

The girls scampered off to do it, and we slipped away.

Scarlett led me through Hawthorne Tower with a familiarity I tried not to dissect the origin of. Thinking of her and Cami together now was so strange, but I knew it was a part of their complicated history, long done.

We stepped out onto the roof. It was twilight, the sun dying behind heavy gray clouds. The white tint of snow still kissed the tops of the towers around us, the roofs of the buildings in the Midlands and beyond. Despite all my feelings about Vires, the city was beautiful.

I clung to the railing looking down at it, taking it all in. Scarlett stepped up behind me. I heard her unzip her jacket. She draped it around me over my sweater and held it closed in front of us. She felt warm against my back in comparison to the cold air. We stayed like that for a long time. She swayed us back and forth, and I leaned my head back on her shoulder and let her, content.

"Did I scare you earlier?"

Her voice was soft, and I knew she was referring to her interaction with her nieces.

"No." It was the truth. I turned in her arms and she let me go. She slipped the jacket off her shoulders, wrapped it around mine, and used it to pull me close to her as she pressed me back into the railing.

"Good," was all she said in response before she kissed me, soft and slow, sweet and hot.

"Do you want kids?"

I blurted the words out without really meaning to, my heart rate picking up with nerves once they had left me. The question hung in the frigid air between us. She studied me, and I felt her hesitation, her quiet hopefulness and the fear that came with it.

"I never thought that could be my life, that it could even be an option for me."

It was half an answer and I kissed her lips, turned colder by the freezing air.

"Let's say it is an option, because you're great with them and you have a huge heart and despite your broody, moody vampire thing, you're the glue that holds our family together..." I stumbled a bit over my own words. "You, me, Cami and Jade, I mean..." I hadn't meant to imply family when it came to Scarlett and myself anytime soon, unsure if it was something she wanted.

She laughed and kissed me, took a deep breath, and told me, "Yes."

I swallowed hard.

"Maybe one day, maybe with you there's a future where we'd have a child, if that's something you also want."

I hugged her tight, feeling what the admission had cost her, how hard it had been for her to take the unchartered step into letting herself hope.

I nodded into her neck and I knew she felt it.

There was so much more to consider than just if we wanted children, but for now, the simple fact we did was enough.

"Take me home?"

It was a selfish request, but I wanted her all to myself while she was like this, soft and warm and open, playful and even hopeful. The light in her eyes cast a beautiful glow on the outlook around us that was usually so bleak, and I wanted to bathe in it for a while longer.

"Why run all the way home? I happen to know of a few spare bedrooms right here."

She swept me into her arms and I laughed as we moved through the halls, fast enough to disorient me, until she was laying me on soft pillows and climbing on top of me.

WE MADE LOVE for what felt like hours, and when we returned downstairs, I could tell it had been.

April and her brood seemed to be gone—or had moved to another part of the tower at least—and Camilla was alone by the fire, staring into the flames.

"Where's Jade?"

Scarlett's question made her jump so hard the liquor in her hand sloshed over the side of the glass and onto her pants, making her hiss.

"When did you get back? She went home to see if you two wanted to come up for air and eat with us. I figured you'd all just decided to stay home. Seems that was over an hour ago."

Scarlett's fear shot me in the chest when I was too slow to make the jump before her.

"We didn't go home."

Cami jumped to her feet and was in front of us before I could blink.

"She's probably fine. Let's just go check."

Scarlett tried to calm us all, swinging me up into her arms again, before we were running.

Chapter Nine

CAMILLA UTTERLY REFUSED to scale the building, and as worried as we all were, as eager as we all were to get to the thirteenth floor, I was glad. The height made me nauseous. So, we took the elevator like civilized beings, Scarlett's foot tapping the whole way, her unease mixing with mine, making the small space stifling.

When the doors dinged open, she was gone before we stepped out, leaving Camilla beside me, her hands gripping her thighs. She muttered, "She's not here, she's not here," over and over with increasing pitch and panic.

"She's not here."

Scarlett's words sent my stomach plummeting into my sneakers.

"Could there be a logical explanation?"

I tried to be reasonable. Camilla was already at panic station ground zero beside me, looking around wildly like Jade might appear out of thin air.

"Maybe she went back to Hawthorne Tower, or to the market to get something for dinner and bring back to yours." Scarlett took my idea and ran with it.

"Camilla..."

She grabbed Camilla's arm and held it until she met her gaze; I realized it was the first time I had seen them touch in so long.

"Stay here with Rayne. I'm going to go take a quick look for her in case we missed her on the way back."

She waited until Cami nodded and then she was gone. Down the hall, the drapes billowed in the wind through the open window. I moved on autopilot to close it all but a crack, to be sure she could get back in, knowing her patience for the elevator was long gone.

Cami still stood in the foyer, the most undone I had ever seen her. I approached her cautiously and took her hand.

"Can I make you some tea?"

She nodded, looking far away, so I tugged her along with me to the kitchen and left her by the bar. I set the kettle to boil. Our relationship was a strange one. When we first met, she'd hated me, disapproved of my relationship with Scarlett deeply, and I had been jealous of her and threatened by her, as silly as it seemed. When Scarlett was sick and unreasonable, she became an unlikely ally, a friend. As much as we had our differences, I had come to love her as a member of our messed-up little family.

"We'll find her."

My reassurance was quiet, and she looked up at me with empty eyes.

"You don't know that." It was true, I didn't, but I did know something.

"If Wilfred has taken her somewhere, he won't hurt her. She's too valuable to him when it comes to Scarlett."

Cami didn't seem to hear me, and I left her to her brooding, remembering how terrible I had felt when Scarlett disappeared into the bunker, and we were left behind to wonder if we would ever see her again. I desperately wanted Jade home, safe, out of Wilfred's terrifying clutches, but I was also confident that she was too valuable to him for him to do any real harm to her and risk retaliation from Scarlett.

The kettle came to a boil and I poured two mugs of tea, choosing a peppermint bag and adding a huge amount of honey to Camilla's in the hopes of helping her out of the current shocked, and possibly tipsy, state she seemed to be in.

I had just set the cup down in front of Camilla when Scarlett appeared behind me.

"Has she come home?"

I shook my head.

"Where did you go this morning, Scarlett?"

Camilla leaped to her feet, sending her stool spilling back across the tile floor and colliding hard with the wall, surprising us all. I jumped at the sudden movement and Scarlett's hand closed around my arm. She pulled me back away from the angry Camilla.

"That's none of your damn business," she snarled, the tension in the room ramping up with every passing second. With both of them emotionally compromised by Jade's disappearance, they were fanning the flames of the old grudge between them that I had hoped was finally beginning die.

"You went into the fucking bunker, didn't you?" Camilla roared the words and the curse sounded so wrong in her voice. "You stuck your stupid, reckless nose into things you shouldn't and got caught, again!"

Everything unfolded fast before me, and all I could do was watch. Scarlett rose up three inches beside me, and I waited for them to collide.

"That is none of your business!"

I could hear the restraint in her voice and silently I begged Cami to sit down so we could talk through this reasonably. I almost suggested as much, but Camilla spoke again.

"It is my business when it means Jade gets pulled into all your bullshit. We get it! You have a shiny new toy now, and finally you have taken your claws out of Jade and let her be her own damn person, but really? Even after he threatened her, you're still on this suicide mission, all for what? So you can keep playing power trip with your breakable little human girl, even at the expense of the sister who was your whole entire world five minutes ago, so much so that she was practically a prisoner in this tower at your beck and call?"

The slap rang out loud and Camilla's head whipped around with the force of it.

A low rumbling hung in the air and I realized Scarlett was growling. I hated the sound.

"You don't know the first thing about Jade, Cami, and so fucking help me, perhaps it's time I educated you."

"Stop it."

I stepped between them, because this was devolving, spilling and spiraling and descending into madness. I was not going to let Scarlett drop *that* truth on Camilla, not now, not like this.

"You're both scared for her, I understand, but fighting each other won't bring her back. In fact, it only makes us even less likely to find her."

"We'll never fucking find her!" Cami was hysterical.

"I knew you were stupid—you have to be to come here of your own free will—but wake up! Look at what he did to Scarlett, she's a psychopath, and you know something, so is he, but he's worse, and he has Jade. Jade who couldn't whip a stupid little Fringe girl to save her own silly skin!"

There was a flurry of motion and a thud, and Camilla was on the floor, Scarlett on top of her, her hands tight around her throat, her face twisted into something I recognized by now, but never wanted to see here, in our home. Cami looked up at her with dull brown eyes, stunned.

"Don't ever talk to her like that."

Cami tried to push her off. They struggled for a second, but Scarlett held firm.

"It's fine, Scarlett..."

Scarlett turned those dark eyes to me and silenced me.

"It's not fine, you're mine!"

She hissed the words and I knew she was in a dangerously dark place. Hurt and fear wafted off her in waves. She felt powerless, and I was quickly realizing with her, that was the most dangerous emotion of all.

"Let me up, Scarlett."

Cami's voice was a hollow monotone. They stayed frozen for a few more seconds until finally Scarlett clambered off her and Cami hauled herself to her feet, straightening her hair. Something hung between them I wasn't privy to.

"I'm sorry, Rayne."

I shook my head, not feeling owed an apology—she was probably right.

We were quiet for a few moments.

"What do we do?"

Cami sounded smaller than I had ever heard her, and Scarlett looked broken. I hovered by the bar, my tea cold on the counter beside me, unsure how to help, how to even open a conversation without risking another nuclear explosion.

"We do whatever it takes." And just like that, Scarlett rose. She was the flower that had bloomed in adversity, a phoenix that had risen from the ashes of her manipulated, twisted life, and I watched her now, beautiful as her back straightened.

"We do whatever it takes." This time she seemed to be saying the words more for herself than for us, and the sentiment scared me. I knew I was powerless to stop her; she would walk through hell willingly for Jade. I wanted her home too, but not at the expense of my girlfriend, the center of my universe.

A cool breeze kissed my cheeks as Scarlett disappeared, leaving Cami and me to stare awkwardly across the kitchen at each other until she returned.

"Where did you go?"

"To summon my father."

"Are you crazy?" Camilla's hissed response pretty much summed up my feelings on the matter.

"We all know that's where she went, what's the point in pretending?"

Still rattled from our last encounter, I was loath to see Wilfred Pearce again.

"Princess..." I knew she was going to send me away, but the elevator dinged, and it was already too late. Her frustration told me she hadn't expected him to arrive so quickly.

"Scarlett, and Camilla... And Rayne." He surveyed us from the doorway. "What seems to be the emergency?"

"Jade's missing."

It was Camilla who spoke, seeming to come back to herself, taking over the interaction before Scarlett could start. I had no idea what angle she was playing.

"How unfortunate." There was no trace of concern in his voice. "I'm sure she'll be home when things settle down..."

"What did you do with her?" Scarlett cut in, and finally, the pretense fell away.

"I have no idea what you're implying, Scarlett."

"Cut the bullshit, *Daddy.*" She spat the word and it sounded vulgar in her mouth. "Tell me what you want, tell me where she is. You want to make a deal, give me your terms, but I want her home tonight."

She released a controlled breath after the words had left her. Wilfred was silent for a moment and then he laughed, long and low and unnerving. It was a play straight out of Scarlett's own book, and it was totally jarring.

"You want her home tonight?" He was mocking her, and she practically shook with rage beside me.

"What do you want?" She repeated her earlier question.

"Why? Because you would do anything to save her? Absolutely anything?"

"You know I would." She spat the words back at him.

"Fine, a trade then. Your hybrid for your sister."

My blood ran cold. Scarlett hissed, and I pushed past her, forcing myself to find my voice.

"Fine."

He studied me with great interest before she pulled me back roughly, spitting a venomous "no" over my shoulder.

"Interesting." He observed it all, the light back in his eyes. His obsession with her was clear in that moment. I glanced over to Cami and saw she was entranced by it too. This was the man who had broken Scarlett, without the mask.

"And say, Scarlett, if I had taken her, and put her somewhere for...safe keeping, what do you think might have motivated me to do such a thing?"

He posed it like a math question, a science question, like asking for the time or about the weather. His voice easy and cool, not in the least rattled even as he discussed kidnapping someone and holding them against their will.

"How would I know?" She spat the words at him, vibrating with an energy that grew darker every second.

"Think."

His tongue clicked on the "k" and then he was beside me and I was yanked back, standing across the kitchen with him, one of his arms pressed tight across my neck.

"What could you possibly hope to find in the bunker archives? I received a very unhappy phone call after your little excursion this morning. Even though you were already warned to mind your own business."

She took two steps forward and stopped, her composure starting to shatter.

"Let her go."

Her voice lacked its usual strength.

"Why?" He questioned her again, his arm squeezing tighter around my throat, beginning to restrict my air supply. I stayed quiet, still in his grasp, flashing back horribly to my own father and the many times he had choked me, beat me, bruised me before Scarlett had saved me.

"Why is she still a human?"

"Wilfred, please..."

Camilla tried to cut in and he silenced her with a look.

"Welcome to the family, Miss Hawthorne. Consider this your first lesson. Stay out of things that do not involve you."

"With all due respect, sir, Jade is my partner. I love her."

He laughed. "While I approve of the alignment of our families and I'm glad the girl has finally proved useful, you'll also eventually learn love is weakness. Isn't that right, Scarlett?"

I jumped as his cane clattered to the floor, his cold fingers clutching my chin, the position he held me in strange until I finally recognized it. He was going to break my neck.

Scarlett crumbled in front of me, melted, broke down into a desperate, frenzied mess.

"No, no... Please. Please! I'll do it, whatever you want I'll do it, just let her go!"

He held me still, and together we watched her, hands raised in surrender, trembling, before she seemed to steady herself though the fear never left her eyes.

"I'll do it. Just let her go, please, whatever you want."

"Kill Camilla."

The words rolled around my head, strange and meaningless in my adrenaline-filled brain, until finally they took form. Camilla shrieked and was already running. He laughed, cold breath on the back of my neck, before I was tossed forward hard. Scarlett caught me before I hit the ground. When she pulled me tight to her, she was crying.

Wilfred returned to the room with a screaming, kicking, fighting Camilla in tow.

"Enough!" He roared at her, and she stilled, looking down at Scarlett and me, fear clear in her eyes.

"I was joking."

He was the only one who found it funny.

Scarlett wiped roughly at her eyes, forcing herself to her feet. She pressed me back against the counter and smoothed my hair before she turned to him. When she stalked forward, she seemed bolder. She yanked Camilla from his grasp and shoved her in my general direction.

"How do I get Jade back?"

She balled her hands into fists at her sides.

"What are you looking for in the bunker?"

She sighed.

"I heard a rumor about Jade, that we're only half-sisters. A human in the Fringe said he had a relationship with a scientist twenty years ago, that she'd told him. I knew it was a lie and I killed him, but then... I just... It's such a strange lie, so specific. Ever since I haven't been able to stop thinking about it. I need to know it's not true."

The relief was visible for the barest moment on Wilfred's face before it was gone.

"And this is why you've been so distracted, why your hybrid hasn't been turned, or trained, why you're sneaking around deep in the bunker?"

The ends of her dark hair danced as she nodded, and then there was a thud. When I found her again, she was crumpled against the refrigerator, blood dripping down her chin, one hand over her mouth where he had struck her. The shock hit me like a physical blow, and I almost ran to her.

"Childish distractions, Scarlett." He hissed the words. "For the record, it was a lie. As much as you wouldn't think it, sadly, Jade is a Pearce. You will put this to bed."

She nodded, looking shamefaced. Camilla shuffled closer to me and grabbed my hand, pressing it between our bodies and squeezing it tight out of view, keeping me from going to Scarlett just yet. As much as I ached to, I knew this had to play out.

"Turn your hybrid, and handle your business, Scarlett, or I will start to handle it for you."

She said nothing, and finally, some of the crushing weight, the dread, began to rescind as I sensed his anger waning, satisfied with Scarlett's lie.

"Jade will be back before midnight. Clean yourself up. I expect to hear your name in the announcements tonight."

She nodded and then he was gone. I rushed across the space and fell painfully to my knees on the hardwood floor, going easily when she pulled me to her and held me tight.

Across the room, Camilla cried silently.

"Scarlett..."

Scarlett stuck out her other arm, and in a flash, Camilla was beside us. I wrapped my arms around her too, and we all sat there for far too long, just breathing.

Chapter Ten

JADE HAD RETURNED unhurt, and Scarlett's busted lip had finally stopped bleeding. We sat together in our room, face to face on the bed.

"You have to stop looking."

She shook her head.

"If anything, I have to find something. We're running out of time."

With only two weeks left, I knew she was right.

"Just turn me..."

I didn't even get to finish before she silenced me without words.

"Would you have killed Cami?"

She let the question hang unanswered for a few long moments.

"Not if there was any other way. I was going to try to kill him first, I just... It's like he paralyzes me."

"He tortured you for years." I held her face in my hands, looking deep into her oddly colored eyes until they would hold mine. "He broke you, baby, it's logical to be afraid."

The endearment was new, but she didn't seem to mind it, though she did take exception to something else.

"I'm not afraid, I'm just...stuck."

I breathed out, content to let the topic die and go back to trying to convince her to give up her insane plan to take down the government, when a knock at the door interrupted us.

When it opened Camilla appeared, puffy-eyed and pale.

"Come in..."

I invited her when Scarlett remained silent, avoiding her eyes. Scooting over, I motioned for her to sit beside me and wrapped an arm around her when she did. For all our history, she was my family too.

"Scarlett, I um..." It was one of the first times I had heard her stutter, her voice raw and cracked. She cleared her throat and tried again.

"I need to ask you something." Her lip trembled, and tears spilled from her eyes when she looked up at her best friend, waiting for the other woman to look back.

"What you said to your father..." A sob broke the words and she took a moment to collect herself. I squeezed her tight, trying to lend her some strength.

"Before Leo died, he told me something, and I just... I never thought much of it at the time, but he said we had another sibling, a sister, April's age... That there was some sort of mix-up."

Another hacking sob cut through her words. My heart plummeted.

"Scar... I need you to be honest with me." She swiped roughly at her eyes. "Is Jade my...sister?" She started to cry, and my heart broke for her. "I know you hate me, and you think it's weird and that she's a child, but I love her, Scarlett. I love her like I used to talk about when we played house as little kids. I want to spend my life with her but ever since you told your father that I just can't stop thinking..."

She wiped at her eyes again and I studied Scarlett's face.

"Our children would be... and I just... If she was my sister. This is everything I ever wanted, finally, but I can't marry my sister... I just... Just tell me please..." She sobbed. "Just say it?" Camilla cried harder.

"Cami, stop it, Jade's not your sister, she's mine. You're not related."

Camilla looked up, tears still wet on her cheeks.

"Really?"

Scarlett looked at her, and with all the sincerity in the world she told her, "Really."

Cami cried harder and to my surprise turned and hugged me tight. I hugged her back and offered Scarlett a questioning look over her shoulder, as she sniffled into mine.

"I checked. There's no blood relation between you and Jade."

I heard the relief in Scarlett's announcement.

Finally, Camilla pulled back and wiped her eyes, another sob taking over before it turned into a laugh.

"You must think I'm so stupid."

I reassured her that we didn't, but Scarlett shrugged, which made her laugh.

"I wasn't going to kill you, you idiot."

Despite the macabre situation, we all laughed at that.

"Any sane vampire in my shoes would have run. I hoped for the best but prepared for the worst. We all know you're crazy for this one."

She patted my cheek affectionately and I reached up and squeezed her hand.

"There you are!"

Jade appeared at the door. She rushed over to Cami and wrapped her arms around her neck, kissing her sweetly on the forehead.

"I was looking for you. Why are you still crying?"

"It's nothing, darling."

She smiled at each other, and the sight was so sweet I wasn't sure if I wanted to cry or hurl. I sensed a wedding on the horizon. Scarlett looked at me and nodded ever so slightly. I smiled back.

"Where did he take you?"

Her voice cut through the moment, back to business, and the sweetness that had lingered around me evaporated. She was still hell-bent on getting herself killed for me.

Jade clutched Cami close to her chest, and Cami rested her head there.

"To the bunker. I sat in a room, nothing happened, then he brought me home."

"Why would he take you to the bunker?"

Camilla asked the question we were all thinking, and it reminded me of a question of my own.

"I meant to ask you what his involvement with the Government is. How does he know whenever you're doing something you shouldn't?"

Scarlett shrugged.

"He has friends in high places. I figured they call and tattle."

"Someone on the council?" Jade questioned.

Scarlett nodded.

"Probably."

"Or he's on the council himself."

My idea was greeted by silence. Scarlett shook her head, but Jade interrupted.

"It would make a certain kind of sense, though... He always knows what you're doing, he took me to the bunker today. No one questioned him or asked if he had orders or permission to be there."

"No one questions me either..."

"That's because they're terrified of you," Cami supplied helpfully.

"I mean I guess it's possible...and if it was true it would definitely be a start in dismantling the Government to know who one of them was," Scarlett conceded though she still sounded skeptical.

"Let's ask Mom?"

Camilla snorted. "Oh, this is going to be good."

Scarlett grit her teeth.

"Is it really worth upsetting her over a crazy theory, a hunch at best?"

"A hunch that makes sense!" Jade supplied.

"You have a mom?" I couldn't keep the surprise from my voice.

"Ever heard the expression it takes two to tango, Princess?" Scarlett joked.

Jade kissed Cami again and then pulled away. "I'll go and get her, let's meet in the living room?"

Scarlett nodded and then Jade was gone.

"Go ahead and get us a good sofa, sweetheart, we'll be there in a minute."

Scarlett dismissed me. I didn't mind. As I turned to close the door behind me, she was pulling Camilla into her arms, Camilla going willingly. As I walked down the hall, I was proud of myself for how much I had grown, proud of all of us for what we had overcome, and strangely optimistic about this new crazy idea that somehow Wilfred Pearce was more involved than he seemed. I had no idea what we would do if he was, but for now, it made me feel like we were making progress.

I went through the motions of remaking my tea and sipped from my mug as I perched on the sofa.

Camilla and Scarlett joined me first, the latter sitting beside me and winding herself comfortably around me, while Camilla reclined at the other end of the sofa, looking tired but relaxed.

The elevator dinged, and voices and footsteps floated toward us.

"But I don't want to be a dancer, Mom."

"Yes but, darling, you'd be beauuutiful. Wonderful. And besides what else are you doing with your life?"

Scarlett rolled her eyes and Camilla snickered.

"Oh my God, she still hasn't realized she has two left feet?"

They appeared at the doorway as Scarlett shook her head.

"Hello, Mother."

"Scarlett, darling, Mommy's here!"

There was something off about Scarlett and Jade's mom. Her hair was jet black, with one thick gray streak running from her crown back into her slightly lopsided ponytail. Black work boots poked out from under her flowing black dress.

"Mrs. Pearce..."

Camilla greeted her cordially.

The woman studied her.

"Camilla, is that you? I have to say you look wonderful even though I know you're defiling my daughter... The other one this time!"

Camilla shifted uncomfortably as Jade groaned.

"Mom..."

"Now don't you Mommy me, young lady." She turned back to Camilla. "Are your intentions pure, Camilla Hawthorne?"

Camilla sat up straight, and I could see somewhere deep down she was fighting a smile.

"Yes, ma'am."

"Well, all right then, I suppose." Mrs. Pearce sniffed again, lifting up her skirts as she plonked down into a recliner and crossed her legs in a very unladylike fashion.

"Mother, I can see your underwear," Scarlett declared dryly, and sharp dark eyes turned to her.

"And what about you, Scarlett? I can't keep up with your toys. Which one is it that has Daddy so wound up now, hm? The nurse?" Her eyes landed on me, and she tilted her head, one hand thankfully yanking her long skirt down over one knee. "Plain, but pretty," she observed aloud.

"Mother, this is Rayne." Scarlett took my hand. "She's not my toy, I love her."

The woman just continued to stare at me.

"Sweetheart, this is my mother, Helena Pearce." Scarlett spoke quietly, squeezing my hand.

"Oh, don't whisper, Scarlett! For goodness sake, we can't take any more of your whispering. I still haven't forgotten what you did to poor Alfie!"

"Oh my God..." Scarlett flopped back in her seat defeated, glaring at Jade. "Why did I let you convince me this was a good idea?"

"Speak up, child!" Helena grumbled.

"Who's Alfie?" I couldn't help but ask, though I was unsure I wanted to know.

"Scarlett's toy." Mrs. Pearce turned her attention back to me. "Stand up, girl, and let me have a proper look at you."

Blushing, I did as I was asked. She hummed as she appraised me. Scarlett looked embarrassed and Camilla was hardly containing her laughter.

"Hmm, yes, a bit skinny, decent chest, nice derriere... Blonde... Scarlett, did you say she was a vampire, dear?"

"No, Mother, she's a hybrid."

Mrs. Pearce seemed suddenly lucid.

"Did you sire her?"

Scarlett seemed to sense the switch too. Her reply was more careful.

"No. ma'am... She was like this when I...met her." I knew she'd had to fight the habit of saying "acquired" or "came to own."

"Impossible. Someone has shared blood with her. Hybrids don't just happen. Is she a Delta hybrid or a non-Delta? Someone's head is going to land on the chopping block for this..."

That seemed to spark something in her, and she set off singing a bizarre little song, while Jade and Cami stared at us, questions in their eyes.

Jade cleared her throat.

"Mother..."

"Call me Mommy, dear." Helena cut in, before she went back to her singing.

"Mommy..." Jade stuttered out the word, embarrassed. "Used to be a Government scientist, one of the best. One day there was an accident...and she...um..."

"Oh, it wasn't an accident, darling. Wasn't an accident at all."

"What do you mean?" Scarlett humored her.

"When you know too much, you know too much."

"What did you know too much about, Mommy?"

She ground out the word, and it sounded odd in her mouth, but all of us were eager to hear what the woman had to say.

"We don't talk about that, Helena!" She barked out the words and I jumped. Her voice was deep and decidedly masculine, and we all exchanged a glance as we realized she was imitating her husband. "Jade darling, why don't you do a little dance for us? I dreamed last night you were in the ballet."

I watched Helena. As strange as she was, beneath the neurosis there was something sad to her. I wished she could tell us her story.

"I don't dance, Mom..."

Jade squirmed uncomfortably as her cheeks were pinched.

"No of course not, dear, that's why I always did like Alfie best. Until Scarlett killed him!"

"You killed your brother?"

I asked the question quietly, and Scarlett's irritated mismatched eyes met mine, but before she could respond we were interrupted.

"Oh yes, she killed him, ding-dong dead! Dead as a doornail, completely and utterly *dead*!" She screeched the last word at a pitch that made me cringe. "She's very good at death." Helena whispered the words like a secret and it was haunting.

"For the millionth time, Mother, it's not my fault he jumped out the window..."

"You threw him into the sky, toward the sun, and he fell like a star..." Helena swung her arms dramatically, and I imagined talking to her was something like attending a poetry reading. The dialogue just kept taking twist after twist.

"Poor Alfie!" Camilla chimed in, a wicked grin on her mouth.

"Oh yes, poor Alfie, poor Alfie..." Helena echoed her words, while Scarlett flipped her best friend off.

"So, your brother fell out of the tower window and...died?"

"Yes!"

"No."

Mother and daughter answered at the same time.

"He was the light of my life, the only consolation after Jade was such a disappointment to us all."

"That's enough!" Scarlett's demand was harsh, and Helena jumped, pressing her fingers to her lips as if she had been scolded. "Enough about the damn dog!"

Alfie was a dog? Beside me Scarlett was cold and hard, and her mother looked afraid of her. I couldn't help but pity Helena.

"What happened when you had your accident, Mom, or your not-accident?" Jade lifted her chin trying to put on a brave face, but it was obvious the remark had cut her.

"Well, it wasn't an accident. I just... Quiet, Helena!" Her voice once again imitated a familiar one.

"Is Mr. Pearce involved with the Government, Helena?" Cami tried.

"Well, darling, he is the Government!" She laughed long and hard at that and we all shared a look.

"What do you mean, he is the Government?" Scarlett asked when she finally stopped laughing. Jade took her hand.

"Explain the science to me, Mom. How does he relate to the um, organism as a whole?"

She seemed to come back to reality a little, and it was so easy to imagine her as a brilliant scientist, making it even sadder to see her reduced to this half mad wreck.

"He's the nucleus." Her voice was quiet, no trace of humor. "He controls the cell, the channels that bring in and the channels that go out. Scarlett is the mitochondria, the powerhouse, and he made her that way to serve his purpose."

"Is Wilfred on the council?" Scarlett asked the question. Helena took a breath, lifting her chin, and as her lips parted, fear in her eyes, I was sure she was about to say something profound, something that would change the face of the game we had been playing for too long now.

"My poor Alfie."

"Take her back, Jade."

Scarlett's disappointment echoed in her tone.

"You were really helpful, Mom." Jade patted her hand and stood though her mother made no move to follow.

Something struck me.

"Mrs. Pearce," I began politely, "can it be reversed? Whatever happened to you that made you forget—can we change it? Is there an antidote or a cure?"

She studied me.

"No." The reply was sad. "My brain chemistry is altered forever; the reaction is irreversible. Might be better just to end it all. A failed experiment."

I swallowed hard, and Jade and Scarlett shared a long look.

"Why don't you come upstairs, Mom? I have a new dance I wanted to show you."

Jade and her wonderful big heart, and the sadness around Mrs. Pearce's situation, made tears sting my eyes.

"Scarlett, change the world, my darling."

We all looked up at her as she lingered in the doorway. The remark was disarmingly poignant given what we all knew Scarlett planned to do.

"I'm going to try," she replied to no one in particular after her mother was gone.

"So, what now?" Camilla asked.

"I'm not sure. I need time to think over what she said again, to try and make sense of it."

Scarlett's reply was strange because there was no confusion in her emotions, only a grim determination.

"You're lying." I called her out easily. Noticing Camilla's eyes on us, I tried not to let my cheeks burn, sure she knew now that we were blood bound.

"What makes you say that?"

Scarlett asked the question coolly and I shrugged.

"There's no way you need time to think about it. What she said isn't going to change, she all but told us he's involved. My question is, what are you going to do about it that you don't want to tell us?"

She sighed heavily, caught.

"What else is there to do but act? I'm thinking follow him, try to find out how involved he really is..."

"And if he catches you?" I asked, trying to keep the fear out of my voice.

She shrugged.

"Don't ask me to turn you, Princess, it's not going to happen. I didn't come this far to quit, and it's beyond that now."

"How so?" Camilla piped up before we could get into an argument over making me a vampire.

"If what my mother says is true the Government is more corrupt than any of us realize. Plus, I'd like to find out what really happened to her...if there's any way we can help her. If I blow this thing open, that may be an option."

"And if you succeed, you'll take over as the leader of the city?"

Scarlett nodded, looking her in the eyes.

"Yes, with my family to advise me."

"You're planning to kill your father?"

Scarlett nodded.

"Can you?"

I asked the question I saw lingering on Camilla's lips.

Scarlett was quiet for a moment before she took a deep breath.

"For my family, yes."

I wanted to believe her, but after seeing the videos, watching her crumpled in front of Wilfred when he threatened me, I wasn't convinced.

"What if there was another way..." Cami offered but Scarlett didn't want to hear it.

"There isn't, Cami, and we all know it."

She sighed. It sounded like the weight of the world rested on her shoulders, and in a way, the weight of the city did. I ached to be able to carry some of it for her; Wilfred's words still kept me up at night.

"I have to go to work or else he'll be back here. We sit tight for now, and tomorrow I'll see if he leaves the tower and plan to go with."

She kissed my cheek and disappeared down the hall, presumably to change.

Camilla's eyes blazed with determination, and I knew in that moment she loved Scarlett.

"We have to try to help her. Even if she's not interested right now, it could save her life later. I'll go tomorrow to Chase Tower and see what information I can get from Drew. Draw me a map, and write down the combination to the safe, anything you can think of that might help, and I'll read it over later."

I nodded.

"Of course."

"Tell Jade I went to take a shower?"

She squeezed my arm as she passed, and once again I was left alone to wonder.

Chapter Eleven

SCARLETT HAD DISAPPEARED with the setting sun, intent on her mission to follow her father through his night. Camilla had also left not long after to head to Chase Tower in search of anything that could help us. Alone in the tower, and both half mad with worry, when Jade had suggested we go for a walk around the inner city, I had jumped at the idea.

The night was cold, a hard frost already forming over the last layers of snow. It crunched under our feet and I had to catch Jade's arm when she slipped on more than one occasion.

Jade talked when she was worried, anything from the weather to the history of the City, old memories with Scarlett and her future plans with Cami. I loved that about her because it meant I could listen, tune into her and not the static in my head that whispered constantly about what-ifs and worst-case scenarios, keeping me on edge and worried about Scarlett.

An older vampire interrupted her chatter, stopping to greet her politely, and making the usual inquiry about "Scarlett's hybrid" and my transformation. He eyed me uneasily, but I had grown so used to it now that the discomfort which usually accompanied such an appraisal barely registered. As I watched the man limp away, I couldn't help but wonder about him.

"Why was he turned so late? And your mom and dad too... I always meant to ask one of you that. Surely if you can be frozen in time forever, you'd want to be in your twenties or something, not your fifties?"

She laughed.

"My parents did look much younger for many years, but as society evolves and goes on people want to change. They want the superiority that age brings, to be separated from the 'young ones.'" She rolled her eyes.

"But how?"

She waved at someone across the street and we carried on walking, making a huge lap around the circle at the heart of the city surrounding the bunker. I tried not to think about what was happening beneath us currently.

"Science. If a vampire reaches a point in their life where they don't identify with their body, they can request to be aged up. I've never experienced it, but I know a lot of people who have. They don't really remember the process, but it involves lying in a sort of light chamber and they make you unconscious for the duration."

She shrugged. I was fascinated.

"Can they de-age people too?"

She made a face. "Who would ever want that? Just sounds sort of creepy, being three hundred years old and being de-aged back into a child's body."

She had a point.

"Vires is strange."

She nodded her agreement.

"I can see why it would look that way if you're not used to it, and after experiencing some of your world I know it's very different. Here, science is king, not nature."

Her words brought me to another topic.

"So, if you all start as humans and get turned, why don't you have your children before you transform, rather than going through the whole surrogacy thing with the humans?"

She eyed me, the corners of her lips pulling down, her hazel eyes bleached pale under the bright streetlights.

"Scarlett explained it to you?"

I nodded.

"I guess it could work; it's just not the done thing. I mean, why go through that pain and wreck your body unnecessarily? Plus, most vampires don't find their mates until much later in life, long after their bodies would have expired if they remained humans."

"It's just so sad. April was nice, but the lady..." It was easy to talk to Jade about these kinds of things, things that for Scarlett and Camilla were just commonplace. She could view them through a different lens and tended to be more compassionate.

"Yeah. I hate that part too."

We walked along in contemplative silence, my mind mulling over the new information I was learning every day. I tried to imagine what my teachers might have made of this, the kids at the high school, my father. I remembered with a jolt that he was dead thanks to Scarlett, remembered my gratitude over the matter, and I wondered if perhaps I had always been a little dark in some ways.

"Miss?"

I let Jade pull me to a stop and turned with her in the direction of the voice that called, expecting to see someone wanting to talk to her. Instead, Zoe eyed me warily.

"Hi... How are you?"

I forced myself to play it cool, remembering the stony receptions I had received previously, and expecting another after the mess Scarlett made of her sister, Hannah, the night that felt so long ago.

"We're managing." Her smile was tight but present and I nodded. "I just wanted to say thank-you, for bringing the pills, and for stopping her before she could..."

She cleared her throat.

"I was watching from between buildings. I was about to come out and try to stop her myself when I noticed you."

"I'm really sorry, Zoe."

I was. Deeply, truly sorry for what Scarlett had done.

Something flashed in her eyes and I could tell she wanted to say something, but she seemed to swallow it down.

"I don't understand you, Rayne. You seem nice, normal, decent, and yet you... I get why you wouldn't want to be one of us, but I don't think I could literally sell my soul to the devil for an easier life."

She was owed her anger, so I kept my mouth closed.

"But that wasn't why I came. Just, thank you, okay? Really... The pills saved Silvie's life, and Hannah's and others too. If I can ever help you, not her, you know where to find me?"

I nodded, and she eyed Jade warily.

"Do you know Christian Hart?" The words tumbled out fast and I knew Jade had been waiting for her moment to ask.

"She's dead." Zoe's tone was sympathetic but firm, and I was sure she blamed us for that too.

Jade stumbled over trying to ask what happened as bodies continued to pass us, the humans all heading back to the Fringe for the night.

"It's really not my place to share that, it would be up to her family, and I really have to go. Thanks again, both of you."

Jade watched her disappear down the street, and I let her for a while, before I tugged her hand gently, urging her to walk on.

She sighed heavily.

"I know I have Camilla now, and I'm happier than I ever was, I just... I wanted to think she was happy somewhere too, you know?"

"Maybe she is?"

It was way too cryptic and philosophical and even too optimistic for typical me, but it seemed to give Jade some peace, so I just went with it.

"Wanna head back? Cami's been gone for like three hours now, she might even be home."

Jade agreed, and we set off walking again. I had to ask her to slow up more than once. Her long legs eating up the ground, combined with her vampire stamina, had me trailing behind her halfway to a stitch.

We moved back into an area that was familiar to me, weaving in and out of the innermost circle of towers, the largest belonging to the Delta families and the non-Deltas just outside them.

"Camilla..."

Jade took off at a run which was more like a flash. I ran awkwardly after her, lost for a moment, searching the streets until I spotted her outside a doorway I remembered well.

Chase Tower loomed above us and I tried not to think of my many days and nights spent there, waiting for Scarlett to find me, as I came face to face with a very drunk Camilla.

She swayed on her feet, Jade holding her around the waist, her hair mussed, lipstick smeared, mascara leaving tracks down one of her pale cheeks.

"What did he do to you?"

Jade was hissing at her, trying to get a word of sense out of her, but Camilla wasn't even coherent.

"Rayne!"

Several people turned to stare at Cami's overly loud greeting.

"Jade, we have to get her home, now."

Cami was a mess. I'd known her to be many things but never sloppy, and judging from Jade's reaction, the same was true for her. As much as I wanted to know what had happened inside Chase Tower, I also knew the last thing we needed right now was a public spectacle.

"What if he drugged her?"

Jade's brown eyes were dark with panic, and she seemed so young in that moment, odd given she was older than me, significantly.

"We aren't going to find out standing here. We need to go home and figure things out, okay? People are staring."

She glanced around us and seemed to understand. Together we towed a very out-of-it Cami back towards the tower.

Cami's dress was skintight and ridiculously slippery, and after having to pull it down in the back and up in the front several times in an attempt to preserve what little modesty it offered, I resolved to talk to these vampires about their stupid impractical wardrobes... Maybe not Scarlett because, well...I was only human.

"Rayne."

Jade was holding up Cami, one foot stuck in the elevator door waiting for me to get in while Cami was attached around her neck, half asleep on her shoulder.

"Sorry!"

We ascended quickly. I grabbed a glass of water while Jade deposited Cami on the sofa. I offered her the drink, but she didn't seem to notice.

"Got the treasure!" she declared proudly, hoisting her ridiculous little designer purse into the air and smacking Jade in the face.

I grabbed the bag from her clutches and rifled through it, setting three vials of the toxin I knew to be fatal to vampires carefully on the coffee table.

"Think Scarlett will consider making a new plan now?"

I looked up excited, but my hope turned to ash in my mouth. The front of Cami's dress had slid down again, and I watched as Jade tugged it a little further, the tips of a very distinct hand-shaped bruise visible over her breast.

"Cami, what happened?" She took Cami's face in her hands, and my stomach rolled at the implications.

Dark hair fanned out on the sofa, and Camilla seemed perfectly content just leaning back there, her face between Jade's hands, looking up at her and saying nothing.

"How do you sober up a vampire?"

It was a genuine question. Jade jumped to her feet and disappeared in a blink. She so rarely used her vampire abilities around me that it startled me.

When she came back, she had a glass in her hands full of a thick dark liquid.

"Is that...?"

"Blood." She confirmed. "Scarlett got it for me."

She held the glass up to Cami's lips and Cami gagged.

"What..."

I was suddenly worried this was another symptom of something horribly wrong.

"No, it's fine. When it sits for a while it gets...sort of gross, and it's cold. Most vampires find it disgusting. I do."

Blood sloshed out of the glass, onto Cami's dress, her chin, her chest, but with the patience of an absolute saint, Jade wrestled two full glasses down her and she started to slowly become coherent.

"I got it."

It was half a question half a statement. Jade paused in what she was doing, wiping her girlfriend's face with the throw off the sofa.

"How much do you remember?"

"Enough." Camilla offered her a smile, though even I could see right through it.

"You have bruises on your chest, babe..."

The words were quiet and suddenly I felt like an intruder in this moment. I thought about getting up to leave but figured it would only disturb them more, and selfishly I really couldn't stand the thought of being alone while Scarlett was still out there playing chicken with her father.

"It's nothing, I'm fine. I got more of the toxin."

Camilla tried to soothe her, reaching up to brush back a lock of long dark hair that hung in Jade's face, but Jade batted her hand away.

"I'm not a child, Camilla. Don't treat me like one. I'm done with people trying to protect me. What happened?"

Tense silence hung over them.

"Were you attacked?" Jade tried again, her voice quieter.

"I spent all night helping him get roaring drunk. Unfortunately, that included a lot of drinking myself. He was pushing the boundaries all the time, despite knowing I'm with you."

Jade swallowed hard.

"He got too forward, I got what I needed and left. There's really nothing more to say."

They stared at each other.

"Cami, did he rape you?" I didn't mean to come out with it quite so bluntly, but it wasn't a dirty word. A sad one, a tragic one, one that shouldn't exist, yes, but if we couldn't open that dialogue, who could?

Dark eyes turned to me.

"There was a time when I was quite attracted to Drew."

That I did not expect, and judging by Jade's furrowed brow, neither did she.

"Tonight, however, I was not interested. I haven't been interested in many of the people I used to find attractive in a while." She smiled at Jade, though a sadness tinged it. "I couldn't make that clear until after I got what we needed, so unfortunately there were some...unwanted advances, but to answer your question, no he didn't. I was wasted, but I stopped things from going too far. I got what I went there to get and got out before the liquor completely took over."

Jade hugged her, and Cami offered me a half smile over her shoulder as she hugged her back.

"I'll go fix you another cup."

I took the crimson-stained glass and headed out of the living room, sensing their need to be alone, the weight of the conversation hanging grimly around me.

Something wrapped tight around my waist as I reached the kitchen bar. The glass fell from my hands and shattered on the floor. I spun around. Scarlett was behind me, a terrifying fire burning in her eyes.

"You're back!"

Jade was beside us before I'd sucked a breath into my fear-emptied lungs. Scarlett continued to look at me for a long second, before finally, she came back to herself.

Cami stumbled in last.

"What the hell happened to you?"

"Hello, Scarlett, lovely to see you too."

I inserted myself between them, not ready to listen to another round of their bickering.

"What happened?"

Darkness settled over her again.

"Wilfred isn't just cozying up to the Government, he's in it."

"What?" Jade and Cami asked at the same time.

"I followed him out of the house, through the Midlands, and watched him doing shady deals with Dimitri and Sage."

The others hummed at this, though I didn't understand its significance.

"Then he went back to the bunker, he almost caught me twice. I lost him inside, but only after he changed...into council robes."

"Oh my God."

The room was quiet for a long beat.

"What do we do?" It was me who finally broke the silence.

"We don't do anything." Scarlett's eyes studied me, stern. "You, Cami, and Jade just need to stay out of the way and let me handle this."

I was about to object, but Cami was already there.

"And how exactly are you going to handle it?"

"Are you drunk?"

She rolled her eyes. "Tipsy, maybe, but sobering up rapidly. Now answer the question."

Scarlett squared her shoulders, and if she succeeded in hiding her apprehension from the others, she didn't from me.

"I'm going to kill him."

"Can you do it?"

I thanked God for Camilla and her straightforwardness, her ability to say what we were all thinking but didn't know how to approach.

Scarlett was quiet.

"He's head fucked you for as long as I've known you, Scarlett. He knows where every single mine in you is because he put most of them there. You'll get one shot and if you miss..."

"He'll kill me, or worse."

Her eyes flashed to me.

"We can use the serum!" Jade cut in excited. "Camilla went to Chase Tower and found the last of Evan's vampire killing toxin. We have three vials!"

"I thought the Government cleaned house on that?" She seemed genuinely confused, and I noted her surprise that Camilla had tried to help her. It stung and not for the first time, I wished we could do more for her.

Jade shrugged.

"They obviously didn't get it all because there's three vials of it sitting in our living room. You can use it on Dad and nobody has to get hurt!"

She was so excited, so naïvely hopeful, and I felt Scarlett's sadness at having to crush that.

"It's too risky, Jadey. We don't know how much he knows about the serum, he could smell it or figure it out before it had time to work, or before I could get it on him or into him. Not to mention it's dangerous for any of us to handle."

Adrenaline shot me in the chest.

"But not for me. At least, I don't think so."

"You're half vampire now, and I won't have you anywhere near this."

She infuriated me at times.

"So, I can't decide if I can even try to help, but I have to let you run off on suicide missions every other night and be okay with it?"

She disappeared, a ghost into the wind, and just as I was ready to scream, full of nervous, anxious energy and frustrated by her ridiculous double standard, my feet were carrying me out of the room and I recognized her compulsion in my mind.

I had enough time to tell the other vampires I'd be back soon, before I was striding down the hall, only stopping when I was in our room, and she was looking up at me with her odd colored eyes from her position on the bed.

"This is my fight, Princess. He's my demon and it's time I faced him. There's no reason for you to be involved."

Her voice was tinged with sadness, and I hated how beautiful she looked held tight in its grasp, bound and determined and broken.

"He's your demon, but you're my everything, yet you expect me to just stand back and let you walk into this alone?"

She laughed, a soft, sad sound.

"Sweetheart, since I met you I've forgotten what it's like to be lonely, to be alone. Before I had Jade, but other than that it was just me and all this...blackness and blood. Now, even when I'm gone, I'm never alone because I know I have something to come back for."

It was sweet, but it didn't change anything.

"And what if I don't want to be something you're always leaving behind? What if I want to be with you, like a partnership?"

"Rayne, if I have to fight with you in the room, I'll die. One threat to you and I'll break. I can't worry about saving you when I'm trying to overcome the person who...broke me."

She stumbled over the words, and the show of weakness was so rare, it was beautifully heartbreaking.

"I don't want to live in a world where you're fighting beside me or pulled into the dark. I want to live in a world where we don't have to fight, where we're safe. Where Jade and Cami can have the big ugly wedding I know is coming, and a brood of adorable kids, and I don't have to leave you alone every night because my hands are always tied."

"And you think being in control of the entire city will do that?"

Her dark eyes blazed into mine.

"I feel like freeing us of my father, and the Government that wants you dead and turned within the week, is a good place to start."

I couldn't find a suitable argument to that truth, and the fight began to leave me. Defeated, I plopped down on the bed beside her.

"Are you sure you can...? I mean... I'm so scared for you..."

She reached out for me, her sadness, her fear, her love shimmering soft against my skin, and I turned and hugged her, feeling my tears, warm against her cool neck. I couldn't lose her. I couldn't unsee the little girl on the tapes, begging and terrified and the man who orchestrated it all, cool and uncaring.

"Are you sure we can't use the toxin somehow?"

She pulled away and brushed the pads of her thumbs softly beneath my eyes, wiping my tears.

"You know we can't, sweetheart. I know you understand this is the only way, as much as you don't want it to be."

A fresh wave of tears flooded my eyes. I hated how much this felt like a goodbye to me.

"When are you going to...?"

"Over the next few days, an opportunity will present itself or I'll create one, soon. Everyone is already talking about how close we are to the deadline for you to be turned."

I tried to tell myself all of this wasn't for me, that there was more at stake, but I knew it mostly wasn't true.

Honestly, I just didn't feel worth it, worth the weeks of worry I knew we had all felt, worth Camilla getting assaulted by a drunk, Jade getting taken by Wilfred, worth Scarlett risking her life.

"Stop it."

Her voice cut into the nosedive I was taking, her palms on my cheeks.

"I wasn't living before I met you, it was half a life, revolving around keeping Jade safe and trying to hang on to some echo of humanity. Then there you were, you were supposed to be an easy target, but I killed the old man and you were just looking up at me, all beautiful and ruined, and thanking me."

I'd never heard the story of how we met from her point of view and goose bumps rose on my arms.

"I knew you were going to be something to me, even then. I just knew. I told myself I was exhausted from traveling and you were too pretty to waste. I drank from you a little, fixed you, and tried to leave you behind. It didn't even occur to me we could become blood bound until I was back in the city."

She slicked her tongue across her lips and paused just for a moment.

"You were so lonely, Princess. I didn't think anyone in the world had ever felt as lonely as me, but then I met you, some silly little human girl. You'd seen the darkest part of me, and you hardly flinched. I tried to forget you, but we both know how that turned out."

She kissed me softly.

"You're my everything. I'd do all this again, a million times over, for one more day with you."

I wasn't sure if my heart was mending or breaking, but everything was bitter and sweet and raw.

Warm tears rolled down my cheeks.
"I don't want to live in a world where you don't exist."
It was my biggest fear, finally voiced.
She caught the tears in her hands.
"Trust me, Rayne. Believe in me one last time."

Chapter Twelve

I MOVED THROUGH the house quietly, surprised to find someone else out of their room. The vampires didn't have to sleep, Scarlett was living proof of that, but I knew some of them liked it. Jade kept almost a human schedule, on the nights she had nothing else to do.

I cleared my throat as I stepped into the kitchen, and Camilla appeared from her spot behind the refrigerator door. I wondered how long she had spent staring into it.

"Don't worry about sneaking up on me, I heard you coming down the hall."

Right, vampire hearing.

"Sorry, I wasn't sure if it was you or Jade or..."

"Scarlett left hours ago, probably the minute your head hit the pillow."

I swallowed, my mouth dry.

"Could you pass me a bottle of water?"

She complied, and got one for herself too, hovering when I sat at the bar. I wondered if she sensed my need to talk or if she had a need of her own. When she didn't start, I broke the silence.

"Is Jade asleep?"

She nodded.

"Are you okay?"

She shrugged. This was worse than dealing with Scarlett on one of her off days.

"Did you guys talk through everything?"

I knew she knew I was talking about what happened in Chase Tower.

She sighed, moving to sit beside me. She picked at the label on the water bottle, the brand familiar to me from the outside world. She looked strangely human in her designer pajamas.

"Not everything, but enough to put it to bed. Jade is wonderful, but she's naïve in so many ways. I love that about her."

"What do you mean?"

She was shredding the label between her fingers now, lightning fast, and all I saw was the little scraps of paper fluttering down onto the counter.

"I didn't want to have sex with Drew, but when it became clear that was the means to an end, I didn't stop it either. He didn't rape me, but I didn't allow it because it was what I wanted. Sex is a powerful weapon, not the same kind Scarlett uses, but still..."

I reached out and stilled her frantic hands.

"I'm just not built for this life, always struggling, always threatened... You've been to my tower, you've met my sister, my family. We're not like the Pearces. All I ever imagined my life to be was much of what April has now. And then I met Scarlett."

There was a fondness still present in her voice, but surprisingly, it didn't bother me like it once would have.

"I love her, and Jade... And I suppose I care for you too."

The admission made me smile, though her dark gaze on my face convinced me to try to fight it down. When I failed, she just rolled her eyes, the ghost of a smile on her lips.

"I'm not saying I would change it. Well, I would, I would make things easier if I could, but I don't want to be anywhere else. Sometimes it's just...exhausting?"

I understood the feeling.

"I think it's okay to be tired."

She shrugged.

"Camilla, so much has happened. We've had so many scares lately, everything changes around us constantly, and Scarlett is this insane driving force and we all sort of try to live in her wake. It's hard."

She studied me.

"How do you love her like that?"

I swallowed, suddenly nervous, shy in my response. Before I could continue, Camilla spoke again.

"There was a time I loved her, beyond being my best friend, being like my sister too. It was like chasing a ghost—she was only ever half there, half gone—and there was always something she would love more than me, something I could never compete with, long before you."

"What?" I forced myself to ask.

"Her blood lust," she answered as if it was the most obvious thing in the world.

"For a time, I hoped she would settle down, and one day we'd have what you have with her now. But she gets this look in her eyes when she's doing...that. And I just knew she would never look that way or feel that way for me. Is it different for you?"

I stumbled over my answer.

"Rayne, I will always love Scarlett, I'll always think fondly of that time in my life, but I have no desire to go back into that mess with her. Everything I really wanted was in front of me for years, and between feeling like a pervert for lusting after Scarlett's *little* sister..." She lifted her hands, making air quotes around the word. "And all the other distractions I used to tell myself were important, I just never took my chance. I'm curious, I want to understand you a little more."

I took a deep breath.

"I think that will always be a part of her. I'm not really sure what to say..." I struggled to explain it without revealing that we were blood bound. "I think she's happiest when we have a balance. Sometimes she needs to be dark, even when she's happy, and I just sort of go into the dark with her... Sorry if that doesn't make sense."

My cheeks started to color as I thought about the frenzied, bloody nights we'd shared, and the soft contentment that lived in Scarlett's eyes for days after. She needed that too.

Camilla studied me.

"I've thought a lot about when Helena said that day. I've only ever read about being blood bound, but it doesn't sound terrible."

We looked at each other in the dim light leaking in from the hall.

I could feel she knew, but out of habit or the strange secrecy and possessiveness that had grown within me around the information, I was not going to admit it aloud.

"I imagine in the right situation, between the right individuals the phenomenon wouldn't be so bad. It might even help two guarded, complicated beings come to understand each other on a very deep level, from what we read about it."

So Jade probably knew too.

I shrugged but held her eyes when I replied.

"I think that's true."

She nodded, and we didn't say any more on the matter. A companionable silence hung over us, until the thought that had been on my mind since the decision to kill Wilfred was made finally left my lips.

"Camilla... How do you kill a vampire?"

I knew there was a time when she never would have answered. It had taken her longer to warm up to me than the Pearce sisters. For weeks, months even, I was nothing but a liability in her eyes, likely to land her best friend in a ton of trouble. I still wasn't sure she would share the information with me now.

"What are you planning?"

Her eyes were suspicious as they studied me, though I knew she was asking more out of concern for my safety than distrust.

"Nothing, I just want to be able to do something, if it comes down to it, if I need to help Scarlett."

She stared at me and shook her head.

"You really think you can take on a vampire, and her father no less?"

I shrugged.

"Probably not, but if she's losing, I also know I can't stand there and watch her die either. I'm just trying to be prepared."

Something in her eyes softened.

"Rayne, she's not going to let you anywhere near that fight, not within this lifetime or the next. Not while you're so breakable, and probably not even if you weren't."

She did have a point, but I still wanted to know, to at least have a chance to be forewarned and forearmed with some knowledge. I was about to explain that to her, but she must have seen the determination on my face.

"There are numerous ways. Severing the head from the body is the most effective and only way to kill us indefinitely."

"No wooden stakes then?"

She scoffed.

“Perhaps it would slow us down—the same for silver bullets, knives, weapons—but unless you get the head, the fight will continue.”

My mind mulled over her words, and I tried to imagine any way I could possibly achieve that. No weapon came to mind to give me an advantage against creatures so much faster and stronger.

“How about a bullet in the head?”

I heard my own words and marveled for a second that I was sitting here in the middle of the night, talking to an honest-to-God vampire about taking a life. My own personal change was brought into stark perspective for me before Camilla hummed.

“Not guaranteed, but it might put them down long enough for you to finish it.”

A gun it was.

She studied me in the low light.

“Rayne, don’t do anything stupid, okay? Scarlett’s like a cockroach, bless her. She doesn’t die, even when there have been more times than I can remember the odds have said she should. I know many strong women and men who would never have survived what Wilfred did to her. She’ll survive this too, and when she does, she’s going to need you.”

I nodded my understanding.

“I think the one thing that would actually finish her off, is losing you.”

The admission was quiet in the darkness, and in that moment, I ached for Scarlett to be there.

“Do you really think she’ll make it through this?”

She took a long sip of her water and considered her answer, and that scared me as much as it comforted me. With Camilla, I knew I would get the truth.

"Her father has controlled her since she was a child, he has manipulated her mind on a level I don't think even she understands. I want to say yes, because I know Scarlett, I know she's a zealot when it comes to protecting and fighting for the things she loves, but part of me is scared. None of us knows how deep his hold really runs, and I don't think we'll find out until she's staring him in the face ready to kill him."

My heart sank, and my next question was the only logical jump I could make, faced with the very real prospect that I could lose her.

"Do you think it would be easier just to turn me?"

She nodded instantly.

"You would be infinitely less fragile; no one would have to die right this minute. I think things still would have to change because the city is too interested in you and Scarlett would never let you become like her, but we would have time."

"But what if I did?" The question was almost a whisper, and I saw the search for understanding in her brown eyes.

"What if I was turned and I did become like her? She wouldn't have to be ashamed all the time, to always feel like part of her isn't good enough for me. We could just be that, together."

Camilla smiled at me soft and sad.

"Rayne, it's a beautiful and terrible dream, and I understand it, but you will never be like her. Do I need to remind you of some of the things she's done? You don't have the stomach."

She was right, and I knew it. I was just grasping at straws, dancing with the devil.

"You should try to sleep. Things are only going to get more hectic as the week wears on, you'll need your strength."

She surprised me by pulling me into a hug. She smelled like some expensive perfume I would never remember the name of and faintly of Jade. The cool expanse of her body wasn't quite right, but comforting still, pressed against me.

"I'm glad she has you."

She let me go, and I squeezed her hand, my chest full.

"Goodnight, Cami. Don't spend too long alone out here, okay?"

She nodded.

As I retreated down the hall, I was happy to notice Jade's bedroom light was on. As I passed by, she appeared in the doorway, giving me a sad sort of smile before she headed to the kitchen, no doubt to retrieve Camilla.

IT WAS WITH Camilla's advice on killing a vampire ringing in my ears that I walked through the city the next night. As soon as Scarlett left for the punishment center after a day of the stoic introspection that seemed more common as we approached the deadline for my turning, I set out on my own errand for the night.

Rain had finally come, the snow turned to mush under my boots, though with another hard freeze in the air, soon it would be glacier slick, ice.

One of Scarlett's thick winter coats hung slightly too big on my frame. Even beneath its downy weight, the cold still seeped into my bones.

I walked quickly, not stopping at any of the stalls in the market, though I scanned their offerings as I passed—clothes, shoes, and food, even electronics. Vires amazed me, and I longed for the day there was time, safety, a second just to breathe, so I could learn more about its infrastructure. It had occurred to me in one of the few moments when I could see beyond the daunting task ahead, that if Scarlett succeeded, she would need to continue to run the city, right down to the small things like this. When I asked her about it, she'd brushed it off saying that everything was already in place. I hoped she was right.

Somewhere in my periphery, a word caught my attention, followed by another and another, as the people around me finally realized they were in the presence of the hybrid. I ducked my head, walking faster, realizing now this was the first time I'd ventured out into the city alone, ever. With the Government at the center of our focus, suddenly the danger of the streets was dulled in comparison. As I walked, the chatter around me increasing, it occurred to me that perhaps I'd underestimated how safe I would be out here alone.

Someone called out in the distance and I picked up a jog, careful to pay attention to where I was putting my feet, trying not to panic. I wanted to make it home without Scarlett knowing I had ever left. The square was large enough that moving around it was fairly easy. Groups of vampires stood together in front of stalls and around the benches lining the bunker, the occasional human dotted between them. I made it through the more populated area, finally dropping back down to a walk when I was confident I had left those who recognized me far enough behind.

I tried to calm myself. The nerves of being out in the city alone, plus the freezing cold air in my lungs and the light jog, all left me short of breath.

She was there, standing beside the long table looking in my direction almost as if she'd been expecting me. Shikara was beautiful—long dark hair to match her dark almond shaped eyes, her kimono style dress and weapons belt making her resemble the fierce warrior woman I was pretty sure she was.

"Still not a vampire?"

The question wasn't impolite, and more of an observation. I shook my head in response.

"Not yet, but soon."

She studied me, and for a long moment she said nothing, leaving me suddenly nervous about having come out here to find her.

"What can I help you with, Rayne?"

There was something calming about being in her presence. Her voice was rich and smooth, each word carefully chosen and clearly enunciated.

"I was hoping to acquire something for personal protection."

She licked her lips but said nothing. I took that as a need for further explanation, fighting the urge to ramble, and trying to avoid lying as much as possible while hiding the fact that I intended to kill a vampire with said something.

"I've been getting a lot of attention, and Scarlett's not always around. I was hoping to find something to help me feel safe."

Her face said she didn't buy it, and as she disappeared below the desk housing her impressive collection of weapons, I wondered if she was going to refuse to help me, or worse, call Scarlett to come get me. Was it some sort of violation for me to try to buy a weapon as a human, or at least half one? Not for the first time, I wondered if this plan had been too brazen, too rushed, too desperate? Everything hinged on her accepting that I would pay her through whatever means Scarlett used, and Scarlett not noticing what I had added to her tab.

I jumped when Shikara popped back up and pushed some ornate-looking knives aside to create a space on her table where she set something down.

"Do you know how to use this?"

I shook my head, suddenly scared. It was the first time in my life I had seen a gun.

"You have no experience in hand to hand combat."

It wasn't a question, but I shook my head anyway.

"All weapons require some level of skill, all should be wielded only after training, but since you came all this way and have a need for something immediately, this is the best compromise."

She picked up the gun, without hesitation, and it looked like it belonged in her hands. She raised it up and pointed it toward me. My heart beat harder in response.

"Breathe in and focus, breathe out and pull the trigger."

I tried to listen while she showed me how to take off the safety, how to put it back on, and how to use two hands to steady the weapon because it would kick back. I tried to soak up her words and tried to process. When she placed the gun in my palms all I could think about was raising it up and trying to shoot Wilfred Pearce, to shoot anything. My hands were already shaking.

Shikara corrected my hold on the handle, knotting my fingers around it and each other in a way I knew I wouldn't remember.

"Practice with it, handle it, let it become part of you, because in a situation where you need it, there's no time for doubt."

I nodded studiously, almost certain that I was going to rush home with it and hide it somewhere and hopefully never look at it again. The idea had seemed solid at the time, consumed as I was by my determination to have some way to help Scarlett, some way to protect her like she did me, but watching my own pale fingers tremble, terrified one of them was going to pull the trigger without my permission, terrified of the power in my hands, I realized the flaw in my plan.

"Will this be on Scarlett's tab?"

I nodded, pleased she had jumped to that conclusion without me having to ask. I waited patiently while the small gun was wrapped in cloth. She watched with uneasy eyes as I shoved it into one of the large pockets on the coat.

"Thank you..." I stumbled over whether to use her name or call her "ma'am." She didn't seem to notice.

"Rayne, if you have to use it, one thing is very important. You mustn't hesitate."

Her words rung in my ears as I rushed home, back through the cold night, both glad for, and annoyed by, the bright lights around the bunker. They lit my way but also illuminated my face enough that more people recognized me. The gun was heavy in my pocket, the weight of it burning my thigh every time it bumped against it as I jogged. I told myself it was a good thing, at least I had a chance, over and over, trying to drown out the anxiety around the weapon that threatened to consume me.

The exercise was cathartic after too long stuck inside, and I vowed to do it more, though I knew perhaps next time I should take someone with me. Pearce Tower loomed ahead like a beacon, beautiful and resplendent, elegant even flanked by other impressive structures.

I slipped by the doormen with little more than an exchange of glances. The elevator came in moments and I was eager to be back on the thirteenth floor, to hide the gun deep in the back of Scarlett's closet in the spot I had already chosen, and just forget it existed.

The doors opened, a soft ding announcing my arrival. I hoped Jade and Cami were still as occupied as they had been when I had left, though perhaps being a little quieter about it.

I stepped into the foyer. All the breath was knocked out of me as something collided with me, slamming me back against the wall. Panic shot through me, spilling into my veins and bleeding away as I looked up to see who had accosted me.

"Where have you been?"

Scarlett was frantic, caught somewhere between staring me down and checking me over, her hands like vises around the tops of my arms as she held me there.

I sucked in a breath, still winded from her rough handling.

"Scarlett..."

"Where were you?"

Her grip loosened marginally, but not enough. I tried to pull away, but she held me tight.

"Do you have any idea what I thought had happened to you?"

Intensity burned bright in her eyes, her face too close to mine, and I tasted her fear. I understood I had scared her, but I could also feel her annoyance at my leaving, something darker and possessive, and tonight, I wasn't in the mood to submit to it.

"I went for a walk."

I pushed against her and she let me go, seeming to come back to herself. She followed me as I moved past her. With the gun still in my pocket I wanted nothing more than to be left alone to hide it.

"You can't just run off into the city."

Something was off about her, something was wrong, and it clung to her like smog. I slipped out of the coat and hung it in the closet for now, relieved to have the weapon off my actual person at least, then I turned to face her. Her irises swam slightly, dazzling green and rich brown, and my heart fell.

"You've been drinking."

I didn't mean liquor. The disappointment that I wasn't enough for her, the jealousy, the feelings of inadequacy crashing over me, drowned me unexpectedly and completely.

"Don't look at me like that. I needed more than you're able to...donate."

There was a softness to her voice, but she was on edge, and the way she glossed over the topic, the lack of apology, cut me even more. I tried to rise above, to tell myself it was childish, impractical to want to be everything to her, but some things were sacred, and for me, sharing blood was one of them.

The betrayal rankled and hot on its heels was the guilt. I knew whoever she had fed from was dead. I tried not to imagine faces—Zoe, Joseph, Hannah—a sick carousel of people I knew from the Fringe cycling through my head as I wondered who had died to sate her.

"I'm sorry I wasn't enough." The words were immature even to my ears, but I couldn't keep them in.

She let out a breath, still watching me intently.

"Rayne, I need to be strong, the strongest I've ever been, and to do that I have to feed, a lot."

I moved to sit on the bed, the previous days of distance between us cast in an entirely new light. I wondered how many more nights she had been out drinking and killing. I struggled with the laces on my boots, my cold fingers still slightly numb, before they were batted away and more nimble ones unfastened the knots with ease. She looked up at me from her knees, her bottom lip drawn in between her teeth. I could feel there was something else she needed to say, and selfishly I didn't want to hear it. I just wanted to be left alone to the tears that were becoming increasingly hard to fight.

"Princess..." Her voice was scratchy, more so than usual, and she cleared her throat before she continued, "Are you mad?"

I swallowed hard, a hot lump in my throat. I didn't think anger was exactly the right word for what I was feeling, but I wasn't sure what was.

"Not mad, no..."

She looked up at me. Thick lashes, dark crimson lipstick and heavy makeup made her the Scarlett she was out there. When she spoke, her voice was hard again, cold.

"There was an announcement tonight. The Government has set a date for your turning. They're making an event of it to force my hand."

My eyes found hers, my own insecurity momentarily forgotten in the face of a much bigger problem.

"It's the day after tomorrow."

Chapter Thirteen

SHE PACED, A frantic back and forth for the rest of the night. I was convinced she was going to wear a hole in the carpet. Our five days had just become less than two. Scarlett had told me to get some rest, helping me into some sleep clothes and tucking me under the covers when I didn't move on my own.

I lay still and quiet, caught between waking and uneasy dreams. The sound of voices filtered in and out as she talked with Jade, with Camilla, the reality of the situation settling over us all. We were out of time.

The first time I asked her she had ignored me, and through the course of the night, watching her pace herself into a frenzy, the reaction was more and more negative every time I tried to suggest she should just turn me.

I honestly didn't want to be a vampire now. I had watched Jade struggle too many times, seen the torment in ten-year-old Scarlett's eyes. The government scared me. Wilfred Pearce terrified me. The blood, the death, and even Vires itself was frightening to me; the thought of losing our connection was so painful it made my teeth ache. More than all of that, though, I feared losing her. The more frenzied Scarlett became the less she controlled her emotions and the clearer picture I got of where she was mentally. This was not a fight I was sure she could win.

By the time the sun crested the horizon she was still. As she perched on the edge of her vanity, her eyes were haunting, set to blazing gold as she watched the sun rise outside. I noticed she'd discarded her clothes sometime during the night. Only thin black lace covered her, her mahogany hair wild, and death in her eyes.

"Scarlett..."

I'd been awake for hours. I couldn't sit any longer and watch her break.

She didn't answer so I pulled back the covers, leaving the warmth of the bed for the coolness of her skin. I padded across the floor to stand between her knees, my fingers brushing smooth tan skin.

"Baby..." The word was soft, and she closed her eyes, leaning into the fingers I wound through her hair. When she opened them, she was looking at me.

"Just turn me...please?"

She tried to look away, but I caught her chin. The movement made her breath catch, and I marveled at her in that moment—beautiful and tormented, and mine.

"Make me like you...please?"

Finally, I had accepted my fate. Wilfred's words that strange day on the fifteenth floor had stayed with me, followed me, and haunted me more than I had admitted, even to myself. Like this I was a burden, and I was going to be the burden that cost her everything. The future was uncertain, the path descending into darkness, bloodiness I wasn't ready for, but was ready to accept. I wouldn't let her die for me.

She still didn't respond. I leaned in and kissed her softly, my lips featherlight against hers until she came to life beneath them, closing her fingers tight around my throat.

"You want to be like me?"

She dipped her eyes to my neck and my heart beat a dizzying staccato in response. She was terrified, half-crazy with the days and weeks spent pushing herself toward a hurdle even she didn't believe she could clear. She loved me, but in that moment, it was a bruising kind of love, dark and claiming. Her grip tightened, making it hard to breathe.

"Yes..."

I wanted to be good enough for her, and I wanted her to live. Maybe I couldn't be the person standing beside her like Wilfred had wanted, but perhaps as a vampire I could be something better, something just as strong as her, equal and opposite and tempering.

"Just do it."

I ground the words out, and no sooner had they left me than we were flying backward. My back hit the mattress before she was hovering above me, her eyes wild. She tore at her wrist with an abandon I had never seen, chunks of flesh hanging messily from the wound, blood running in a bright trail down her dark skin. She pressed it against my mouth.

"Are you ready for this to be the last time?"

She asked the question against my neck, and I wasn't, I would never be ready to give up being with her like this.

Wet droplets were running down my neck, soaking my chest, and I didn't know if they were tears or blood, or both. Her bare legs were tangled with mine, the long sleep shirt I wore pulled up around my hips as she pressed our bodies together.

"If I bite you, there's no going back."

I felt the press of her teeth against my neck.

"Tell me to do it..."

The words were almost a growl and I felt her tears, tasted them in my blood-filled mouth more than I saw them.

I wasn't ready to say goodbye to this, I wasn't ready to say goodbye to my life as a human, but more than anything, I knew I would never be ready to say goodbye to Scarlett.

I wanted to drink from her forever, acutely aware it was the last time. Instead, I forced myself to yank her mangled wrist away from my mouth. My fingers were covered in blood, and it was thick and sticky and cool on my lips, my chin. She looked down at me like the sight was a revelation.

"Change me, Scarlett. Like this, just you and me, our choice."

I felt it coming, everything building in her head, her chest, the fear, the pain, the anger, the love, and the dark. The weight of it stole my breath. Her lust for this moment, all the ways she had wanted it, they swallowed me.

She pulled her wrist away from me, using that hand instead to hold my chin. We studied each other for a long moment, and I watched the bloody tears roll down her cheeks, acutely aware these would be my last moments, my last memories of my human life. I couldn't think of a more beautiful way to spend them.

She bit me. It was hard and deep, and her mouth was flush against me, the pain white hot and so much more than I expected, but it filled me up, the strangled scream from my mouth as pornographic as it was pained. This was everything I had ever wanted.

The tide started to settle over me, and I grappled for her wrist, wanting to take from her too and feel it run both ways, but she held me down. A million memories flashed through my head. I saw myself through her eyes, lying broken at the bottom of a staircase, caked in my own blood. I saw myself in Chase Tower pressed against the wall and wanting her. I saw the fear on my face when she made Aria kill herself, and the desperation in my eyes when the virus almost took her life.

Our life together, a million little moments, they filled me up and tore me down, and if this was the last time I would ever feel our connection, ever feel her like this, I couldn't have asked for anything more. As she pinned me to the bed, keeping her own bleeding arm away from me, and just letting me feel, I finally understood this was her gift.

She drank until I was dizzy, and when she pulled back, her mouth bloody and her eyes full of tears, she was scared.

"Is that it?"

She laughed softly, sad.

"No, Princess. You have to die with my blood in your system."

I swallowed hard. I was scared.

"Are you ready?"

I nodded, and she pulled me up into a sitting position, moving too quickly until she was behind me against the pillows, one arm across my chest holding onto my shoulder, the other under my chin. The realization crashed over me that she was going to break my neck. I started to cry in spite of myself, horrible racking sobs swallowing me. She held me still against her cool body. The familiar scent of blood and her shampoo would be the last thing I would smell, and I squeezed my eyes shut, waiting.

Her hands were shaking. I wished desperately that she would just get it over with, and I wished I could open my mouth and scream for her to stop. The wound on my neck was bleeding profusely, thick ribbons of blood running over my collarbones and soaking the neck of one of Scarlett's sleep shirts.

We were silent save for my sobs and it was too late to turn around. The marks on my neck would damn us even if we could.

"Just do it."

The words sounded like a battle cry and I grit my teeth, ready for the pain. Her grip on my chin was bruising, but her hands were shaking hard.

She took a deep breath and I held mine, hoping desperately that it would work, that I wasn't broken, that I would come back to continue my forever with her like we had planned.

I screamed when she moved, my eyes clenched closed tight.

When I opened them, breathing hard, she was across the room, pressed against the wall, her chest heaving too.

"I can't. I'm not going to kill you."

My heart soared and plummeted. This was the only way to save her, the only way to avoid sending her out into a fight she couldn't win. But I wasn't ready to die.

She looked like a wounded animal, pressed into the corner, bloody smears left behind from her hands on the light gray walls.

"I'm not going to kill you."

She repeated the words again, and again, coming back to herself more and more each time. My voice was lost to me, my psyche so ingrained with hers that I had trouble sorting out what was mine and what was hers. I felt her refortifying, steel and fire and ice spilling into her veins. She was hard and abrasive, and she was soft and scared and broken, and once again her hands were tied.

Her gaze caught on my bleeding neck, and I knew she had left herself no choice. Neither of us would survive unless she killed me now. There was no more hiding the fact I had been bitten. Her only alternative was to fight Wilfred and the Government, and to somehow win.

"You are mine."

I screamed again, surprised when she was already across the room and on me, the pads of her fingers pressed painfully against my neck.

It was her battle cry.

"I'm yours."

She was raw and powerful, and a little bit terrifying, and the time to subvert her had passed. I could already taste the fight.

She kissed me hard and I lost myself in it, my blood and hers mixing together in my mouth. By the time she pulled away she had already pushed me down again and we were too close to losing ourselves.

She stopped, pulling her hand out of my underwear with a look that left my insides molten.

"Afterwards," she promised me, and all I could do was breathe and nod.

She healed my neck and her wrist using our blood, and when she pulled me up on shaking legs to take me to the bathroom, I followed obediently. She positioned me in front of the sink and slipped behind me. Her cool fingers brushed my neck as she pulled blood-matted hair back behind my shoulder.

I watched with interest as she turned on the faucet, my eyes never leaving the girl in the mirror, pale gold hair and deep blue eyes. She looked like me as much as she was a stranger.

Scarlett wiped the blood from my mouth and chin, before she washed it from my neck. I flinched, the flesh still tender. When she was done, red-tinted water ran down the drain, and I raised my eyes to the twin puncture scars that were silver on my pale skin.

Behind me, she was still caked in blood, eyes intent on the scars.

"You're mine, Princess."

"I'm yours."

Her lips over the little marks sent a jolt through my body, pleasure and pain, and I had to push her away before it became too hard to stop.

"Get dressed."

I did as she asked, tugging on my jeans and a T-shirt, braiding my tangled, crimson-stained hair out of the way, watching as she slipped into a tight dress and sky-high heels. She pulled on her leather jacket and I knew—this was it.

She took her time over her makeup but left my blood dried on her lips and chin, a macabre display to match the punctures on my neck, unapologetic.

"What are you going to do?"

She didn't answer, taking my hand instead and leading me to the living room. She tugged me inside, grabbed her phone, and tapped out a message I couldn't see. When I looked up Camilla and Jade were both staring at us, mouths agape.

"Scarlett..."

Camilla sputtered the word. Apparently done with her phone, Scarlett threw it aside.

"She's mine. We're blood bound, and I'm going to fix this now. Take care of her and Jade, Cami."

They exchanged a long, meaningful look before Camilla nodded. I took too long to catch up, my mind still caught on the fact that finally, our secret was out there.

"Wait..."

Jade seemed to come back to her senses at the same time as I did.

"Where are you going?" There was a desperation in her voice, tears already in her eyes, as it settled over all of us that this could be the last time we would see her alive.

"To end this. I love you forever, Jadey."

Jade collided with her with a soft *oomph*. I was already crying, not equipped, not prepared, not ready for this goodbye, not in this life or the next.

They pulled apart and Jade was crying hard. Tears shone in Scarlett's eyes but she didn't let them fall. She kissed me. For a moment it was everything before it turned cold and sharp and she was already falling away, going to that dark place in her psyche, the one she was counting on to carry her through this.

"Come back to me..."

I managed to force the words out.

"Always."

She turned to leave, and I pulled her back, feeling weak, feeling broken open, already aching at the thought of letting her go out there and do this alone, useless.

"Rayne..."

My name was as beautiful in her voice as it had been the very first time, and it crashed around me.

"You're mine."

It was my promise to her.

"You're mine too."

Something burned in her eyes, bittersweet, and a smile touched the very corner of her lips.

Panic was already rising as, once again, I felt her preparing to leave.

A slow clap interrupted us, and we all turned to the doorway.

"Touching. So touching. I got your message and figured why meet in the bunker when we could meet right here, Scarlett?"

Wilfred Pearce stood at the mouth of the room, amusement and something darker shining in his eyes.

"Cami, take them to your tower."

Any pretense was gone. We all knew exactly why he was here, and I wondered if he had known her plan to challenge him all along.

"No one's going anywhere." It was an easy declarative, leaving no room for argument. Camilla stayed frozen on the sofa, Jade pulled back down beside her.

With a growl Scarlett shoved me in their direction as he stepped toward us.

"This has nothing to do with them..."

"I'd think the bite marks on your pet's neck say differently."

His eyes flashed with something as he glanced at me, before again he was looking at her, and we were all spectators as he stepped closer to her still.

"Is that what you wanted to tell me? Could you not go through with it? Is that why you called me down here, to kill her and finish the job?"

Something in Scarlett's jaw clenched.

"I'm not turning her."

She was cool and detached as him on the surface, but beneath a storm raged.

They remained in a silent standoff. Standing three steps away from the sofa, I didn't dare to move. I caught Camilla's eyes, questioning, because surely, there was something we could or should do. She just barely shook her head.

"What is it you want to say, Scarlett, because there is something."

"How long have you been a council member? How long has this city been built on lies...? Camilla."

She didn't take her eyes from him, the last word unrelated, a command, and then I was flying, too fast to stop or resist until she put me down. Jade and I were slung together in the back of Scarlett's closet, the door already locked from the inside, three deadbolts I had never noticed, then Camilla turned to face us. Jade was already in front of her, trying to get around her.

“We can’t just leave her! I’m not going to leave her to die for us!”

I watched them grapple, numb, until something awoke in me, and my eyes landed on that familiar winter coat I had worn to the market. I slipped it on, my heart beating fast though the seconds slowed down as they passed. I was forming my plan.

“I have to do this for her!”

“What, let her die?”

The vampires were screaming at each other, Camilla stronger, easily holding Jade away from the door, though Jade was struggling, valiantly.

“She’s not going to die.” I took a deep breath. “Camilla, open the door.”

She hissed.

“Are you fucking crazy? If she dies it will be protecting you because you gave him everything he needs to control her like he always has.”

A loud thud muffled her words, followed by the faraway shattering of glass.

“Camilla, let me out.”

I tried to channel Scarlett’s cool, calm exterior, to subvert the terror that had gripped my insides the minute those locks had clicked into place, and for whatever reason, I couldn’t feel her anymore. I needed Cami to trust me more than her own judgment, and more than Scarlett’s unspoken request to take me away.

Jade grabbed my arm and tugged me back from the door.

“Rayne, she’s right, he’s just going to use either of us to control her. But someone has to help her.”

Her dark eyes fell on Cami, and Cami balked visibly.

“Jade, I’m not her, I don’t know how to fight... I’ve never had to.”

"Because Scarlett has always taken care of all us, and now we're just leaving her to die? She can't beat him!"

They devolved into bickering. Pain spilled across my vision, almost sending me to my knees, before it was gone, and of course the stupid vampire was still working to block our connection while having the fight of her lifetime.

"Stop! Just stop." I looked at them both, letting my determination burn hot in my eyes. "Only one of us has to die to end this. I've had enough of her blood that I'll be fine."

It was still strange to say that aloud.

"He's not going to kill you now and call it all good, she knows too much."

"He won't have to. Camilla, this is my decision to make. Just let me out, please, she's hurting."

It wasn't a lie.

"Cami, let her go." Jade's voice was soft from behind me and I turned around to see tears in her hazel eyes. "If anyone can save Scarlett it's her. I know how crazy it sounds, but just let her out, please."

Indecision warred across Camilla's face, torn between what she thought to be best, between Scarlett's request of her, and the request of the woman she loved, plus the fierce determination I kept careful on my face.

"Do not die." She hissed the words as she flung open the door and tossed me out before again it was closed and I heard the struggle on the other side. I was sure Jade had hoped to go with me.

I stumbled to my feet, carpet burns on the palms of my hands, having used them to slow my fall. Paying them little mind, I reached into my pocket, pleased to feel the cold weight of the gun still there. I had to take it out to unfasten the safety. My hands were steadier this time. The gun still scared me, but losing her scared me more, and with it done I shoved it back in my pocket and started down the hall.

Everything was silent for too long, still. Just as fear that I was already too late, that they had left or worse, she was dead, began to choke me, I heard something move.

I froze, five feet from the doorway, footsteps across the tile audible beside the sharp click of his cane on the floor. My stomach dropped into my boots.

"Now the question is, what do I do with you, child?"

I reached for her desperately, pressing myself back against the wall. I willed her to let me know she was okay, to tell me what to do, because honestly, I wasn't sure. Camilla was right: even if I died and was turned now, we all knew too much.

A soft strangled sound broke the silence, then another, and to my horror, I realized she was crying.

I rushed forward, torn between my need to get to her and to be quiet enough, hoping Wilfred was so distracted he wouldn't hear me coming.

My breath felt frozen, heavy. I fought to breathe, to drag it in and out of my aching lungs as I hovered beside the kitchen door, terrified by her sobs and the silence that hung around them. Holding my breath, I leaned forward, peering around the corner and into the room.

Devastation met me. The counters were cracked, broken, cabinet doors missing or hanging from their hinges. China and utensils littered the floor, and blood, so much blood. Wilfred's back was to me. He leaned heavily on his cane and my stomach turned as I noticed one of his legs was bent at a jarring angle. He was standing over her. I saw her two bare, bloody feet, the rest of her obscured by his body.

"You're mine, Scarlett."

Those words turned my blood to ice and raised as many questions as they answered about Scarlett's own obsession with the term.

"I was never yours."

There was no strength in her reply, and just for a second, I felt a flash of what she did. I had to bite my lip to stay silent, pulling back behind the doorframe and leaning against the wall to take a shaking breath that was not as quiet as I'd liked.

"Do not forget who built you, and now it seems it's time for me to end you. Yours will be a reign that is hard to recreate, but I already have the perfect candidate. After all, with you gone, what else will she have? I'll complete her transformation, with your blood of course, and she'll wake with new eyes and the echo of everything you were in her veins. She will be magnificent."

An inhuman noise ripped through the air, followed by the scuffle of moving parts. I steeled myself and stepped back around the door, pushing my mind forward and through, around the fact that he planned to use me to replace her and back to stopping him, stopping this, saving her.

They moved too fast for my human eyes to follow, and giving up trying, I reached into my pocket. The gun felt lighter in my hands now, in the face of absolutely everything being lost.

Scarlett screamed, and they were still. I raised the gun and stepped around the door completely. The sight that greeted me knocked all the breath out of me.

Leave.

Her eyes never met mine, but she knew I was there. The command was desperate, the last wish of someone who had accepted her fate, and in the face of her weakness, I was somehow strong.

"Hello, Rayne."

Wilfred spoke without turning around, and the hairs on the back of my neck stood.

I tried to pry my eyes away from her, from the odd angle of her broken arm, the blood seeping from too many places, but most of all, the thick handle of the butcher knife protruding from her shoulder, for all intents and purposes pinning her to the wall.

She was screaming in my head, *run, run, run*. I flipped a switch and she was gone; my mind was quiet and focused, and mine.

"Hello, Wilfred."

I felt none of the bravado I projected, but perhaps that had been her gift to me too.

"You have something that's mine."

He laughed, and if Scarlett was ever scary, he was terrifying. The sound sent ice crawling down my spine, but I held my ground, letting him finish his showpiece while I watched her, frantically willing her to lift her head and meet my eyes.

Fight for me one last time.

I begged her silently, pouring everything I had into the command, and then Wilfred's laughter was dying cold in the dusty air of the kitchen, and he was all I could see.

"Yours?"

"Yes. Mine."

In my periphery, I saw her head come up. I played the only ace I had.

"I've considered your offer, and I will accept it, but first I have a few conditions." The gun was gripped tight in my hands, I knew he had seen it, but he said nothing about it, leaning instead on his cane and tipping his head.

"Please do tell. This I must hear."

I swallowed down my fear, cold and hard in a way I didn't understand, but somehow, I was ready to sell this.

"You wanted someone to work beside her, to take some of the weight. I don't want to work with her, I want to *replace* her."

He must have liked my words as his eyes darkened and he leaned forward ever so slightly, listening.

"I don't care about the Government, or the bunker, *or you*, but I will do what you ask, and I'll do it better than she ever has. You need an insurance policy—well, she's mine, she lives, she will stay quiet, and we will all get on with our new lives. For Scarlett, that will be as *my pet*."

I spat the last words, a smile I was sure was terrifying twisting onto my mouth, as I realized she was inside my head, and she was directing.

"All my life I was broken, and now, I'm ready to break. You can teach me."

That line was all my own, and he nodded, though something in his expression told me he had not quite swallowed it, yet.

"I like you, Rayne, I like what we could accomplish together. You have an affinity for darkness; you fell in love with my darkest creation after all. I believe you could fall in love with it all by itself, but first, a test, to be sure we are on the same page."

I lifted my chin at Scarlett's bidding. The fight was slowly leaving me, but buoyed by my distraction, maybe inspired by my plan, she was with me again, pushing me through this, forcing me to believe just a little longer that somehow, even with her broken and bleeding on the kitchen floor, we could still win.

I watched as she yanked the knife out of her body and out of the wood, with a gargantuan effort. The pain I felt for the flash of time she lost control sent bile spilling scolding up my throat and into my mouth, and I was scared I would vomit.

She slid down the cabinet, leaving a bloody trail behind her, crying softly.

"Pathetic."

Wilfred hissed the word, his attention turning back to me.

"If we are going to do this, prove something to me."

Scarlett was crying still, but I could feel her will inside my head, holding me in place, fortifying me when I was ready to shatter.

"If you are to obey me let's begin with this. Take your pretty little gun and shoot Scarlett, now."

I balked, bidding Scarlett to take the reins because I had run as far as I could go, ridden this bluff all the way to its end, and I couldn't go any further.

I spun around, and pulled the trigger, stumbling back two steps from the recoil before Scarlett was hissing in pain.

I tried to drop the gun, desperate, frenzied, frantic, panicking so hard I was struggling to breathe. She held me still with iron focus, my face impassive and the gun held tight in my hands.

She was inside me, and I was powerless to fight. I couldn't look away from Wilfred's dark eyes. They held me, enchanted. I couldn't even check to see where the bullet had hit her.

"Welcome to the family, Rayne."

I slicked my tongue across my lips and smiled, though inside I was screaming.

"Thank you, Father."

I lowered the gun and let it fall to the ground with a clatter. We stepped closer to each other. I was unsure if we were going to embrace, or if he was going to break my neck right then and there.

His eyes were obsidian, his breath was cool on my face, and as he reached for my throat, I closed my eyes.

The minute Scarlett's will released me, I flopped, falling back onto the floor, landing hard on my backside, a whoosh and a thud. I looked up to see Scarlett with the butcher knife. Blood rained down over me, stinging my eyes and staining my lips. I wiped it away as more fell down, a bloody crimson tide as she sawed off his head.

Her broken arm hung bizarrely, her legs wrapped around his waist as he bucked and jerked and tried to dislodge her. When he fell forward we were at eye level, and then his head was gone.

I screamed and screamed, the edges of my vision already spilling into black when she crawled off him and descended on me.

"You are mine." She was growling, hissing, still crazy, covered in blood. She half crawled half dragged herself atop me, and bit me hard, harder than she ever had. Tears spilled down my cheeks, but with her mouth around my throat I was powerless to move.

She was too dark. I tried to push her off, but she pinned me easily, even broken as she was. The wound from her shoulder dripped onto my chest, coating me in a cool, thick, sticky liquid that for once held no appeal for me. She scared me in that moment more than she ever had.

"Scarlett, stop... Stop... Please..."

She was too far gone, I could feel it pouring off her like smog. She was too hurt, too broken, too deep into a place in her psyche where even I couldn't bring her back. I cried, truly, genuinely terrified of her for the first time. She had lost herself, and she was going to kill me.

"Scarlett!"

Another voice joined mine and then another. I saw the flash of feet passing by my head and then they were trying to haul her off me—a snarling, spitting, growling mess, eyes wild and blood matted into her dark hair. It hurt when they pulled. She clung tighter, bit down harder, and when she finally let me go, I was dizzy and sick and too lost to scream.

My vision swam but I could see Camilla holding Scarlett tight. Jade appeared in front of me.

"She needs blood to heal, Jade, now."

Camilla's voice was urgent, and Jade fumbled.

I tried to open my mouth to tell her I was fine, but I couldn't move, realizing she was the only thing holding me up.

Scarlett roared and Cami yelled back.

"You're going to kill her, you fucking idiot. You're going to kill her, Scarlett."

Jade was busy trying to position herself so that I could bite her neck, my own neck too limp, my head rolling to the side when my muscles no longer had the strength to hold it up. I watched Camilla press her fingers deeper into the wound in Scarlett's shoulder, the only reason she was able to hold her.

"Scarlett, stop, come back to us. Fight, for God's sake."

Jade's neck bumped my lips, her dark hair tickling my cheek.

"Go ahead."

It was all-wrong, and I struggled to move away from her, wanting to keep my eyes on them instead. The darkness wafting off Scarlett made me irritable and I knew I would shove Jade off me if I could.

"Cami, she won't..."

"You have to cut yourself... Scarlett, please, come on, please, she needs you, she is dying. Scarlett, do you understand me? She's honest to God dying."

There was a thump and another and then Scarlett was standing over me again. When Jade's cool weight left my back to be replaced by strong arms around me, for the first time since she tried to say goodbye to me, I could breathe.

"Princess?"

She studied me with frantic eyes, and I watched sharp teeth rip open the skin on her wrist, fascinated. She hissed her pain when I grabbed her broken arm but said nothing. Cool liquid rust filled my mouth, slicked through my insides, coating me, fixing me, replacing everything she had taken, and I took it back, greedily.

I drank until I couldn't force myself to swallow more, but still I clutched her arm to my mouth, enjoying the drip of her blood onto my tongue, the relief, the contentment she was feeding me.

"Scarlett, are you okay?"

Jade's voice was quiet, hesitant, and I watched her hover beside us. Suddenly aware that Scarlett was still hurt, even with the huge volume of my blood she'd taken, I reluctantly let her arm go.

I groped around my neck while the others watched. I found the bloody mangled bite, gathered some of the blood on my fingers and pressed them up to her ruined shoulder. She had to guide my hand after I missed the first time. Jade screamed when she jerked her arm hard and it reset, and my stomach rolled as she dug the bullet out of her leg.

After her wrist was pressed to my neck and neither of us were bleeding anymore, the room stayed silent around us for a long time.

"I almost killed you..."

I surged up and kissed her, tired but strong again with her blood inside me.

"You saved me."

I forgot about our audience, lost in the feedback loop we shared.

"You saved me first."

She kissed me desperately like it was the first time and the last time, and I clung to her tight.

Her fingers were rough in my hair. I was debating taking off my shirt, wanting to feel her blood-encrusted skin on mine, when someone finally cleared their throat. I growled, realizing what I had done when Scarlett snickered. Camilla sighed.

"Not that you two don't deserve this, but there's a dead body in the kitchen, a dead very important Delta vampire body. Probably ought to fix that first?"

Chapter Fourteen

THE WALK TO the bunker felt like a death march, and like a parade. Crowds in the square parted for us, eyes followed us, Scarlett and I still covered in blood, her leather jacket torn through from the knife, her dress ruined by a small bullet hole in the thigh and soaked dark with blood.

Jade and Camilla trailed along behind us, hands clasped together. It hadn't taken us long to convince Scarlett that we were going with her. I wasn't sure if excitement or exhaustion made her agree, but as we marched through the square, her anticipation was making me giddy. In her mind the long coming battle was fought, and won, and she was ready to be crowned queen.

After the sweetness of our reunion, of the realization that we had survived, the reality that she had almost killed me had crashed around me hard. The memory of her darkness, and the way she had totally lost herself to it, was salient. I resolved to talk to her about it later, but as we entered the bunker, I feared what was to come if she succeeded in overthrowing the Government and becoming the ruler of the city, and I feared what would come if she failed.

The sack on her back bounced, thrown together haphazardly from Jade's light gray bedsheets. They dripped a bloody crimson and I walked over the trail uncaring. The cargo Scarlett carried was no secret to anyone who dared to look.

She reached back for me and took my hand in her cold one, pulling me closer to her as we walked deeper into the structure that had been my home those first days or weeks in Vires. Guards watched us as we passed but no one interfered, and we descended deeper, the air taking on the same heaviness that still haunted my dreams.

We entered the council chamber without knocking, the click of Scarlett's heels ringing us in, the pad of our boots and sneakers following behind her.

Five hooded figures greeted us, sitting in their places across the platform. My cheek burned at the memory of the last time I was here. Scarlett dumped the sheet onto the floor with a thud. She yanked it open without preamble, leaving the contents on display, before she stepped back, close to me.

"The game's over. Take down your hoods and let's put an end to this sham..."

There was a flurry of motion and I jumped back, finding safety huddled close to Camilla and Jade. When the room stilled again two of the figures were on the floor, presumably dead. Scarlett wiped fresh blood from her mouth. It dripped, black as tar in the dim light.

"And you three?"

One stood, throwing back his hood.

"Good to see you, Scarlett. I had wondered when you'd finally overthrow him."

That voice, the day in the market, the man who was so familiar and the time in the bunker when he had put the long scar across my cheek. She remembered it too, apparently, because she lunged forward. Luke screamed and when she stepped back, his right hand hung limply in her left, detached. His ragged breaths filled the silence.

"Never touch what's mine."

She was a goddess, a dictator, giving her commands, and I felt a horrible sense of foreboding for what lay ahead now it seemed she would indeed succeed in taking control of the city.

"Now. Will you join me or be the next to die?"

He bowed low in front of her, though resentment still burned in his eyes as he cradled his gushing wrist to his chest.

"It would be my privilege."

I tried to ignore the satisfaction, the thrill wafting off her at his agreement.

"And then there were two..."

Another hood was thrown back and I recognized the scientist who had conducted the tests on me the last time I was here.

"River."

"Scarlett."

They appraised each other for a moment.

"We were figureheads, nothing more. Your father ran everything, he consulted us for some things. For example, I made many of the decisions for the city's agriculture and tried to advise him as best I could on matters of science."

She was cold, logical and rational but not unkind. Honestly, I was sort of relieved this was going so well, and relieved that it seemed Scarlett would have help from people who knew about keeping Vires running day to day.

"Would you do the same for me? I assure you, I'm a much better listener."

The scientist nodded, and they exchanged a look I couldn't understand, before the woman took her seat.

"And you?"

The final figure lowered their hood, and the betrayal Scarlett felt shot through me.

Shikara held her eyes, unblinking, and Scarlett faltered for the very first time.

"It's not what you think."

Scarlett swallowed and any trace of the emotion that had played on her face at the reveal was gone.

"It rarely is, my friend. We have a lot to discuss, but for now, will you pledge yourself to my cause, or will you die for his?"

Shikara laughed, a dry, humorless sound.

"I have loathed your father for years. I will join you, and perhaps one day you will come to understand that I haven't betrayed you as you believe now."

Scarlett tipped her head, her eyes still wary.

"Vires is mine. My family will be protected at all costs. Disobey me, try to cheat me or move against me and you will die. Help me as I learn how the city is run, work with me, and you will be rewarded."

Luke was the first to recover from that space.

"Perhaps an announcement then, if I may suggest such a thing?"

He was still clutching his arm to his chest, and I hated how he simpered, catering to Scarlett in a way I felt stroking her ego. Camilla and Jade were silent beside me and I wondered if they shared in my dread of what this would mean for her.

"Perhaps." She neither agreed nor contested. "But first, how long have you been the council, how long has my father been running the Government?"

Shikara was the one to answer her.

"Since before you were born. The five of us, three now, were his original placeholders. Before us there was an impartial council, they were old and tired, and as Wilfred dismantled them, we took their places. He planned everything, the icing on the cake being raising you as the ultimate enforcer for his law."

I noticed that Scarlett still couldn't look her in the eye.

"And the guards, will they obey me?"

Shikara nodded, dark hair brushing her elbows.

"They are duty bound to the bunker, most of them leveraged one way or another. Most of them want to keep the lifestyle their work affords them. You shouldn't have a problem."

Scarlett glanced back at me. The ghost of her longing kissed my skin before she spoke again.

"Call four of the best and have them escort my family home. We have much to discuss."

Luke flitted forward to talk with Scarlett, stealing her attention just as I was about to storm over and tell her we were not leaving her here.

"Rayne..." Camilla pulled me back. "We need to let her do this. They need to respect her, and she still needs to set the board, or this could all still play out horribly. We need to go home, for now."

I heard Scarlett giving her permission before Luke disappeared to go feed and heal, taking his severed hand with him. Morosely, I wondered if it could be reattached. Shikara too disappeared after excusing herself.

"Scarlett..."

I felt her flash of annoyance as I interrupted her, and I knew she felt my answering frustration. For a minute our fires burned hot and hard against each other, before she pulled back and I was left with nothing but a cold stone wall.

There was so much unresolved between us, so much left to work through, but as much as I hated it, Camilla's words made sense. She had to get things under control here.

"Come home tonight?"

She tipped her head, the only concession I was going to get, and anger bubbled beneath my skin. I ached to kiss her hard just to let her feel it, to remind her that I wasn't going to lose her to the dark.

She crossed the space between us in two long strides, and her lips crashed into mine. Realizing I had compelled her I tried my best to undo it. Even when I was counting frantically in my head to distract myself from compelling her, she was still kissing me, her lips bruising. When she pulled away my body burned. I could taste the promise of more on her lips. She was dark but she was still mine, for now.

Camilla cleared her throat, and when I looked to my left, both the other vampires were staring at us, Jade's cheeks beet red.

"Wait here for the guards?"

Her voice was rough with something that did nothing to quell the fire burning inside me.

"Okay..."

She moved back to the scientist who had watched our entire exchange with eager eyes. They talked quietly about something I couldn't hear before they were moving away, leaving Jade, Camilla, and me alone in the room with the strange stage and Wilfred Pearce's beheaded body.

"I hate this place. Do you think she's going to be okay?" Jade asked.

Cami shook her head, telling her silently that here was not the place to talk. Seconds later, the thud of boots announced the arrival of the guards.

"Ma'am?"

They addressed Camilla who treated them as nothing more than her staff and asked them to lead the way. As we walked, flanked on all sides by armed vampires dressed in black, I was glad I had upgraded from the bag-over-the-head treatment I had enjoyed from them in the past.

The walk back to Pearce Tower felt long, much longer than the victory march to the bunker had been. With every step between Scarlett and me, I grew tired, and I ached for her more.

They accompanied us into the elevator. I jammed myself between them and Jade, pushing her against the wall, Camilla slipping in behind me. Once in the apartment, we walked to the kitchen, Jade stopping so short that I plowed right into her back.

Cami stepped around us and closed the door.

"I'll send for someone to start...fixing it."

It was a ruined bloody mess, like something from a horror scene. I wondered absently how much of the blood coating the previously beautiful tile floor was mine.

We moved back through the hall, the guards already gone, presumably to head back to the bunker, to await their next orders from their new leader. Something inside me shuddered at the thought. I followed Cami and Jade into the living room and plopped down into a recliner, too tired to care about my dirty clothes, my bloody hair.

They sunk down together on the sofa, Jade falling in Camilla's lap, long legs tangling with long legs as she leaned down to kiss her. I leaned my head back, closing my eyes and letting them have their moment. I desperately needed one of my own, but unfortunately my girlfriend was off learning how to run our city when morally, I was not entirely sure she was qualified. I sighed, telling myself she couldn't make it any worse than Wilfred had.

My mind ran lazily back over the events of the last six months, the times "the Government" had ordered punishments intended to hurt us, to hurt Scarlett. It had been Wilfred all along. Everything was just crashing together, bleeding into a picture painted with a sick sort of symmetry that all made sense now, when Camilla, finally done getting lost in Jade, interrupted my thoughts.

"Rayne, are you okay?"

I opened my eyes. Both of them were watching me.

"I think so. Part of me can't believe she did it. And part of me is worried about what's going to happen now she did."

Camilla nodded, and Jade looked conflicted.

"She has the keys to the kingdom now. It could be dangerous for her, yes."

That was the last thing I had wanted to hear Camilla say but as always, she was honest.

"All we can do is try to temper the dark, to keep her human, remind her. I was actually hoping you would have some way to rein her in, honestly."

Me, rein in Scarlett when she was on a roll. The thought was funny, and I was about to laugh when I realized what she was talking about.

"It doesn't always work like that."

"So it's true?" Jade cut in. "You two are blood bound?"

I nodded, watching the fear and awe that played across their faces.

"We have been since before you met me, apparently. I didn't know until she was sick."

"What's it like?" Jade was curious as she asked; she almost looked excited. I guessed finding out your sister and her girlfriend had been doing something forbidden by law, by history, by nature, would be something out of the ordinary.

"Like knowing someone intimately, I guess. Sometimes I can feel what she's feeling but she's better at blocking it than me. We can compel each other, but again, she's way better at it."

Camilla leaned forward.

"So, you drink her blood."

A blush bloomed across my cheeks as I nodded. Jade made a face.

"That night when she was going to kill the girl in the Fringe you stopped her?"

I nodded again, tired, content to sit back and watch them fit the pieces together rather than playing Twenty Questions.

"So then why are we worried?" Camilla asked. "If you can compel her then that means you can bring her back if she's going too far. Usually when you take her out of the moment she understands later, right?"

"I won't be her father."

It was something that had already crossed my mind many of the nights I had laid awake waiting for her to get home. Back then it was just a what-if—*what if this crazy plan of hers succeeds and I start to lose her?* Now it was real, and I was even more determined.

"I'll help her to make the right choices—not that I know what they are, but I'll try. I won't ever control her unless it's an emergency. I hate the thought. We've both done it, that's how we survived Wilfred, but it's not something I want to do to her. I guess we just have to believe in her?"

I didn't mean for it to come out as a question, but Jade was all teary-eyed and nodding along like I'd said something profound anyway.

"She can do this. I know it."

Camilla seemed less convinced but was eager to hear about exactly what had happened while she and Jade were locked in the closet. I was halfway through recounting it all, when a loud thud from above made me pause mid-sentence.

"What was that?"

Jade jumped to her feet.

"My mom is up there. She probably doesn't even know my dad is dead or anything."

She took off in the direction of the elevator and was gone in a flash. Camilla grabbed my hand and shot after her, leaving me sort of sailing through the air behind her as she pulled me along. We made it into the elevator just as the doors closed behind us, and I crashed into the vampire, unable to slow my body from the horizontal free fall it felt like she had tugged me in. She grumbled as we collided and set me on my feet.

"Remind me why we didn't just make you a vampire again?"

There was a smile in her eyes that I returned in full force.

The elevator doors opened, and we crept toward the sound of movement, soft thuds and scuffling. I wondered if the fourteenth floor was being robbed.

"Oh my God, Mom!" Jade stopped in a doorway, and I peered around her.

"Shikara?"

Looking as composed as ever, Shikara sat up atop Helena Pearce, her dark hair wild as it tumbled loose down her back.

"What...you can't... She's crazy... You can't do *that* to her..."

Jade sputtered out the words.

Helena popped up from beneath her lover, giving me an eyeful that I never, ever wanted to see.

"Jade, darling, why don't you wait downstairs and we can talk in a little while?"

She was lucid.

"Mommy?"

Jade sounded so very young, despite the bizarreness of the situation, that the single word almost made me cry.

"I'm fine, honey, Shikara fixed me." She looked up at Shikara, who looked much younger than her, adoringly, her eyes filled with too much love, too much memory for this to have been a spur of the moment fling.

"Babe..." Camilla started to steer Jade away. "Maybe we should just go wait downstairs?"

I turned to leave, but Shikara's voice called me back.

"Rayne?"

There was a softness glowing in her eyes that I had never seen before.

"Would you close the door on your way out?"

Dumbfounded, I did.

SCARLETT CAME BACK to me just before the sun crested the horizon, just before she would break her agreement to come home. It had been a long night of hearing about Helena and Shikara's romantic involvement and the heartbreaking story of how Wilfred had kept Helena crazy this entire time because she was once a brilliant mind on the verge of exposing him.

After everyone dispersed to process, Cami had loaned me her phone, showing me the messages that served as announcements to the vampires throughout the city. Apparently, in the Fringe they had speakers. Through the announcements I had tracked Scarlett's activities, listening to a macabre display in the punishment center where Luke was named as her successor, though it was made clear Scarlett would not be giving up that domain completely anytime soon. She threatened Vires into compliance under her hand and then promised a brighter future as she swore to uphold the values already held dear.

I heard a voice I didn't recognize announce that at least three people were dead for moving against the Government, the Government which I knew now consisted of Scarlett alone.

I fell asleep to the sound of static and woke to the ticking in the pipes as the shower was turned off. She appeared minutes later, a silhouette in the dim light of dawn at the foot of the bed.

I reached for her and felt nothing. Frustrated, I reached again with more intent and took a dizzying and unexpected trip through her emotions from the night, ending on the fear she held in that moment, which surprised me. She snarled at the intrusion.

"What are you afraid of?"

I couldn't see her face, and somehow, that made it easier. I pushed myself up until I was sitting and drew the covers down to my waist, letting the chill in the room wake me.

"I'm not afraid of anything."

I exhaled and waited. The cool hardness, the grandiose confidence in the words had no place in our bedroom.

Just when I began to worry she was going to leave, she spoke again.

"I'm afraid of losing you."

The stoniness that had risen into my chest thawed at the words.

"I'm afraid of losing you too." My reply was a whisper, but I knew she heard.

The towel hit the floor and she crawled to me. Her skin was cold when she settled beside me. I pulled her under the covers, not caring that she was damp, eager to warm her back to her usual tepid temperature.

"You're never going to lose me, Princess."

She leaned back into the pillows beside me, the ends of her wet hair tickling my neck. Soft cold lips pressed just below my ear and I felt the apology though I wasn't ready to accept it.

"You almost killed me today. When Luke bowed, you liked it. You've been running around killing people and having them swear fealty to you all night... Scarlett, all along you've said you needed power to protect us, but honestly, you need power because it makes you feel good, and I'm so afraid to lose you to that."

"I need you more."

The whispered words sounded so broken, and I almost, almost gave in and turned my head to kiss her like I knew she wanted.

"I don't want to lose you to the dark."

She took a deep breath.

"I know I frightened you today. I hardly remember... I'm so sorry. I was hurt and stuck in combat mode, I didn't realize; it was pure instinct."

"You told me I was yours, right before you bit me."

She let out a shuddering breath.

"That's instinct too. You're mine, Princess, right down to the core of me. That doesn't make it okay."

She sounded ashamed.

"What would have happened if Cami hadn't stopped you?"

Both of us already knew the answer, and it hung between us until finally she said it.

"You would be a vampire."

She swallowed hard and I wondered if she was crying, a veil of dark hair hiding her face from me.

"I understand if you can't trust me, sweetheart. It was a situation I've never been in, and one I don't foresee happening in the future. I never want to hurt you, Rayne. You're my world. Do you understand that I'm sorry?"

"I do." I did. It was never so much that I wanted an apology. I wanted to know she understood there was a problem, that she recognized the seriousness of the situation, and it was an isolated incident in an extenuating set of circumstances that wouldn't be repeated.

She moved away from me, pulling back the covers, and my heart fell as I realized she was leaving me.

"I'll give you your space tonight..."

I reached for her and pulled her back before she could leave. She landed beside me on the pillows, tears shining in the first light of the sun on her cheeks.

"Scarlett... I don't want you to beat yourself up over it. I just wanted to know you were aware of it. We have so much to talk about, and we will, but I...want to be with you for now?"

She nodded, fresh tears in her eyes, and I laid my head down on her shoulder, her cool arms wrapping around me. The covers were pulled up over my back.

She threaded her fingers through my hair and finally, I exhaled, relief crashing over me, the first semblance of peace, in far too long.

"Can you believe we did it?"

She sounded almost childlike in her wonder and it was impossible not to love her like this, as she really was when it was just the two of us.

"You did it."

She laughed softly, breathy at the correction.

"I think we did it together. Things weren't going all that well when you showed up."

"Seeing you like that..." The memory assaulted me, the strongest person in my world head down, sobbing, her arm broken, a knife through her shoulder. I slid my arms around her neck and held tight. It was so easy in moments like this to feel her mortality though she spent most of her time acting as if she was infallible.

"I almost killed you and you're upset I got hurt?"

She was working through, trying to follow the tracks of my emotions that I knew were sometimes hard for her still, after a life of being twisted by one of the few people in the world who should have loved her.

"No matter what you do, I will always hurt when you hurt... I'll always love you."

The admission was quiet, and I tipped my head back, finding her eyes. She was nervous still, soft, tentative waves that lapped at me, love and apology and uncertainty.

I watched her watch me, waiting. The deeper I got inside what she felt, the more I sensed the weight of her guilt, her shame, her self-hatred. She blinked, and I felt her pull everything back, not completely shutting me out but balking at the intrusion.

"Have you looked in the mirror?"

I nodded and said nothing more. The sight of my neck after my earlier shower had been unexpected, but not terrible. The twin puncture marks she had originally left there had become a tender raised crescent, still sore to the touch, and not unlike my face after Luke had scratched me. In time it too would flatten and contract into another pale silver scar on my skin. She swallowed thickly. I felt the ice-cold kiss of her self-loathing before she locked me out again.

Her cheek was cool under my fingers, and I stroked it until she looked at me.

"I'm not saying it's okay that you lost control, I'm not saying you didn't scare me, but I do know you would never hurt me on purpose."

She just looked back at me, still somehow, wrong, and I realized she wasn't breathing. It was jarring.

"Why do you breathe?"

She shrugged, taking a breath before she replied. "Habit mostly. Speech requires it too."

"But you don't have to?"

She shook her head no and I marveled at all the things I still didn't know about her.

"I'm sorry I shot you... Or you made me shoot you..."

"I could kill Shikara for giving you a gun, you're dangerous with the damn toaster oven, but I suppose that's the least of her crimes."

I cringed.

"Did you talk to Cami before you came in?" Cami was usually awake while Jade slept, and I figured after the stress of the last twenty-four hours, she was likely to be up when Scarlett got home.

"I did, and she told me all about your unfortunate meeting with my mother."

"Did you know..."

"Hell no. I'd always suspected something happened to make her crazy, but I didn't know it had anything to do with my father. And I had no idea she was ever involved with Shikara. For a long time, I considered Shikara a close friend, though she always tried to fulfill more of a mentor role in my life. Guess now we know why."

"You and her weren't ever...involved?"

Scarlett chuckled at my discomfort.

"No, sweetheart. Although it had crossed my mind, but she never seemed interested and so it stayed as just an errant thought. I haven't had many ongoing...arrangements aside from Camilla. The rest were mostly human and all just for a time."

I tried not to let the information worry me, tried not to acknowledge the jealousy that still lingered at the thought of her last human "arrangement," the thought of her with anyone else.

"Your insecurity baffles me."

I grumbled at her to get out of my head.

"Is that why you were so upset when I had to feed before fighting with Wilfred?"

I had almost forgotten about that and although I had been upset, I was suddenly embarrassed.

"Jealousy is supposed to be an ugly emotion, but I don't see it like that."

Her voice hovered on the edge; it was almost molten, liquid sex, though she held herself back. The hesitancy I'd felt earlier was still present. She didn't want to upset me, didn't know if she deserved to go there with me yet.

"I'm not jealous."

I was ragingly, blindingly jealous. She kissed me, and my own hatred of the idea of her drinking from anyone else was reflected back from her to me.

"It wasn't for pleasure. In fact, there was no pleasure in it."

Her eyes burned up at me, turned gold in the morning sun.

"No?" I hovered over her, watching her bite her lip as she shook her head. I knew already where this was heading, what she wanted, and I needed the release too.

"You're mine, Scarlett."

I leaned down to kiss the corner of her mouth and wrapped my fingers gently around her throat. She blinked and her eyes closed for a long beat. When they opened her irises danced for me.

"Always."

Chapter Fifteen

THE FIRST WHISPERS of spring were in the air, and once again I was walking through the square alone. Unease hung heavy on every corner, whispers of a new regime and Scarlett Pearce quieted as I passed each stall. Some people still recognized me, some didn't, or maybe they just didn't care anymore given the bigger news that the Government was overthrown and the woman many of them feared the most had appointed herself their new leader.

The scar on my neck itched and I tugged the thick wool scarf tighter around it, already anticipating the day it would fade some as the one on my cheek had and no longer be so sensitive. Humans manned the stalls, and it was nice to be out in the daylight, the vampire population in the market significantly lessened, only the occasional Delta perusing the offerings or moving through the area on their way to wherever they were going.

"You shouldn't be out here alone."

I jumped sideways. Shikara caught me easily around the wrist and held me steady.

"I thought you were going with Scarlett?"

Fear shot hot through me; the fear I had been doing so well at distracting myself from, until now.

"She decided to go alone. She didn't want to risk any of us."

I cursed her silently.

"Rayne." Shikara's eyes found mine, a certainty there that soothed me somehow. "You know she's no stranger to your old world. It's a simple business meeting and then she'll return. Riley has a group of guards at the wall on standby."

I swallowed, forcing myself to nod.

"Okay." It wasn't okay. I was still reeling from Scarlett's flippant reveal this morning that the human world knew about vampires, and apparently the government had some sort of arrangement with them that meant both parties could coexist.

"Where are you going?"

When I started to walk again, she followed me, keeping pace.

"I wanted to buy some clothes."

I waited for her to either continue polite conversation or excuse herself, but she strode beside me still. Finally, she seemed to sense the awkwardness.

"Do you mind if I accompany you? It's best you not wander around alone and I was going to head to Pearce Tower soon anyway."

I sort of didn't want her to come, not because she was poor company—honestly, she intrigued me—but more because I wondered what she would think when she found out I wasn't clothes shopping for myself.

"Going to see Helena?"

She dipped her head, a smile playing on her usually stoic face.

"What's the story with you guys, if you don't mind me asking, I mean."

She was oddly easy to talk to, easy to be around, and I had been curious about her relationship with Scarlett's mom ever since we had walked in on them.

"Our story..." She mulled over the words. "Many years ago, we were lovers. She was the most brilliant scientific mind in the bunker. I was the official weapons mistress of Vires, so we both worked for the Government. She worked for Mark Chase for a long time, and eventually the student began to surpass the master which became problematic for Wilfred when her silence couldn't be bought in the same way his could."

The words sounded too easy, rehearsed almost, though I wondered if that was just a product of all the time that had passed.

"They were close to discovering how to give the Delta gene to any vampire. Helena told me at the time she was weeks away. Then of course there was the accident and suddenly she was someone else. I never understood the details, but it was Wilfred's doing. Mark came to me not long before he died and gave me an antidote and apologized for his part in it all. Genetic technology I don't understand changed her."

My blood ran cold at the thought.

"So, Wilfred forced her to be with him all this time, to have kids with him?"

Something dark flashed across her face that I couldn't decipher.

"As far as Helena understood she loved him. They were married not long after and then the girls came along. I don't know if she consented to their creation. It's really as simple as a few hair follicles."

We were getting too far out, far away from the bulk of stalls, but walking and talking and learning more about the man who had apparently not only ruined Scarlett's life but the lives of everyone around him, suddenly seemed more important than my purchases.

"The years wore on and whatever they did to her began to break her. Her reality shattered."

Shattered seemed like a fitting description for what I had witnessed of the woman before Wilfred's death.

"I remember, she was pretty cold to Jade and obsessed with her dog."

Shikara looked up. "Alfie?"

I nodded.

"Her dog."

She laughed, and I thought I saw the thin sheen of tears in her dark eyes.

"Alfie was our son." The words were quiet like a confession. "He disappeared not long after Helena was taken from me, and left with nothing, I accepted Wilfred's invitation to sit on his sham council. We hated each other, but we were also dangerous to each other. I suppose we both wanted to keep the other close."

"Shikara..." I didn't know what to say. *I'm sorry* just didn't feel like enough.

"I guess when she couldn't remember why she was so distraught over Alfie he bought her the dog. She has a lot of remorse over her relationship with the girls, with letting Scarlett get so twisted and Jade growing up like she did. She wants to make it right but doesn't know if it's too late."

This was all so broken, and it made my chest ache.

"And the two of you?"

She smiled at that, small and sad, but it was something.

"I've waited hundreds of years for her. Once Scarlett is settled, I plan to get aged up so Helena and I are around the same age physically, and just enjoy the rest of our lives together. I'll continue to work on the council, if only to look out for Scarlett. Perhaps Helena will return to science, who knows. The beauty of immortality is that we're not too late, no matter how much time he stole from us."

It was a beautiful sentiment against a backdrop of blood and inequality and all the other things vampirism had started to mean to me, and I savored it.

"Didn't you want to pick up some new clothes?"

She gestured back to the stalls. I nodded, and we turned.

"Actually, I wanted to get new clothes for some of the staff in the tower. I know firsthand that conditions are pretty bad on the servant floors. Some of the people who came up to rebuild our kitchen didn't even have shoes."

I waited, testing her reception to that information.

"It sounds like yours and Scarlett's story is just as interesting as Helena's and mine. I could show you to a good stall to purchase some uniforms. They only sell beige, but they are good quality. If you want something fancier like the Hawthornes, you'll spend considerably more."

"The beige is fine." I was already unsure how Scarlett was going to feel about me doing even that much. Now the Government no longer loomed over us and she had all the power she could ever want, I really didn't see what we would lose by making living conditions better for the humans—not that I had understood it before either.

I followed Shikara to the stall and ordered what I hoped would be enough for everyone to have a few clean shirts, a pair of pants, and a thick winter coat. I worried about the cost, but Jade had told me weeks ago not to. I still didn't understand the currency in Vires, but apparently Scarlett would never worry about it in this lifetime or the next thanks to all her work for the Government. I suspected Wilfred Pearce had left behind a small fortune too. Thinking of this as spending his money made me feel better.

"Rayne..."

Shikara's voice was urgent at my back.

"I need to take you home now, then I must leave."

Dread crept into my veins.

"What happened?"

She tucked her phone away and spoke quickly to the stallholder, arranging for my purchases to be delivered to the tower, before she replied.

"There was an incident on the south side of the bunker, some of the humans tried to revolt. All I know is Jade was involved, she's fine, but Scarlett is making an example of the people responsible."

"I'm not going home."

I set off in the direction I thought was south. Shikara stopped me with a steady hand on my arm.

"Stay close to me?"

I nodded my compliance and she tugged me back in the opposite direction. We trudged around the bunker at a grueling pace, and as we walked it dawned on me how much I was slowing her down. Glancing sideways I could see the effort on her face as she kept herself at a punishing power walk beside me.

We had just passed Hawthorne Tower when I stopped short.

Scarlett was striding toward us, eyes down on the ground in front of her heels, her bare arms and chest flecked with blood, her hands dipped crimson. Jade trailed behind her, tear tracks on her face and what looked like a nasty busted lip, Cami half guiding her half carrying her.

"Scarlett?"

Her eyes flicked up and her murderous expression did not clear.

"What are you doing outside?"

She snapped the words and I stopped short, staring her down until finally she swallowed and carried on walking. I figured that was all the apology I could expect.

"What happened?"

I rushed to Jade, concerned when fresh tears leaked from her eyes when she saw me.

"Let's get inside first?" Camilla's tone wasn't unkind but the strain around her eyes was obvious.

"Can I help?"

Shikara interrupted from behind me and suddenly I was reminded of her presence.

"I think I can make it upstairs but thank you." Jade shared a watery smile with her and my heart swelled. The Pearce family was far from perfect, but perhaps this was a new beginning for us all, in more ways than one.

I followed behind them back through the foyer and up to the thirteenth floor, sad to say goodbye to the sun before it was fully set but worried about Jade and Scarlett.

"What exactly happened?"

I was surprised when Shikara got out with us rather than continuing up to see Helena.

"We were shopping, and some humans grabbed Jade. They had a silver shard, couple of pieces of pipe... I was trying to take care of it."

The resentment was apparent in Camilla's tone and I sensed that once again she and Scarlett were butting heads.

"What did they want?" Shikara's dark eyes were cool as she gathered information. I liked her, I liked her ability to keep her head and ask questions where I knew Scarlett would simply leap. I was grateful she was going to be around to help us through whatever came next.

"To talk to Scarlett. Apparently, they want some improvements in the Fringe, and for whatever reason they thought snatching her sister might make her willing to talk. As you probably can imagine, there wasn't much talking. Screaming yes. Talking no."

In between listening to Camilla relay everything and watching Shikara take it in, I noticed Jade hanging her head.

"They went about it in a terrible way, but honestly, would it be so wrong to let them live a little more comfortably, give them enough food, medicine, reward them honestly for a day's work?"

Seconds after Jade voiced the question that was on my mind, a voice answered from the doorway.

"Yes, because they can't be trusted. Give them an inch and they want a mile, as they demonstrated today. I've been out of the punishment center for a few days trying to get things situated and look at what happened."

Her hair was wet, her bloody dress replaced by sweats, her tanned skin scrubbed clean, but murder was still dark in her eyes.

"Do you really believe that?" Shikara was the one to question her, though everyone in the room took a collective breath at her statement. Scarlett moved, three graceful strides bringing her to my sofa where she sunk down beside me, a careful distance still between us.

"I believe our system has worked well for hundreds of years. We have nothing to gain by changing it and have everything to lose."

Camilla snorted.

"Says the woman who bent, cheated, and broke the system in every way possible. According to your system, Rayne would be half starved to death and suffering God knows what living in the Fringe."

Scarlett glared at her.

"Rayne's a hybrid."

"But I wasn't always." My response was quiet, but I knew everyone heard it. I reached for her hand and she didn't pull away. As flawed as her logic was, I knew a lot of it stemmed from fear and what she'd been conditioned to think—not that it made her right.

"What would you have me do, Princess? We're vampires, we feed on humans. There's a circle of life, natural order situation in play here."

Suddenly on the spot, I was unsure how to answer.

"Nobody is contesting that some sort of power dynamic has to remain. Nobody is even suggesting any radical change in the way the city is run, but could it hurt to improve their living conditions, really?"

Shikara was the one to speak up and I was grateful for her. I knew Scarlett respected her deeply and she was more likely to consider the words carefully coming from her. I felt her playing with the idea in her mind, the possible outcomes making her more anxious than I ever would have guessed. Responsibility was a heavy weight on her.

"Our workers would be healthier, the city would look cleaner, and maybe if we just try this and make things a little better for them we could avoid issues like today."

Jade spoke up, tears still in her voice. I felt them thaw Scarlett almost completely.

"Wouldn't you rather provide them with some building materials to work on the Fringe and increase their percentage of the food allocation just a little than have to murder twelve people in the street?" Camilla asked bluntly. "Well...maybe not would you rather, but wouldn't it be easier," she amended. Scarlett was still glaring daggers at her.

"I would rather you kept her safe." The words were cold and venomous.

"You think I didn't have a plan?" Camilla's voice got an octave higher and my own tiredness of their bickering was reflected on Jade's face. "Just because I didn't wade right in all psychotic laughter and slasher movie doesn't mean I wasn't going to keep her safe at any cost."

Jade laid her hand on Cami's arm and Cami deflated, though I could still tell Scarlett bristled beside me.

"Scar... We love you, we all know you're doing the best you can, and you have a lot of stuff to deal with right now. But would it hurt to try and make the city a little bit of a better place, when finally, *finally*, we have that option? I get that the old way was okay, at least for us, but it was Dad's way. Do we really want to be like him?"

Jade's big hazel eyes held Scarlett's, and even secondhand I felt her winning the battle.

"This is our home, Scarlett." Cami's voice was softer now, tired as she held Jade's hand tight in hers. "This is where we will spend the rest of our lives, raise our families. Wouldn't it be nice to make it a better place for that? Isn't it time for a little civilization? No more murders in the streets if we can help it, no more humans walking around filthy and sick and in rags. Perhaps we have to give, in order to gain?"

Shikara bowed her head in agreement.

"Fine."

Even though I had felt it coming, her concession surprised me. I knew what a big leap this was for her, and I was thrilled to see her take it.

"We can try. How they respond is on them."

For the first time all day, Jade smiled.

IT WAS DARK by the time Scarlett led me up to the roof. Things had settled again between her and Camilla, and I figured it had a lot to do with the future she and Jade had made clear they wanted together. I knew Scarlett struggled with accepting them at times, but I also couldn't imagine anyone else trying to date Jade and living to tell about it.

"What are we doing up here?"

She was restless, and I felt her relief finally come when we stepped out into the cold night air. I pulled my jacket tighter around myself.

"I just wanted to get out for a while."

Her eyes were wistful, a hundred tiny stars dancing in them from the city lights of the towers and the Midlands. She hopped up easily on top of one of the AC units and then pulled me up too and onto her lap, my legs sideways and my feet flat on top of the large box.

"What happened outside the wall?"

I watched her study the scene before us and wondered how much more her eyes could see than mine.

"Nothing exciting. Lots of old men. Most of them were as turned on by me as they were terrified of me."

She snickered, a wicked grin on her face.

"Is that what you like now, old wrinkly politicians?"

She licked her lips, turning her gaze to me.

"Oh no, Princess. I like pretty girls with blonde hair, blue eyes, and a little bit of a blood fetish."

The last part caught me off guard and I spluttered out my reply.

"It's not a blood..."

"Fetish." She interrupted me, the word all tongue and teeth, her eyes shining as she played with me.

I blushed, and she laughed.

"We can call it whatever you like, sweetheart, but you're my particular brand of wholesome, sweet and surprisingly kinky."

"I'm not kinky..."

She snorted.

"Don't make me fuck you on the roof to prove a point, it's far too cold." She pressed the tip of one of her cool fingers against my lips, and when I opened them, she pushed it into my mouth. I let my teeth graze it lightly as she pulled it away.

"I love you."

The levity still sparkled in her eyes but there was a sincerity there too.

"I love you too, I know you're trying."

She shrugged, suddenly interested in staring out into the night again.

"It's not a weakness to want to make things better, Scarlett."

There was the faintest hint of vapor left behind by my breath.

"Honestly, I don't. I want to make you happy, and Jade and even freaking Cami. None of it's for me."

She was drifting, uneasy; she just felt lost. It dawned on me that for the first time in a long time, she was truly her own person, able to make her own choices.

"Aren't you happy you don't have to worry about your father anymore?"

She shrugged.

"Yes, because it means all of us are safer. No, because now it's all me. I killed twelve people today, nobody made me, it's all mine now." Her voice was quiet. "As much as they deserved it and as much as I know it was the right call, I'm scared you'll finally see me for what I am and being blood bound won't even be enough to make you stay."

I sighed, exhaling some of the irritation that came with hearing the argument used to defy the possibility our relationship could be real or last, again. She didn't need my anger right now, and it would prove nothing. Her insecurity lapped at me, and I licked my rapidly chapping lips and tried to find the right words.

"You've never been an angel. As much as he was a factor, I've known on some level this is a part of you. It doesn't change anything for me." That sounded a little too lenient, so I amended myself. "I never like to hear you did something so terrible. It turns my stomach to think of some of the things you've done, honestly, but I understand."

I touched her cheek and she looked at me with unreadable eyes.

"I know you from the inside out. I'll always hope for you to be your best, but I understand you're not the same as me, and I'll be here for the worst too. I want you to try, and I don't want your life to be so violent and so heavy, but I'm here and I promise I'll never let you get lost in the dark."

She hugged me tight, her face disappearing into my neck. We stayed like that for a long time, Scarlett threading her fingers through her hair. Half of me was reminiscing on my words. Half of me was wondering if she was okay because she wasn't breathing, though I could feel the catharsis of her working through what I had said.

"For better or for worse... Is there something you want to ask me, Princess?"

Her voice was rough when she pulled back, a welcome peace in her eyes beneath the glitter of her teasing.

My heart beat fast and suddenly I was nervous, breathless, because I did want that. I wanted forever with her, with her family, and as much as she was joking, I felt the faint glimmer of hope beneath it too.

I took a deep breath, suddenly ready to be brave, but she pressed her cool finger against my lips before I could speak.

She knew what I was going to say. Her eyes shone with the first echoes of tears. She studied me intensely, looking at me like I was something unusual, something fascinating, in a way that reminded me so much of our first days together.

"Soon." It was a promise, and it hung between us for a few seconds before finally her finger fell away only to be replaced by her lips.

"Might as well get married. After all, I've heard it's quite a common problem in your world, your significant other spending your money while you're out of town."

I shoved her away, licking the taste of her from my lips, caught between apologizing and laughing.

"What's yours is mine?" I tried.

She laughed.

"Fine, but I'm still giving Shikara a hard time about letting you do it. I've been calling her Mommy at random, and it freaks her out like you wouldn't believe."

I loved her like this, head back and laughing, light in a way she so rarely got to be.

Finally, the laughter subsided, and I kissed her cheek, unable to resist.

"And how about your mom, how's that going?"

She shrugged, but her optimism bubbled below her apathetic exterior.

"We both got head fucked by him, maybe there's something in common there. She wants to make up for lost time, I'm open to spending some time together. Jade is still struggling with the fact that she didn't really want either of us to be created, but I think she'll come around. Shikara has been helping her a lot. I think Cami might actually be jealous."

She snorted.

"Still glad you live with a bunch of crazy vampires?"

I twirled the ends of her hair in my fingers.

"Every day."

She smiled at me like I was the most precious thing in the world, and with contentment flowing back and forth between us, my own insecurity was too far away to question it. She pulled out her phone and lit the screen, and for a second, I worried she was going to leave. She put it away and I held my breath, ready for her excuse.

"Do you know what day it is?"

"Wednesday?"

She laughed.

"It's midnight, Happy birthday, Princess."

"What... Really?"

She nodded.

"It's today? That means I'm nineteen. I can't believe I lost track of the date, though I actually can."

"Well, technically you're eighteen, and you'll probably always be eighteen. I don't know if aging up works the same for hybrids, but I'm okay with that."

She gave me a smoldering look.

"You remembered my birthday?" I was not immune to the darkness in her eyes, the coarseness of her voice, but somehow the emotion was stronger. Before Scarlett I was invisible; a slew of horrible birthdays I tried to ignore spanned behind me. The fact we were up here because she remembered made my chest warm and my heart hurt with too much happiness.

"Of course." She said it as if to her, a three-hundred-and-seventy-year-old vampire who had just overthrown an entire regime for me and was running a city and dealing with a total family upheaval, remembering my almost irrelevant birthday was the most obvious thing in the world.

Chapter Sixteen

SHIKARA HAD JUST finished moving the last of Camilla's things into Jade's room, apparently taking it as some sort of personal challenge to do it all by herself. Given the amount of boxes, it had definitely been challenging, but Shikara seemed barely out of breath, though I guess that meant nothing.

"Mom, you're being gross."

Jade's relationship with Helena was steadily improving. She came down every so often to spend time with her daughters, and while Scarlett was civil enough but closed off, Jade's careful optimism about the whole thing was a joy to witness.

"Helena, you are ogling Shikara something fierce," Cami agreed.

"They're right, my love, you have been staring..."

They all laughed. I hovered by the doorframe of the living room, enjoying the sweet moment.

Helena's eyes fell on me.

"Rayne, dear, why don't you come and sit down. She'll be home soon. We were going to look at some of the new agriculture plans if you're interested?"

Somehow, without Scarlett, I didn't feel quite like I fit. It wasn't that they made me feel unwelcome; in fact, it was the opposite. Everything in Pearce Tower had been so warm lately, so open and welcoming and so much was changing, and evolving for the better. The domesticity surrounding me just made me ache for Scarlett. She was home much more than she once had been, but she was still gone too often, especially now the plans to improve the city were finally being put into effect.

I plopped onto the sofa, Camilla and Jade on one side, Helena on the other with Shikara perched on the arm beside her, running a whetstone absentmindedly along the blade of a knife.

"Not in the house, darling." Helena chided her gently, before she unrolled a large diagram of the Fringe and the surrounding farmlands at the edge of Vires. It was fascinating. I lost myself in it easily, enjoying listening to Helena talk passionately about the science behind the new developments, and Jade and Camilla's input on the social and economic side of things, as well as Camilla's concerns that the "stench" would reach the inner ring of the city.

"Rayne."

Shikara tapped my shoulder, pulling me back from where I had been following along with Helena's explanation of how crop rotation worked.

"Scarlett texted, she'd like to meet with you at the bunker. She said to tell you everything is fine and asked me to accompany you."

She shared a look with Helena that I couldn't decipher but it made me uneasy. Jade must have caught it.

"I could use some fresh air. How about me and Cami come too?"

I nodded my agreement before Shikara could say no and left to get my shoes and coat.

They made small talk around me as we walked through the square. Spring was coming to Vires more and more every day. The market was as peaceful as it had been since the announcement of some of the city improvements. I was pleased that rather than creating anarchy, the improvements we had all become so invested in seemed to be making it a better place.

Helena asked me questions multiple times, and I knew my answers were short and non-committal, but I couldn't shake the feeling of dread hanging over me. I told myself it was just thoughts of descending into the bunker again. As we went down into the stale air, I tried to convince myself Scarlett missed me, or wanted something that probably wouldn't be happening given almost our entire family had decided to tag along.

She was anxious and excited. Her emotions hit me in the gut so hard that I lost my breath when we entered the foyer where she waited for us. Her nervousness frayed mine, before her eyes held my gaze, and suddenly, our connection was blank.

"Hey, Scar, is everything all right?"

Jade asked the question on everyone's minds. Scarlett's smile was big and genuine when she replied.

"It's fine, I just...I need to talk with Rayne alone first. But maybe you guys could wait here, and we'll meet you once we're done?"

My feelings were so jumbled, so blended together that despite the clear happiness I could still see in Scarlett's eyes, anxiety engulfed me. I took her hand, muscle memory knotting my fingers tight in hers as she led me away from the rest of our family. Thankfully, she took me into a room on the same level, and not any deeper in the bunker.

I stepped inside and met the cool gray eyes of the scientist who had tested me the day that now felt so long ago. I knew her to be River, and her presence only made me more anxious.

"Why don't you sit down, sweetheart?"

Scarlett's voice was breathy, and I complied, perching on the edge of one of the chairs that lined the wall across from the desk where River sat, a million questions on my tongue. Tan fingers found mine in my lap and she took a deep breath, licking her lips and crossing her ankles. I knew she was stalling.

"You're scaring me, just tell me, please."

She was suddenly scared. I tried to reach out for her, tried to give her something steady, something calm, but my stomach was in knots. I saw the echoes of my unease on her face.

"Scarlett, would you like me to start?" River's voice cut in politely, and Scarlett studied me for a long moment, before she seemed to find her determination.

"No, thank you. It should come from me."

My stomach plummeted.

"No...Princess, no, it's nothing bad. It's good... I mean, I think it's good and it's okay if you don't, and no one is going to make you be a part of anything you don't want to be."

My heart felt ready to break out of my chest and my anxiety over the whole situation had reached a fever pitch I was struggling to tamp down.

"Just tell me, please." I tried to keep my voice steady but all I managed was a whisper. Scarlett took a deep breath.

"We've been working to clear out the bunker, sort of doing an inventory, making sure everyone who works inside was loyal to us and excavating all of Wilfred's dirty little secrets."

I wished desperately she would stop rambling and just say it.

"We found something in one of the lab communities." The way she blurted the words plus the widening of her eyes once they were out made me realize I had compelled her. I blushed crimson and resolved to get a hold of myself.

She cleared her throat.

"As I was saying, we found something. Another...project of my father's, I suppose. I'm sure he intended it to be a way to manipulate us both in the future if his plan to have you work beside me had been a success."

My mind spun in a horror reel. Genetic weapons to make us crazy or make us forget each other sprung to mind, but why then was Scarlett so quietly excited underneath her nervousness?

"I'm not sure how to tell you this."

I was worried I was going to be sick, so done with Wilfred Pearce and all his surprises.

"Do you remember how Jade and I came to be, and how my mother wasn't exactly an active party?"

I nodded, unsure what she was trying to say. She stared at me for what felt like forever, apology and hope written all over her face. I struggled to put the pieces together until they fit with an astounding pop.

There was no way she was telling me what I thought she was telling me...

"What are you trying to say?" My voice was broken, pitchy with nerves and panic.

"They found a little girl living in one of the communities. My father was the one who ordered her creation." There was already so much warmth, so much life and hope and love in her voice, and I just couldn't process it all. I couldn't keep up. I stood abruptly, the feet of my chair scraping harshly against the concrete floor.

"I just um... I..." I needed to get out of there, out of the thick, sweltering air of the bunker and feel the sunlight on my skin. I was hurting her; the reflection of her disappointment was overwhelming, no matter how hard she was trying to keep it away from me. I wanted to sit down and stay, but I was choking, my body telling me frantically that I was not getting enough oxygen, I was suffocating, so I turned and fled.

I sped past the other vampires in the foyer, ignoring Jade's desperate call asking me what had happened. I ran as fast as my feet would take me, out of the bunker that held so many memories, so many emotional echoes for me. I didn't stop until I was outside, the late winter sun soothing on my face, fresh air cooling my burning lungs. I stumbled on leaden legs to a nearby bench and sat down, letting my head rest in my hands.

I did my best to breathe, vaguely aware I was having some sort of panic attack. Guilt rose up in my throat, guilt for leaving Scarlett standing there, which fed into the panic again, and I was back to listening to my unsteady breaths.

Someone sat down beside me. I felt their presence, the soft whisper of their clothes the only sound. I didn't lift my head, still trying to force my mind through the information, to somehow make it sink in, make it feel real beyond the blinding panic that somehow, thanks to Wilfred, there was a little girl in the bunker who was made from me and Scarlett.

"Beyond the shock, are you afraid of the responsibility or of her?"

It was Helena's voice that spoke to me, steady, soothing, her tone telling me she would wait for an answer if I didn't know.

"Both." I choked on the word, the first prickle of tears in the back of my eyes, even as I covered them with my hands. I didn't want to admit it, but I was terrified. Beyond the implications of having a child, a part of me was nervous about having a child with Scarlett.

"She filled me in briefly, and Rayne, she doesn't expect anything from you, even if she hopes for it. None of us will think less of you if you don't feel ready."

It was all so overwhelming, and again, I was scared I was going to vomit. I scrubbed at my eyes and looked up into the vampire's brown ones.

"You're in shock. Scarlett's never been the best with emotions; she doesn't realize dragging you down here and dropping it on you wasn't the best way. She's trying."

"I know she is." I squeezed my eyes shut, not wanting the tears I wasn't exactly sure why I was crying to fall.

"You feel what she feels, so you feel her hope? Her excitement?"

I nodded, noting the fascination in her voice as she spoke about us being blood bound.

"She tried to keep it away from me, but I knew."

"So, you know she wants this then?" she concluded, and I guessed I did.

"I just...can't imagine it. It doesn't feel real. I know she's more than she pretends, and she's taken care of all of us, but she's so...dark sometimes."

Helena fished something out of her pocket, and I watched her unlock her cell phone.

"Do you think she would ever hurt Jade?"

I shook my head. The question was ridiculous.

"Of course not. Jade is..."

"Even at her darkest, do you think she would directly and intentionally do anything to damage her? Do you think she did a poor job of raising her?"

I could see the words cost her, the weight of years lost, time that could never be turned back, the admission that she had missed so much. I swallowed. Her sadness put my own into perspective.

"Of course not, she would do anything for Jade."

She pressed the phone into my hands. A picture stared back at me. I recognized Scarlett, looking about ten years old, sporting her signature glare and a fading black eye, a little girl with scruffy brown pigtails at her side.

"Shikara took them for me through the years. She gave them to me recently, even after all this time..."

She cleared her throat, coming back to the topic at hand.

She swiped left and there were the Pearce sisters again, older this time, Jade's hair in two neat braids as she stood in front of Scarlett.

"I didn't fix her hair that way, Scarlett did. She knows how to raise a child. Over the years she'd convinced herself the family she had was all she would ever have, and she'd managed to convince herself that was enough, until she met you."

I swallowed hard, still staring down at the guarded eyes in the picture, one green, one brown, small hands protective on Jade's shoulders.

"You expanded her world, made her dare to dream, Rayne. She almost got herself killed going over the wall to get back to you, and when you came here, she drove herself mad trying to get you from Chase Tower... I remember it like I was drunk the whole time. It's blurred and the edges are frayed, but it's there."

She took my hand in her cool one and squeezed.

"We love you, you've been so good for her and nobody is going to think less of you if you don't want to do this. You're so young, but don't let what society tells you a good parent has to be stop you. Scarlett was a good parent, the best parent to Jade. If you think you want to try she'd be there to guide you."

She was quiet, and I let the words settle over me, biting my lip and squeezing her fingers in mine, slowly coming back to myself as the haze of my panic lifted.

"I have faith in her for this, and I have faith in you that you will do what's best for yourself, whatever that is. You're our family, and we all need to find a way to live with this together."

My throat was dry, so I swallowed.

"If I didn't..." I couldn't even say I didn't want her; it sounded so cruel.

"Honestly, I don't know. Perhaps Scarlett could raise her alone, perhaps Camilla and Jade. They're both worried about you but beside themselves to be aunties. If none of that worked, we could look for a family in the Midlands perhaps." All of it sat wrong with me. "You've had a lot to take in, why don't we head home? The others will meet us later. Just take a few days to think it over, sleep on it maybe?"

Half of me wanted to jump on the offer and disappear back to Pearce Tower and away from the madness that had descended over my life in the last half an hour. The other half of me didn't want to leave.

"Can I see her?"

It was a quiet request, and Helena looked at me with so much love, so much longing and the same quiet hope I had felt from Scarlett that I almost bolted again.

"Let's go and find out?"

I nodded, keeping careful control on my breathing as I followed her back down into the bunker. The others were talking animatedly in the foyer, crowded around River. My eyes fell on Scarlett who was pacing, chewing her thumbnail and looking tortured.

"Darling..." Helena stayed between us, and I was grateful to her for managing the interaction, still not feeling capable, still shy somehow, scared. "Rayne wants to see her. Can we arrange for that?"

She nodded and when she opened her mouth to speak, she had to stop and clear her throat.

"Yes, of course, I'll just... I'll..." She gestured over her shoulder, already walking backward. "Maybe River can answer some questions for you or something until I'm back."

She fled.

"Hey, Rayne," Cami beckoned us over, and I went as Helena took me, still holding tight to my hand. Cami squeezed my shoulder and Jade gave me a tentative smile.

"River, why don't you explain to her what you told us about how this all came to be?"

Helena squeezed my hand, and the scientist began.

"From the file it seems Wilfred used hair samples to obtain the DNA. The child was conceived in the lab and implanted into a human. The woman was then aged up to complete the pregnancy and disposed of."

I saw Jade look away. I knew River didn't mean to be cruel, but her words were so clinical, like the invasion of our privacy and the loss of a life were just another day at the office. Perhaps for her, they were.

She skimmed her finger further down the page on her clipboard before she flipped to the next.

"The child was aged up again after birth. I believe physically she's four years old now. There's limited information on her development. I'm not sure who the lead on the project was; the only note I see is that she displays limited social skills and doesn't speak... Yet unsure as to the connection between age advancement and retardation of social and verbal skills, no existing studies to compare data on child age advancement." She broke into reading right from the file.

"It's not legal in Vires to age up a child," Helena explained. "So they had no precedence to know really what to expect."

I wondered if it was bad that I was relieved she wasn't a baby. Before I could ask, the door at the back of the room opened and Scarlett reappeared.

I was vaguely aware of our family around us, Helena letting go of my hand, Jade holding her breath, but all I could see was Scarlett, Scarlett and her worried dark eyes, a little body in her arms, smaller than I had expected, her face obscured by thick mahogany hair that matched the vampire's.

"Sweetheart..." Scarlett's voice was rough and thick with nerves and emotion. I ached to feel it too, to taste the moment from her side as well as mine. She sat on a seat, leaving one conveniently empty beside them, an invitation, and I moved on autopilot to sit down.

The girl clung to her, her face tucked into the vampire's neck.

"Does she have a name?"

I wanted to touch her, to have her raise her head so I could see her face. I needed it somehow now.

"Well, the lab project...had a name. My father called it Dahlia." There were tears in Scarlett's eyes. "Many years ago, I had a doll with the same name. It was very precious to me before he destroyed it."

She loved her already. Her sorrow and love and fear that I wouldn't understand began to leak, quiet at first, touching the tips of my fingers, and I wasn't afraid.

Scarlett moved the child gently, lifting her and turning her around before setting her back on her lap facing me. The difference in their skin tone struck me first. Dahlia was paler than Scarlett, but tanner than me. I watched her tiny hands fist in that leather jacket I knew so well, something old and something new, but suddenly, they were both equally a part of me.

Beneath dark hair and thick eyelashes two large eyes studied me, one a shade of blue I recognized as my own, the other a deep green that was undeniably Scarlett's.

"It's genetic... The heterochromia..." Scarlett's words almost sounded like an apology and I found myself irritated.

"It's beautiful... She's beautiful."

Overwhelming hope crashed over me, still careful, a place uncharted, but Scarlett wanted this, and my heart swelled. Nervous as I was, I wanted it too.

The little girl clung to the vampire, more still than I thought a child ought to be, her cheek pressed to Scarlett's chest, her face half obscured by her hair. She watched with wary eyes as I reached out to touch her, but when my hand brushed soft over hers where it held the jacket she didn't pull away.

I smiled, hardly able to tear my eyes away to look into those of the woman I loved. Scarlett was crying, the sight not as jarring to me as it once was.

"You just keep on surprising me, Princess. Every time I think I couldn't possibly love you more."

I reached up and touched her cheek, conscious of the small body between us.

Seeing her there, tears in her eyes, happiness and hope and a hundred emotions I knew she had never dreamed she was meant for, our daughter clinging to her chest, the feeling was definitely mutual.

Epilogue

"OKAY, MAMA, OPEN the door!"

Somehow over the past two weeks, that title had come to belong to me.

I pulled open the door to the newly redecorated room and let Scarlett and Dahlia step inside, our family crowding into the doorway behind them.

"What do you think, baby?"

I crouched down, and she ran to meet me, laughing when we collided. Her hair was pulled back into a long braid down her back, neater but matching mine—Scarlett's handiwork.

The walls were a darker gray than I had liked, everything accented with a rich royal purple in the once guestroom now bedroom, right beside ours. Scarlett had insisted on letting her pick the colors.

"Do you love it? Are you sure you picked the colors and not Mommy?"

Scarlett made a face at me, happiness shining in her eyes, as beautiful as ever in loose jeans and a thick sweater, and I wondered if I would ever tire of this.

Dahlia still didn't speak, but she smiled and laughed and interacted with us more every day. Helena monitored her progress and we hoped soon she would catch up to what was expected for her as a four-year-old.

"Okay, enough waiting, let the fabulous aunts take a look!" Camilla dragged Jade into the room and they took

Dali around, inspecting everything from the new wood furniture to the designer sheets that were of course Camilla's doing.

The room had been a family project. Even Shikara had helped, and as much as she grumbled about being called "Gramma," she'd spent countless hours already making Dahlia a collection of jewelry fit for a princess, after her first offering of a blunt ornate dagger was thankfully vetoed by an anxious Scarlett.

"As much as we want to stay, Grams has to take Gramma and run some errands. We'll be back tonight, just going to check on the new development and my cultures."

We all told them goodbye, and Dahlia waved. This far we'd kept all talk of the Fringe, even of vampires away from her, unsure how much she knew and what her short life in the bunker had been like. Scarlett and I had decided to let her get back on her feet and settle before we added more uncertainty to her world.

A hand reached down for me and I let Scarlett pull me to my feet, surprised when she pulled me into her arms.

"She chose the colors from the swatches..."

Lately she had been so light, free and open and whole in a way I had never known her. I knew running the city, picking up the pieces of her father's crooked regime was hard, but increasingly she was letting all of us share the burden. Many nights were spent after Dahlia was in bed discussing her problems with Cami and Jade, Helena and Shikara in the living room.

"Right, because if you had there would be less gray, more black?"

She laughed against my lips when I kissed her.

There were still dark days, nights she came home having already showered on another floor, her clothes in a trash bag by her side and some of Shikara's sweats too long around her ankles. There were still moments of uncertainty; the first time Dahlia fell on the hard tiles in the kitchen, Scarlett had been moody and full of self-loathing for two days afterward. She was Scarlett, beautiful and imperfect, but mine, ours.

"I never thought I could have this."

Both our eyes were on our daughter, wedged between Jade and Cami on her new little bed listening to Jade tell her a story about the dream catcher that hung on her wall, and the family of Native American vampires in the Midlands Helena had asked to make it for her.

She kissed me, softly at first before her tongue pushed into my mouth. My mind flashed pleasantly back to the night before when it had done the same thing, mixing my blood that coated it with her blood in my mouth. Things were good, better than they had ever been, and somewhere between all the change in Vires and finding Dahlia, underneath we were still ourselves—I was still in love with her as much as I ever was.

"Okay, moms, keep it PG."

Jade made a face, twirling the new engagement ring that shone her left hand.

"Mommy..."

The word was clear, her voice was soft and so unexpected, and in the silence that followed, I heard nothing but her breath and mine.

"Mama..."

Dahlia didn't say anything else, she just smiled, and I wondered if she knew she held the heart of every single one of us, vampire and hybrid alike, as we all beamed back at her, Scarlett's hand tight in mine.

About the Author

L.E. Royal is a British born fiction writer, living in Texas. She enjoys dark but redeemable characters, and twisted themes. Though she is a fan of happy endings, she would describe most of her work as fractured romance. When she is not writing, she is pursuing her dreams with her champion Arabian show horses or hanging out with her wife at their small ranch/accidental cat sanctuary.

Email: L.E.Royal@outlook.com

Facebook: www.facebook.com/le.royal.writes

Twitter: @leroyalwrites

Website: www.leroyalauthor.com/home

Other books by this author

Blood Echo

Also Available from NineStar Press

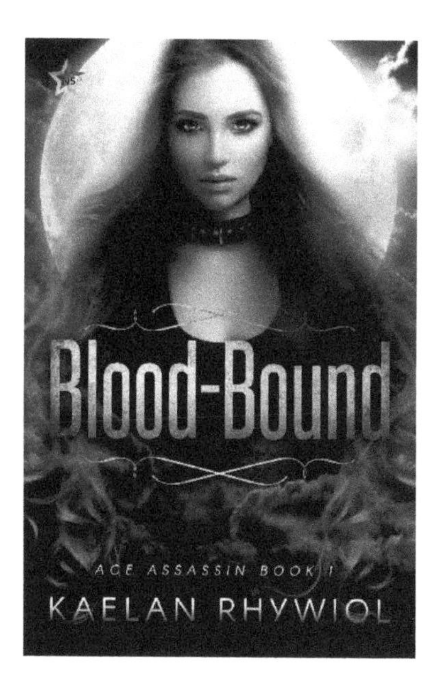

Connect with NineStar Press

Website: NineStarPress.com

Facebook: NineStarPress

Facebook Reader Group: NineStarNiche

Twitter: @ninestarpress

Tumblr: NineStarPress

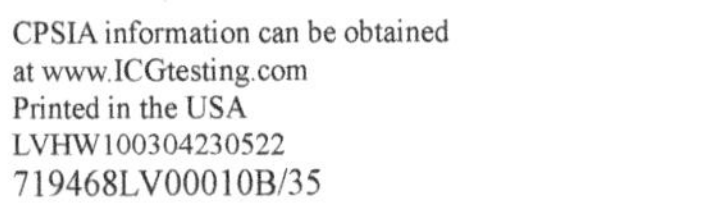

CPSIA information can be obtained
at www.ICGtesting.com
Printed in the USA
LVHW100304230522
719468LV00010B/35